The Prince
and the Patriot

The Prince and the Patriot

John D Rogers

y Lolfa

I Alun, Teiddwen, Aled a Tom
— y cenedlaethau nesaf

First impression: 2009

© John D Rogers & Y Lolfa Cyf., 2009

Cover illustration: Chris Iliff
Cover design: Sion Ilar

ISBN: 9781847711656

Printed on acid-free and partly recycled paper
and published and bound in Wales by
Y Lolfa Cyf., Talybont, Ceredigion SY24 5HE
e-mail ylolfa@ylolfa.com
website www.ylolfa.com
tel 01970 832 304
fax 832 782

Chapter 1

IT WAS COLD but sunny, with little wind: a perfect day for football, thought Geraint, as he avoided the potholes on the cinder track leading to the station. He was pleased it hadn't taken long to thumb a lift for the three-mile journey, having been worried he might miss the train.

Carrying his holdall with his football kit, he had been about to leave the house a little after 9.15, when his mother had asked him why he was going so early. He had had to think quickly. Just to buy one or two things, he explained, and to get some money from his post office account. To his surprise, she had rummaged in her handbag and pushed a £1 note into his hand, whispering, 'Not a word to your father, you know he's still in a bad mood with you.'

'Wow, thanks, Mam. Er, good luck with the collecting.'

She gathered up clutches of labelled charity boxes. 'Got your towel?'

'Yes. See you this afternoon then. I might stay in Mach for a while or look for a weekend job somewhere.'

'You could have your hair cut. You know your father hates it that long.'

Geraint sighed. 'Come on, Mam. This is the sixties, not the fifties.'

'Get on with you. Bye, love.'

And he had gone out feeling guilty at the deception and wishing that his father had not started the cold war between them. If only he and I were still as close as Pete and *his* dad, he reflected.

A distant, wind-blown, two-tone siren announced the approaching train. Near him, in front of the dilapidated, boarded-up station buildings, stood a mother and two toddlers, going shopping in Mach or Aber, he assumed. The sun was warm on his face and he could hear the shouts of lads knocking around a football on the nearby field. 'Must remember to ring Melanie when I get back,' he murmured to himself, and then looked round nervously to see if anyone had heard him talking to himself.

The two dull green coaches slid into the station and the guard jumped out. No one got off and within seconds, the engine rattled and throbbed louder and away they went, a cloud of diesel fumes pumping from the exhaust. Geraint was in the rear coach and sat in the nearest empty seat to the door, one of the few facing forward. He looked for Llŷr and spotted him a few yards ahead near the other door. Surely he's overdoing it, he thought: all this business about getting on at different stations and not sitting together. Who does he think could be watching us? And if I hadn't hitched a lift to Aberdyfi in time for the train, what then? There was no bus at this time of day.

The winding track, squeezed by the road on one side and the river on the other, kept the train's speed down. Normally Geraint enjoyed gazing at the view – the tide-swollen, swirling waters, the clusters of white, huddling yachts straining at the tethered buoys, and the distant sweep of Cardiganshire hills – but this time he looked through the window unseeingly.

As they squealed into Dyfi Junction, he could see the Aberystwyth-bound train already at the opposite platform. Doors opened and slammed. People scurried across – and suddenly, one of the two girls who must have just got off his own train glanced his way. Melanie. For a moment, she halted, staring at him with a hard, piercing look. And then the expression changed quickly to scorn as she moved off. The other girl – he recognised Anna – looked back at her and then they both boarded the other train, slamming the door shut.

Geraint felt dizzy, gripped by nausea and horror. His train began to move off as he strained to see her. Why that look of disgust? What had he done to deserve this?

And then he suddenly remembered the previous night, the glimpse of someone passing near the station in Tywyn, his fleeting suspicion that it was Melanie. Why on earth had he given in to temptation to go out with Bethan? Just because they had bumped into each other that chaotic wet lunchtime in the school corridor, when he had been smarting at what Melanie had said, and ripe for Bethan's eloquent eyes when they had collided. If he was right, and Melanie had glimpsed them, the rift would be deeper.

He was conscious only of a vague blur of fields and hedges as the train completed its final four miles to Machynlleth. Was he expected to avoid the opposite sex just so that Mel had the luxury of trying to sort out her own problems? But then, perhaps he should have phoned her instead of letting things drift.

He made his way over the steel bridge and through the grey stone buildings at Machynlleth station. Standing by a waiting taxi, and blinking in the sunlight, he suddenly heard Llŷr's voice: 'Walk into town, but keep back a bit, behind me. Hang around the clock tower until you see me getting into a Land Rover and then get in quickly after me.' Then he walked rapidly past Geraint and down towards the main road.

As Geraint followed, he still saw Melanie in his mind. She had looked elegant in a close-fitting trouser suit. If she appeared here now, he thought, he'd willingly go off with her and forget all this... this business he was going to.

Still, he reflected, as she's not here, I might as well give it a whirl. Like some spy film. They'll be giving me a password next, something like 'The eagles of Snowdonia have nested' answered by 'And may their eggs be plentiful'. Perhaps they have an M and a supply of exploding fountain pens, just like the Bond films.

And yet, despite it all, he felt excited; he wondered how many other lads of his age had received such an invitation.

In the town square, he crossed over to the carpet shop and ironmonger's and then walked slowly towards the tall, ornate stone clock tower. It stood at the T-junction of the two main streets, presiding impassively over the usual Saturday bustle of crawling traffic and swirling crowds, green Crosville single-decker buses edging past pavements narrowed by green groceries spilling out of shops onto trestle tables, and everywhere, reminders of approaching Christmas. And, reflected Geraint, people doing ordinary, mundane things, whereas I... He felt superior despite his nervousness.

He saw Llŷr standing in front of the tower, looking anxiously up the main shopping street which ran at right angles to the road they had walked along. Funny, he thought, Llŷr almost looks like an eagle in profile, thin and wiry, that jutting nose and piercing eyes. He loitered between two cars parked in front of the shops on the station side of the tower.

'Ger!'

He turned to see Llŷr clambering into the back of a grey, mud-bespattered Land Rover that had stopped a few yards away. Assuming it must have come from the Aberystwyth direction, Geraint rushed over, threw his sports bag in and then climbed over the tailgate, squeezing in next to Llŷr.

The Land Rover swung round and headed back the way it had come. Geraint tried to study the man opposite without making it too obvious. Stocky, almost fat, but strong, with powerful shoulders and arms; a scraggly beard, dark brown corduroy trousers and a navy blue V-necked sweater over a red check shirt. His face seemed somehow fleshy yet at the same time it suggested severity and determination rather than self-indulgence or weakness. Geraint looked back at the receding road, and became conscious of eyes boring into him.

Suddenly they swung off the Aberystwyth road onto a narrow minor road and the engine noise rose as they began a steep climb. To the left was a forest of dense spruce and larch, and on the other side, sheep-cropped, rocky fields. Then the forest ended abruptly next to a barbed wire fence; the vehicle slowed and went through an open metal gate before bumping along a rough, stony track. Two minutes later they relaxed as the Land Rover stopped in a concrete yard in front of a white-painted stone farmhouse. Two black and white collies pranced around them, barking officiously, while a black cat, curled up on a window ledge, merely eyed them curiously.

The driver shepherded them into the house. He was small, wiry, in his late twenties, Geraint guessed, wearing blue jeans tucked into turned-down wellies and a cap worn slightly askew, the peak almost over his left ear. In a blur, he noticed three other people and then all seven sat down round a scrubbed white table in a spacious kitchen warmed by a huge Aga.

Mugs of tea appeared and the farmer, sitting at the head of the table, said in English, but with a strong accent suggesting his first language was Welsh, 'Right, we're all here then, lads. Scouse?'

The one woman didn't seem to object to her inclusion in 'lads'.

Scouse turned out to be his Land Rover companion, and the reason for his nickname was obvious when he spoke.

'Right then, everybody. Let's get down to business – part two, as we had a constructive meeting earlier on.'

Geraint felt the voice was authoritative, despite the thick Merseyside accent.

'Empty your bag on the table, please.' Scouse said this quietly to Geraint, who obeyed without demur. Scouse rummaged through the assortment of football kit and towel and then felt round the inside of the bag before handing it back. 'Why have you brought these?' he asked, pointing at the items on the table. Geraint explained that it was to account for his absence from home, to which his interrogator replied, 'Good thinking – well done.' He gazed at Geraint for a few seconds, as though trying to decide what to do or say. 'We're taking a chance in bringing you here. But yerra patriotic Welshman, and you won't divulge anything you see or hear. Will you?'

Geraint shook his head. Something about the look he received and the way Scouse spoke made him feel he would comply, without any appeal to his patriotism.

Llŷr must have noticed his nervousness and said quietly in Welsh, 'Don't be afraid, Ger. Nothing to be nervous about.'

'Exactly,' added Scouse, sitting down to protesting creaks from his chair. 'Time for cards on the table. Geraint, you are at a meeting of the West Wales Brigade of LAW, the Liberation Army of Wales, which I presume you have heard of.'

Geraint nodded, murmuring, 'Who hasn't?'

Scouse smiled. 'Of course. The LAW has been getting

good coverage on TV and radio and in the papers; pictures of us marching in uniform, urging the nation to revolt and throw off the shackles of English domination and colonial exploitation. And no doubt you've noticed our initials and symbol of crossed swords painted on bridges and walls, especially in your county.' He paused and then went on: 'As for more forceful reminders of our country's plight, there are the explosions – mainly on water pipelines leading from Wales to England.'

Geraint heard someone down the table interject a triumphant-sounding 'Yeah!'

Scouse went on: 'We're always on the lookout for likely young recruits, people who combine intelligence with the courage to stand up for their country. LAW has no time for wishy-washy so-called constitutional methods of trying to win freedom; we believe the only way is by hitting the English hard by direct action and at the same time awakening our people more effectively than by knocking politely on doors or holding middle-class wine and cheese parties. As a long-term aim, we want to force the London government to concede independence for Cymru.' He sipped from his mug and then looked at the woman on his left, saying, 'Mair, d'you want to go on? In Welsh if you wish.'

Geraint thought the adoring glance she gave Scouse implied more than just comradely friendship. An Anglesey accent, he thought irrelevantly, as she began to speak. He noted her short red hair, round face and earnest look. Can't be more than about six years older than me, he reflected.

'... and we are not out to hurt anyone physically, but we do engage in military activities, under cover, against installations of the Crown or the British imperialist state.'

The vocabulary, the sentiments, the serious faces looking

his way – all made him feel uneasy, and conscious that this was serious, deadly serious. And part of him was so impressed that *he* was here, a part of it. Well, almost anyway.

Scouse interrupted his abstraction. 'Those here today are all from these parts. But our headquarters are south, in Carmarthenshire. You may have heard of our commandant, Marcus Owain ab Ifan. Now what we want today is to invite *you* to join us.'

Geraint stared at his face, nonplussed. But why else bring me here, he wondered. It was pretty obvious.

Scouse went on, perhaps seeing his expression as suggesting worry rather than admiration. 'Don't be afraid. We aren't about to shove a recruitment form under your nose and force you to sign in fresh blood from your arm.' Geraint managed a smile. 'We'll introduce you to everyone, talk a bit more about things – and you can decide after a few days. OK?'

Geraint's tea remained untouched before him. He felt all eyes on him and he didn't know what to do with his hands. 'Er, I've not long joined Plaid Cymru,' he said, wondering whether they knew this and whether it was relevant.

Scouse sipped his tea and said, 'Yes, we do know – we know quite a bit about you, or we wouldn't have taken the risk of bringing you here – or asking you to join.'

In the brief silence, Geraint heard the distant bleat of sheep, and then the sudden rasp of a match as Llŷr prepared to light a cigarette.

'Your stand for the Welsh language, staying firm despite being suspended from school, took a lot of guts. You didn't go back and cringe and ask to be forgiven. I think you should remain in Plaid Cymru – it could be handy, keeping us in touch with what the members think, looking out for possible recruits for us, if you do join us. You could also help Llŷr put a bit of backbone into Plaid Cymru attitudes to the Investiture of Charlie boy, get them off their backsides and away from constant committee meetings.' Scouse shrugged his shoulders and added, as though living up to the Scouse image, 'Know warra mean, like?'

'Yes, yes.' Geraint wondered how on earth he could ever explain or justify any of this to his parents.

'Yes,' put in Mair, 'you could march in uniform with us, showing we have youth on our side. No offence to anyone else,' she added, smiling and looking around.

'So,' said Scouse, 'you have until Wednesday evening to make up your mind. Someone will phone you and ask what you have decided. Just answer yes or no, nothing else. Then, if it's yes, we'll be in touch.'

'What then?' asked Geraint. 'If I say yes.'

Scouse drank the rest of his tea and then answered. 'You'll be invited to a meeting soon after and sworn in. Nothing painful. But it will be a solemn oath on the flag – and you'll be told the current password. If, however, you say no, remember you have agreed to keep everything secret about us.'

Mair spoke. 'What about your parents?'

Geraint didn't need time to reflect. 'Well, they weren't keen – to put it mildly – on me joining Plaid Cymru. I reckon anything to do with... all this, would have to be secret. I mean, they'd go up the wall if they found out I had joined you.'

'OK, fair enough,' said Scouse. 'It's up to you; we won't tell them – or anyone else – if you join. If you don't want to march in public, OK, there are other ways you could help us.'

Geraint stayed silent, nodding, but wondering if he should ask what Scouse had meant by 'other ways'. He felt a churning inside of fear and excitement.

Scouse got up and walked over to the window. He looked out, then turned and leant back on it. 'Haven't you ever felt frustrated with conventional politics, with endless talk, knocking on doors, arguing with the serf-mentality or arrogant English immigrants, our very own white settlers? Don't you feel that this has never achieved much, never got us any nearer seeing a truly independent Wales?'

Geraint nodded, murmuring, 'Dead right.'

Scouse smiled. 'I tell you, you'll get some excitement and feel you're doing something really worthwhile for this land of ours, OK?'

He nodded at Carl, who said to Geraint in Welsh, 'Back in a minute.'

The two disappeared through the back door, and somehow the atmosphere relaxed. Chairs scraped back and there was a babble of voices. Mugs were replenished from the chipped enamel teapot on the edge of the Aga, and more clouds of smoke emanated from a middle-aged man's pipe. Geraint coughed and stood up also, glad to stretch his legs and try to think about everything that he was hearing.

Llŷr patted him on the shoulder. 'Congratulations, Ger lad! You've made it this far, then. Now all you have to do is to say yes on Wednesday, eh?'

Geraint just smiled. His head was spinning from the smoke and the implications, from exciting possibilities and instinctive fears.

Chapter 2

Geraint sat on the edge of the table and asked Llŷr, 'So how come *I* got the invitation, rather than, say, oh, I dunno, anyone else in school or the branch?'

Llŷr peeled the cellophane off another packet of Embassy before replying. 'Well, we're always on the lookout for new members, just as Plaid Cymru is. But especially anyone who's prepared to do more than just dress up and march. And you did make a name for yourself back in October.' He put a match to his fag. 'Actually, I think it was Scouse who brought the matter up. Asked if I knew you, what I thought of you. "Not much," I said, "as I'm a Porthmadog lad myself and haven't been working in Tywyn for more than a couple of years." Then of course I got to know you from Plaid Cymru meetings.' He inhaled deeply and went on, smoke funnelling from his nostrils: 'I said I thought you were a bit young for… well, for all this sort of thing. Scouse said if you were old enough to make a stand for the language as you did, well, you were old enough for us. I'm not sure how it went from there. It all sort of became definite we'd approach you. Scouse had done some delving into your background, he said, talked about you with those on high – presumably Marcus down in Carmarthen. And here we are, old son!'

'Sounds like something out of the secret service,' said Geraint, impressed and unable to stop himself feeling important.

Llŷr tapped some cigarette ash off. 'Yeah, well, some things we do *have* to be secret.' And he smiled enigmatically.

'As I said, the trouble with some people who join us is that they're all for banging the drum so to speak, marching down the street. When we do march, there's usually about another ten who are with us – but they were not invited today. Sort of special committee, really, I suppose. If it's anything that might risk arrest, I mean on a serious charge, and affect their job, their mortgage, their bloody wives and so on, I bet we won't see even the backsides of that lot.' He stopped, noticing Geraint's wrinkled brow. 'Hey, don't worry! We don't envisage getting you arrested – at least not for a while!'

Geraint laughed nervously. Llŷr steered him by the arm towards Mair. 'Meet the others. This is Mair, of course, a student at Aber.' She was standing near them, smoking and talking to another man, but nodded at Geraint and smiled. 'And with her, that's Guto Evans of Corris,' he said, looking towards the man of about 30 dressed in scruffy jeans and a tattered sweater. As Llŷr guided him away, he added quietly, 'Used to work in the slate quarry up at Aberllefenni – but is currently on full-time leisure at the expense of Her Majesty's government.' To Geraint's puzzled look, he added, 'The dole, Ger.'

He led Geraint to the other side of the table, passing a venerable Welsh dresser laden with obviously antique tableware. 'And this is Pedr ap Steffan – used to be merely Peter Stevens.'

Geraint thought he detected a flash of annoyance cross the man's face, but he quickly gave a warm smile and shook Geraint's hand. 'Welcome to the club, Geraint, assuming you decide to join.' Geraint wasn't sure what to say, but Pedr sucked on his pipe and added, 'Well, don't rush into it lad. I mean, have a hard think before you make up your mind.'

'Right.'

And Llŷr shepherded him away. 'He works in Machynlleth library, and he's a town councillor. An independent. He doesn't come on marches. Probably lose his job if he did.'

They stood by the window, looking out at the concrete yard and nearby barns.

'What about Scouse?' Geraint asked.

Llŷr was gazing towards some cars parked in front of piled up bales of hay. 'Ah, yes, where would we be without him? Well, he's a Liverpool Welshman. You know what they call Liverpool in the north? "The Second Capital." He understands Welsh fairly well, but doesn't speak it much.' He scratched his chin thoughtfully. 'Anyway, the vital thing is that he knows how to handle the hardware – explosives, guns, et cetera. Foreign Legion experience. Deserted, so he told us. Wanted to come back to Wales to... help.'

'But what's he do now? I mean for a job.'

'Student in Aber.'

'At his age! He's *old*, at least 30!'

Llŷr smiled. 'He's a post-grad student. You see he already has a degree from somewhere else – before he hopped it to France. Lives in a flat in Aber.'

'What's his real name then?'

Llŷr looked round the room and then at Geraint. 'I suppose there's no harm in telling you – it's Arthur Constable.' He inhaled deeply from his cigarette and then added: 'You've probably noticed the signs... bit involved with Mair.'

'Yes, the looks and so on.'

'Mmm, bit obvious, isn't it? She's doing drama at Aber. So you see, you're in distinguished company – no idiots, all good, reliable patriots and no thugs or lay-abouts!'

Geraint was silent for a moment and then asked, 'Carl?'

Llŷr shrugged his shoulders. 'Farmer here. Single bloke,

both parents dead and lives on his own with sundry dogs and cats.'

Suddenly the door opened and Scouse and Carl manoeuvred themselves in, carrying a heavy metal chest and a wooden pole. Geraint said to Llŷr, 'When you spoke to me a couple of weeks ago in the pub, after the Plaid meeting, you said we'd be doing... something... about the Investiture.'

'All in good time, g'boy, all in good time. Our beloved Prince Charles hasn't even arrived in Aber yet. And he'll be the cleverest member of his family by a long chalk if he can manage to learn Welsh in a year!'

Carl and Scouse, meanwhile, had put the chest on the floor and unlocked a padlock on the lid. As everyone gathered round, Scouse took the pole from Carl and unrolled a huge *Draig Goch*, the Welsh flag, with the LAW emblem of crossed swords superimposed on the lower half under the dragon's feet. He leant it against the wall by the window. Meanwhile, Scouse opened the lid of the chest, took out several heavy objects wrapped in canvas and put them on the table.

'Just to show you, Geraint,' he said, 'that we not only want to defend our country but are collecting the means.' He began unfolding the canvas. 'Point-38 revolver and ammo; nine-mil German Luger plus ammo; and a very effective Sten machine gun. And, last but not least, a box of Unigel detonators.' He turned to Geraint. 'You're honoured, wack. We don't normally show these to anyone not in the group.'

Geraint was impressed, awed and a little scared. Yet he longed to pick one of the weapons up. As though reading his mind, Scouse said, 'Here – feel this. It's not loaded.' He passed him the Luger and Geraint cradled it in his hand, feeling the weight, and then held it, pointing it down. 'If you do join,' went on Scouse, 'you'll be able to come with us to a secret location for weapons practice. You'd start off with the Luger. This lot had a session back in August, camping one weekend, up in the hills Llandrindod way. In fact, your mate Llŷr was the number-one marksman. Even aiming through cigarette smoke,' he added, grinning proudly at Llŷr.

'Number one after *you*, Arthur,' interjected Mair, nodding sagely.

Geraint handed the Luger back to Scouse who took it by the barrel and wrapped it again in canvas. He and Carl put everything back into the metal chest which was then locked and taken back out to wherever it was secreted.

'How about that, then?' asked Llŷr, his voice vibrant, almost quivering, his eyes alight with passion.

The others drifted away and general conversation broke out while more tea was poured and tobacco smoke swirled.

'You didn't tell me about your marksmanship,' said Geraint, surprised not only about his expertise but at the fact that it had all been so secret. He also felt a growing inclination to say yes on Wednesday.

'Ah,' said Llŷr quietly, taking his mug over to the sink as Geraint followed, 'there are probably a few things you don't know yet.'

Llŷr swigged the rest of his tea while Geraint wondered what he meant. He said, 'I've heard of LAW of course – and seen pictures on TV of blown-up water pipelines – either blamed on you, or you claim it anyway. Or sometimes they blame it on Plaid Cymru. But I never dreamt I'd be here with you all. I'd no idea it was so... organised.'

'Well, organised up to a point.'

Geraint turned round. It was Pedr, he of the perpetual pipe-smoking. Geraint thought he looked out of place with his small moustache and balding crown, and his ancient, brown tweed sports jacket with leather elbow pads. He reckoned he must be in his early 40s, was plump and somehow avuncular, the sort you'd imagine with a little nephew or niece on his knee rather than crawling through the bracken clutching a detonator. What *was* a librarian doing here? he wondered. And then immediately he smiled, asking himself what on earth a 16-year-old sixth former was doing there.

Pedr patted down some tobacco in his pipe and added, 'Don't get carried away, lad. So far, most us have not blown anything up. And it's not always so impressive, so organised.'

'Why's that?' asked Geraint. Llŷr was leaning against the sink, examining his feet.

Pedr didn't answer until his pipe was drawing well, billows of smoke wreathing his face. 'Oh various things, some minor. For example, the Sten. We practised with it in the summer. Brilliant weapon, we only have the one, but we found out that – what was it called? – the bolt-cocking handle was missing.' He laughed without seeming amused. 'Nevertheless, you could still fire it semi or fully automatic – using a pencil or screwdriver as a substitute for the missing bit.'

Geraint smiled, a bit disappointed, and looked at Llŷr, who merely shrugged his shoulders, looking enigmatic. From behind a cloud of smoke, Pedr said, 'Actually, Scouse hasn't been with us all that long. He sort of, well, arrived and took over. With the blessing of Those of the South.'

Llŷr looked at Pedr and said, with just a touch of annoyance, 'Oh come on, Pedr. He was appointed by Marcus – and we weren't exactly organised or effective *before* he came.'

'Up to a point,' said Pedr slowly. Geraint felt he couldn't imagine Pedr ever losing his temper or yelling. 'Yes, I'll admit he's knowledgeable – though he hasn't yet used explosives in anger so to speak. And none of us has.'

Before Llŷr could speak, Geraint remarked, 'There's another organisation, isn't there? I saw a picture in the paper of people marching with a flag. But not LAW's.'

'Ah, that will be MAC,' said Pedr. 'Mudiad Amddifyn Cymru, the Movement for the Defence of Wales. Don't know much about them. Though Scouse says that the last explosion, the Welsh Office to-do in May, was a joint effort between our Swansea column and MAC. I must admit that I can't see the point of two similar organisations at it. We should amalgamate.'

Scouse and Carl came back in, talked quietly with Mair and Guto, and then Scouse told Geraint it was time to go. He patted him on the back, though to Geraint it was more like a bruising thump, and told him to remember the Wednesday phone call.

This time, Geraint sat in the front of the Land Rover with Carl, with Llŷr alone in the back. Carl babbled non-stop about LAW – their summer 'manoeuvres', hoped-for exploits, the stupidity of the forthcoming Investiture, Plaid Cymru's weaknesses – while Geraint, mind a-whirl, grunted monosyllabic answers and stared unseeingly out of the window. It wasn't that he didn't want to join LAW, just that the waiting, the implications of membership, the secrecy from his parents, all gave him that familiar gnawing of the stomach and entrails, rather like before a major exam or painful visit to the dentist. Then a vision of Melanie's smile came into his mind and he thought about how much he missed her and how unfair he felt she was being. He wanted to grab that Sten and loose off a fusillade of bullets into… something. Or Mrs Archer…

Arriving in Machynlleth, he realised it was too early for the train, so he excused himself from Llŷr and wandered along the main street, having said he might look for a part-time job. But all he did was wander, reflect and cogitate. It was exciting enough to make him want to say yes on Wednesday night – but he told himself he could make a final decision later. And then he remembered with a start he had forgotten about Melanie for at least half an hour.

He got back to the house about four o'clock and had the presence of mind to shove his football shorts, shirt and socks into the washing machine and get it churning and whirring before his mother came in, exhausted but elated and laden with clusters of charity collecting boxes. He had also phoned Pete to check on the score of the game he had played against Ysgol y Gader, the Dolgellau comp.

Chapter 3

DURING THE EVENING meal, Geraint pondered how to solve the problem of persuading Melanie to see him – and sorting things out. He cut the end off a sausage in his mixed grill, only half aware of what he was doing, and scarcely heard his father bark, 'I thought I told you to get your hair cut.'

Taken aback, he was about to fall into his usual routine of pleading or staying silent or making a vague promise, but suddenly looked straight at his father and said, as jocularly as he could, 'Oh, come on, Dad. It's 1968, not '58. It's the fashion.'

His father's fork stopped in mid-flight. His mouth was open, ready for the piece of lamb chop. After a one-second pause, the fork went down and he said acidly, 'I don't care *what* the fashion is. I am *not* having a son of mine going around looking like a long-haired lay-about.' He paused, convinced this sharp remark would elicit the expected submission.

Geraint forced himself to chew on and swallow some food, and then added calmly, his hand shaking slightly, 'Dad, I like it this way. I'd look an idiot if I had what you want, short back and sides.'

His father's plump face seemed to be taking on the colour of what he had poured liberally on his sausages. 'Right! I've had enough of this nonsense. Either get your hair cut, suitably, by next weekend, or... I don't know what the world's coming to!' He stabbed a sausage to death and savagely quartered it.

Geraint felt a strange sense of victory. And yet he was

saddened by his father's stubbornness and square attitude. His mother quickly intervened: 'How did the football go?'

For a moment Geraint panicked, wondering what on earth she was on about. Then he realised and answered, 'Er, oh, we won two-nil.'

'Did you score?'

Geraint regretted not rehearsing the details. 'No-o-o,' he said, trying to sound disappointed. 'I, er, they put me in defence.'

In the past, his father would have taken an enthusiastic part in such a conversation. Not now, what with The Hair, The Row in school over what he'd done, and the general bitterness that seemed to have poisoned relations between his parents lately. For a moment, the idea of divulging the truth occurred to him – but was quickly dismissed. Maybe they would come to terms with his being in Plaid Cymru, but not being involved in LAW. And he was surprised at how he seemed to be accepting the idea of membership of that more militant organisation. The fact remained, however, that he hated the necessity for deceit and subterfuge. He tried to console himself with the thought that he'd been forced to give his word to keep everything secret, but it still gnawed at him. To reward his mother and keep the chat away from dangerous subjects, he asked her how her collecting had gone.

'Pretty well,' she said, her face becoming animated. 'I won't know the total for a while until… well, there's my own tin and two others I brought back, but I'll have to wait for everyone else to bring in theirs before… but I think there's a chance we'll beat last year's amount. It *is* a good cause, such an awful affliction, multiple sclerosis.' And then, turning to her husband, she said, 'Oh, John, Mr Parker, you know, the chairman of the town's Investiture committee, said to tell you he's still waiting for the primary school to give him the exact number of Investiture mugs to order. Did he call in?'

'Oh, er, yes, just before I closed. I'll have to ring the school on Monday.'

'It's handy with the Investiture coming. I mean, it should give trade a boost over the winter, you know, when things are quiet.'

His father grunted. 'Mmm, not many lines moving yet, though.'

'Oh well,' she murmured, patting her lips with her napkin, 'it's early days and there is the school mugs orders.' And then his mother chattered on happily about her day, the people, the gossip.

Yes, thought Geraint, helping to clear the table later, it will have to be a phone call – and not on the sideboard for the world to hear everything. If I knock at her door, her parents might answer and if they send me packing, even if Mel *wants* to see me, she'll find it difficult to get out then. He offered to wash up, but his mother said she would do it. What will I do if her parents answer the phone? Do I pretend to be someone else? Or be brazen?

'What are you doing tonight, love? And move yourself – you're in the way and looking as though you're a million miles from here.' His mother clattered dishes into the washing-up bowl. He said sorry and moved through to his bedroom while his father switched on the television.

After half an hour's fruitless attempt to concentrate on a Douglas Reeman war story he had borrowed from the library, Geraint levered himself off the bed. 'I'm going for a walk, maybe see Ieuan or Pete,' he told his parents, moving off before possible questions. He played with the coins in his pocket and decided to use the phone box on the promenade.

Less chance they'll be occupied, he thought. And less chance of anyone seeing him there. He couldn't explain why, but being on his own and unseen were important.

He walked down past the front entrance to the school and turned left to go under the railway bridge, only yards from the station shelter where he and Bethan... Never mind that, he told himself, nervousness increasing. He rattled the coins in his jeans pocket again and felt his stomach churning. Past the Bay Hotel, and the road leading to the sprawling estate of flats and tiny bungalows inhabited by ageing Brummies. He smelt the salt air but heard no pounding of waves. Tide must be out, he thought.

He turned left by the row of seafront houses, tall, solid and battered by decades of onshore westerlies and spray, then saw the two adjacent phone boxes, both empty, one lit, one in darkness. A car went slowly past, pulsating with the muffled beat of music, several heads outlined by orange street lights. A nearly full moon ghosted in and out of the clouds, glinting silvery light on the restrained and distant sea.

He stopped by the darkened, red lattice booth, his nervousness leaving a bitter taste in his mouth. Christ, get on with it, he muttered. He shivered and heaved open the heavy red door. Was the phone working? Yes. He took two sixpences out of his pocket and put them on the metal shelf.

He dialled. The metal circle clicked rapidly back, each number bringing her nearer. He noticed dusty cobwebs in the corner, visible in the faint light from the nearby lamp-post. With each double *burr-burr,* his stomach seemed to tighten more and more. He closed his eyes, gripping the receiver hard.

'Tywyn four-seven-eight.'

A female. Not Melanie. Too old. Mother – must be.

'Er, is Melanie there please?' What will she say now?

A very brief but noticeable pause before: 'I think she's still in. Who's calling?'

The same sort of English accent as Mel... With an effort, he managed to say his name.

'Oh, just a moment.' A slight change of tone, less neutral somehow. He heard the phone being clunked down on something, a pause, and then the sound of a door shutting, and silence.

A car sped past, its headlights dazzling him for a second. He rested his left elbow on the metal window frame, almost feeling sick, and closed his eyes tightly. 'Just come to the phone. All you have to do is *speak* to me.'

And then a low, cautious 'Hello... '

'Mel?'

'Yes.' She sounded restrained, distant.

'Hi. Er, I just had to call. Mel, I need to see you, to talk.'

'Are you sure you want to see *me*?'

'*Course* I am.' He breathed deeply. 'Mel, you've got to believe I miss you one helluvalot and whatever you think about me, us, well, I just want to see you and... get things sorted.'

Silence. He heard a door shut.

'Why didn't you talk to me on the train, then?'

'Mel, I didn't see you till you were getting off! I got on after you, in Aberdyfi.'

'I noticed.' Another pause. 'Are you sure you've got *time* to see me with all your political activities these days?'

Geraint groaned. For God's sake, he thought. What a stupid thing to say. Then out loud: 'An occasional Plaid Cymru meeting, a couple of afternoons door-knocking. Anyway, I've *had* to keep busy – it takes my mind off... off missing you.'

'Anna's here.'

'Well, get rid of her!' Geraint breathed the words slowly, deliberately, distinctly.

Pause. 'All right. Where shall I see you?'

Suddenly his stomach seemed to unknot itself. 'Anywhere! Say, the Talyllyn, just down by Wharf station, by the booking office.' It wasn't well lit, not far from her house... 'As soon as you can.'

'Yes, OK.' And the phone clicked into silence.

He put down the receiver and pushed hard against the door. He breathed the fresh, salt-laden air deeply. Now, he thought, let's get there quickly and stop this feuding, and sod her parents' block on them.

He walked quickly along the promenade and headed for the two dark, barrack-like buildings at the end. Between them, a narrow road led away from the beach and directly to the meeting place.

What if? Well, what if she changed her mind or what if her parents stopped her or...? 'Oh shut up,' he told himself. He hurried along the dark, narrow road, puffing a bit. A sheep poked its head over the dry stone wall on his right. Others silently munched, heads down, shaggy silhouettes. On the other side, ranks of empty caravans.

He passed the school playing fields on the right and with a return of his earlier tension strode over the main line railway bridge. There. The darkened Talyllyn buildings on the right. Had she arrived? Two cars zoomed past on the main road, but there was no one waiting or walking up and down. Yes, he reflected, another wild, let-it-all-hang-out Saturday night in swinging Tywyn. Still, I'll settle for her head on my shoulder. Excitement enough after this afternoon.

He went down the short, steep drive to the single-storey

building that formed the headquarters and booking office of the narrow-gauge railway. No one. Cursing, he wandered around to make sure she wasn't on the platform or lurking in shadows. Then he leant back against the door and tried to force himself to be patient.

Turning round, he stared at the darkened model railway track in the window, the tiny locomotive and captive carriages lifeless by the frozen figures on the platform, forever waiting, unable to go anywhere even when children dropped a coin in to send the trains obediently round until the current died.

Feeling desperate, he wheeled round and walked as fast as he could, turning right onto Brynhyfryd Road to cut the distance she had to walk. And then suddenly he saw her. It had to be. He knew the outline, the gait.

They stopped about a foot from each other, her face hidden in the shadows. She said, 'Hi,' and stood, as hesitant as Geraint. He noticed she was wearing her flared jeans and navy duffle coat. He said, 'Hello,' and, indicating with his thumb the way he'd come, added, 'shall we walk this way?'

They ambled, not touching, side by side but silent and with what Geraint felt might as well be a mile-wide gap. All his fluency seemed to have evaporated. He had no experience of repairing collapsed bridges between himself and a girl he loved.

When they reached the Talyllyn corner, he said, 'We might as well go down there, it's sort of private.' She nodded and followed him down to the corner, by the door.

Self-consciously, they stood by the wall, and neither spoke, each bursting with accusations and questions and self-righteousness, waiting for the other to surrender. Eventually Melanie uttered a scarcely heard 'So?'

Geraint swallowed and said, 'You said you'd get to work

on your parents to remove the ban on us going out, and that I should leave you alone to let you have time to do it your own way. So I did. And I miss you and it's been ages – and you've said nothing to me.'

She didn't answer for a few seconds while appearing to examine her shoes. Her voice was flat, matter-of-fact. 'I saw you and that… other girl going to the station – joined at the hip. Hope you enjoyed yourselves.'

'That, that was nothing, I mean nothing serious. I saw her that one night and that was that. It's no big thing.'

'Not what *I'd* heard.'

'What d'you mean?'

'You and her. Going out several times, keeping it secret, or so you thought.'

'That's all lies! Who told you?'

'Oh someone. A fifth-form girl.'

'Well it's not true!' Silence. 'Mel, you've got to believe me.'

'Have I?'

'Yes – it was a spur of the moment thing, and even when I was with her, I thought of *you*, missed *you*.' He mentally shook off the fleeting memory of Bethan's beautiful breasts. He looked into the shadow of Mel's face. 'I took her to the caff, then. Anyway, it was just the one night.'

'And the station?'

'Yeah well, there was nowhere else to go. It's over.'

'Why would someone lie to me?'

He snorted. 'Oh come on, Mel! You know this town, the blabber-mouths and mischief-makers. They're just stirrers. D'you believe me?'

She sighed and looked down. 'Yes, I suppose so.'

Geraint willed her to look at him and not at her feet.

Instinctively he put his hand under her chin and gently raised her head until their eyes met. She moved forward at the same moment as he did and they hugged tightly, Geraint burying his face in her soft, fragrant ocean of brown hair. Then he put his hands on her shoulders and they kissed as he moved to caress the back of her head. It was a tender, slow, gentle searching of each other's lips, mouths and real feelings. As they moved apart their hands met, their faces still close.

Chapter 4

S HE RUBBED HER nose against his for a second. 'I *have* missed you, you know!' She seemed to be smiling, thought Geraint, but he felt her warm tears on his cheek. 'You're a brute.'

'Hey, why? What have I done?'

'Oh, I dunno. Bethan, ignoring me all the time, you and your Plaid Cymru meetings.'

Geraint said quietly, 'You told me to ignore you – until… '

'Maybe I did – *then*. But I hoped you'd, well, sort of forget that and talk to me.' She shook her head, sniffed and then smiled again, wiping her cheeks with her hand. She let go of Geraint, undid her duffle coat and Geraint moved forward, putting his hands round her waist and inside the coat. He hugged her and felt an inner warmth he hadn't enjoyed for a long time. 'Come on, Ger – let's go.' She dragged him towards the road.

'Where?'

'Oh, what's it matter? The moon, Saturn, Chipping Sodbury.'

They walked on in silence but more or less at peace, with Geraint beginning to feel that familiar stirring in the groin.

They soon found themselves on the deserted, windswept beach. By silent consent, they turned left onto the soft, dry sand. Each knew they were heading for the spot where they had met by chance on that first night, weeks before.

'No mad dog this time,' said Geraint, laughing.

'My dog's not mad! Pankhurst is lying by the fire, all snug.

I should've brought her with me – she could bite you if you misbehave.'

The clouds had rolled away, and Geraint shivered in the colder air. They plodded through the sand until they reached a wide hollow which they slithered down. He put his arm round her as they sat, immobile silhouettes. He stared up at a billion flickering stars, distant suns, some, thought Geraint, already dead, exploded into nothingness – or was it black holes? No sound of the sea reached them. No breath of wind stirred the spikes of grass that ringed their cold hollow.

Still with her head against him, Melanie asked quietly, 'Ger, why were we so stupid, wasting all that time apart and everything?'

He didn't answer. He couldn't help a tinge of resentment at the 'we' but didn't want to create disharmony again. However, his feelings got the better of his restraint and he said, equally quietly, '*We*? I was waiting for *you*. It was your parents who didn't want me round you.'

Melanie sat up and put her hand on his knee. 'Yes, well.' She ran her other hand through his hair. 'It wasn't easy. I left it a few days and then hinted that I'd like to invite you round. So they'd see you were, well, ordinary, no, I mean, OK, not... well, what they think you are.'

To Geraint she seemed flustered and unusually incoherent. 'What *do* they think I am?' he asked, staring ahead at the rim of their small, sandy world.

Melanie sighed. She removed her hand from his hair and seemed to stiffen. 'You know – a big nationalist, hating the English and so on.'

For a few seconds, Geraint didn't speak. Then he said thoughtfully, 'But I suppose I *am* a nationalist now.'

'Well, maybe – but not sort of *extreme*, the way they think you are.' She leant against him and felt for his hand. 'I suppose if there hadn't been so much publicity for what you did in school... '

Geraint laughed. 'Yeah, and ably helped by you – what I did, I mean.' He kissed her gently. 'So go on. What else have they said about me?'

Melanie moved her hand, perhaps nervously, he sensed, down to his knee. 'They were *awful* – just wouldn't change their minds. And to make it worse, and this is what *really* annoyed me, wouldn't even *discuss* it all. I mean, we've always discussed things we disagree about.' She took her hand off his knee, and picked up a handful of dry, soft sand, letting it trickle through her fingers, and then repeated the action. 'And I kept hoping that as time went on, I would get them in a good mood and they'd see it my way, but they didn't, and rabbited on just like, well, "ordinary" parents. Oh that sounds silly, I know, but I mean ones who don't, who never discuss things the way we did. I didn't want to go against them, but I wanted *you*. I thought that if you came round and knocked, Mummy at least would be courteous and then they'd *have* to be nice to you.'

She sat motionless. Less resentful, Geraint said, 'Well why didn't you say all this to me in school?'

She answered with a touch of annoyance, 'Oh, I don't know. I didn't want to be pushing you. And you seemed so bitter and distant, and you were playing football with that Pete and the others sometimes.' She paused, and then added angrily: 'I don't *know* why I didn't talk to you! But why didn't *you*? You could have sat next to me in English.'

'Mel! You told me to leave you in peace until... '

He leant back and put his hands under his head. Melanie leant over and lay close to him, whispering in his ear, 'I *was* going to say something only I saw you with Bethan that night.'

Geraint said nothing, staring at the stars. 'How come you agreed tonight?' he asked eventually.

'Mummy said you were on the phone and that I should tell you not to ring again or bother us at all. I didn't say anything, but I felt sort of excited – even though I might not have seemed it when I saw you. Anyway, when I came off the phone, I just said I was going out to meet you. They tried to stop me. Oh not physically, just trying to forbid me, then warning me I'd be getting involved with extremists. Anna told me I was silly bothering with you and went off in a huff.' She lightly kissed his cheek.

Any resentment Geraint had been feeling was now draining rapidly away. All he cared about was that they were together, and that simple, quick kiss meant a lot to him. 'So you just walked out, then – like I did when I told Mum and Dad I'd joined Plaid Cymru and was going to my first branch meeting. I was quite surprised how easy it was. I was shaking, you know. I'd never really defied them before. And since then, they've made the odd sarcastic remark about my politics, though Mum's been fairly OK lately – even gave me £1 this morning. You remember Dad stopped my pocket money after "The Incident".'

Melanie laughed, and snuggled closer to him. 'Dad said he'd "seriously consider" stopping my allowance if I went out tonight.' Almost wistfully, she added: 'They scarcely ever have rows, but they seemed to be beginning one when I went out. I think Mum was trying to speak up for me, but Daddy wouldn't have it.'

Parents! thought Geraint with exasperation. He wished he had the courage to slide his hands inside her T-shirt but, thinking it was too risky, restrained himself. 'Where were you going this morning?'

'To Aber, with Anna. Had a look in some clothes shops but didn't really see anything I wanted. Anna bought some things, and then we had a burger and chips.' She put her head on his chest and he felt almost intoxicated by the fragrance and softness of her hair. 'So where were you off to then?'

He groaned inwardly. 'This morning?'

'Yes – on the train.'

'Oh, a Welsh nash meeting as you'd call it.' He tried to laugh.

Melanie was silent then seemed to shiver. 'Come on, it's getting cold. Let's walk back.'

She stood up and heaved Geraint to his feet. He felt disappointed, deprived, but then told himself not to be so selfish. The physical side could wait. He had achieved a lot that night.

As they clambered up the slope, she went on: 'You're spending an awful lot of time on this Plaid Cymru, aren't you? I mean, before that day in school, you couldn't give a damn about politics.'

'I suppose so,' he said, feeling guilty at having deceived her.

'Don't you think, well, it's a bit of a waste? Don't get me wrong. I'm not against people speaking Welsh and having rights and so on, but a Welsh government and all that. It's just never going to happen. I mean, you could be doing something in *real* politics, to change things through parliament, like Labour is doing.'

They walked slowly along the firmer sand, hand in hand. Geraint wasn't sure how to explain why he was becoming more involved. 'I suppose it's partly respect, self-respect.

If you're Welsh, you stick up for your country.' He fell silent, wanting to say more, groping for ideas. And then he remembered a little booklet the branch secretary had given him when he joined. 'Why should little countries like Ireland, Norway, Denmark, Luxembourg, et cetera, even the Isle of Man, have a parliament – and not us?'

'But Wales couldn't survive without England.'

'I don't agree.' Geraint didn't know how to prove this, but he felt it irrelevant. If Wales had a parliament the rest would follow. 'Come on, Mel – let's drop it for now. Tonight's... sort of special.'

They stopped walking and Melanie said yes and put her arms round his waist. They locked each other in a long, passionate kiss, a single silhouette on the silvery beach. Only their tongues moved, gently.

They broke off and breathed deeply.

'Mel, I love you.' The words were whispered and Geraint felt a strange exultation. He had never told a girl this before – though, he reflected almost ruefully, there had never been anyone else who obsessed him as she did. Even now, he was afraid: afraid the words sounded too corny, too sentimental and cheapened. Melanie deserved the best and surely there was a more impressive way of saying it. But he couldn't think of one.

Melanie hugged him tighter and whispered, 'Oh Ger. I love you too.'

Nor had anyone said this to him before. 'You're not just saying it?' he asked, immediately regretting it.

'Course not! I'm not in the habit of saying this to every lad I meet, you know.' Geraint was grateful she sounded amused rather than exasperated. Sensing his doubts, she added, 'I love you, fathead – and don't forget it!'

They walked slowly and reluctantly back towards the world of homes and sanctions and prejudice and ordinariness. As they were passing the Caravan Club, two headlights stabbed the darkness and a vehicle stopped by them. It was a green Land Rover with Forestry Commission markings. A head poked through the driver's window, and a familiar Yorkshire voice boomed: 'That you, Geraint?'

He peered into the lights and then realised. 'Yes, Mr Barraclough… Mike.'

'Thought I recognised you! How's life?'

Geraint and Melanie moved across to the open window. 'Er, fine. Just been to the club?'

'Yes, thought I'd try it. Bit of a hole, although at least it's open on Sundays.' He gave a short laugh. 'Perhaps even the pubs will after the referendum.'

'Huh. Mam says there's no way people here will vote for that!'

'Mebbe. Oh, by the way, saw you in Machynlleth earlier today.'

Geraint's heart began pounding. 'Yes?'

'Yes. By the clock tower. You were getting into the back of a Land Rover. That bloke with you, bearded, well built, who was he?'

'Oh, er, I don't remember his name.'

Mike paused. 'Thought I knew him. But it couldn't have been. Probably just a look-alike. Anyway, must get back. All the best. Night to you.'

He roared off. Geraint hoped in vain that Melanie would not probe.

'Why were you getting into a Land Rover?' she asked, as they moved off down the dark lane.

'Just a lift to the meeting.'

'Oh. Who was he, the man we've just seen?'

'Mike Barraclough. In our branch of Plaid Cymru. Works for the Forestry and lives in Pennal. Single guy I think. Was in the army before. Bit odd, isn't it, now working for the Forestry?'

Melanie didn't answer, but then said, 'Sounds English.'

'He is. Just goes to show, doesn't it?'

'What?'

'*Some* bloody English have bloody sense.'

'Ha ha.'

Geraint remembered his own surprise at coming across a Yorkshire accent at a Plaid Cymru meeting. And yet Mike had shown an impressive knowledge of Welsh politics and had learnt enough of the language to follow most of the proceedings. And then it occurred to him: is Melanie wondering why I was going to a Plaid Cymru meeting when a fellow member knew nothing about it? He drove it out of his mind and concentrated on the present.

They headed for Melanie's house. Walking slowly, sometimes chatting, sometimes just holding hands and enjoying silent, tranquil togetherness through soft, warm fingers. As they neared the house, they slowed and then stopped.

'Scared?' asked Geraint.

'A bit.'

'I'll wait here till you've gone in.'

'OK.'

They hugged and Geraint felt not a tingle of lust this time. He wanted to have her warm, comforting body next to his forever. Just to feel her security, to breathe her perfume and hair.

'Tomorrow?' he asked quietly.

'Yes.'

'When?'

'Say twelve o'clock? Talyllyn?'

'Yes. Unless I see you before you reach it.'

'*Nos da, cariad.*'

Geraint kissed her quickly; she touched his cheek lightly with her hand and then opened the ornate metal gate. Geraint stood back but watched her go up to the front door. She turned and waved, then inserted her key before disappearing into the darkness.

He stood there for five minutes. No light or sound. The lounge was at the back, he remembered. And Melanie's bedroom. He turned and crossed over the road, heading home. What a day, he reflected, what a day. Whatever is happening to this unconfident lad who was content to do his A-levels, be obedient to his parents and for whom politics was one long yawn? he wondered. If anyone had told me six months ago, *three* months ago, that today I would have...

Chapter 5

ON THE SUNDAY, Geraint completely forgot about the significance of the approaching Wednesday with its need for The Answer. All that mattered was that he and Melanie were back together.

He had woken late, about 9.30. He lay there and couldn't at first comprehend the strange mood of pleasure, undefined and shadowy as though he had just jerked awake from a delicious dream. Then with elation he remembered the previous evening.

That afternoon they enjoyed a stroll in the sunshine, then agreed that they ought to try to get down to some homework. As Melanie said, she didn't want her parents to have any genuine excuse to stop the relationship.

On Monday, he cursed the tradition of the two sexes occupying separate halves of the assembly hall. From time to time he turned to peer through the frustrating forest of heads, seeking her, aching for her hand in his.

Willoughby-Smythe, the deputy head, took assembly in the unexplained absence of Caradog, the head. As he couldn't speak Welsh, after the hymn he merely announced, '*Ein Tad...* ' to introduce the Lord's Prayer, then mouthed an approximation of the rest as everyone recited.

When he had finished announcing the weekend sports results, the deputy head blinked behind his large spectacles and said, 'And now it gives me great pleasure to announce an exciting competition open to all of you.' Someone near Geraint groaned. He went on: 'The Post Office has launched a special competition for the design of a first-day cover, that is, envelope, for the Investiture next year.'

From several parts of the hall, but mainly from each end where the older pupils stood, came groans and hisses. A surprising number, thought Geraint, who had restricted himself to a silent obscenity.

'Er, may I remind you this is still assembly?'

The undercurrent of noise and shuffling slowly receded like a tired ebb tide, and silence re-asserted itself. The deputy head went on to give details and to invite everyone to see either himself or the art teacher, an Englishman called Bradman, for entry forms and leaflets.

Just in front of Geraint, Ieuan said loudly: '*Brâd*!' Geraint laughed, the word being Welsh for 'treachery'. As they slouched off to the library, where the sixth form registered, to get their books for first lesson, Ieuan said in Welsh to Geraint, 'There you are, Ger. You used to be a dab-hand at art. A chance for you to glorify our great prince.'

Despite recognising the teasing nature of the remark, Geraint was surprised at how the idea made him angry. He was sure he wouldn't have felt like this if the announcement had been made a few months ago. Now he felt incensed at what he thought of as the entanglement of children in the political, pseudo-sacred, so-called patriotic event planned for 1969... or so he seemed to remember Llŷr describing it recently.

A nudge in the ribs suddenly made his eyes re-focus and his mind tumble down to the here-and-now – Melanie, to whom he gave what he thought must be an embarrassed smile. They collected their books and headed for the English room and a lesson in which Geraint could not give his usual concentration – not easy with Melanie's mini-skirt high up on her thighs, her leg rubbing against his and her hand occasionally wandering.

They restricted themselves to school-time togetherness and walking back towards Melanie's house. Neither wanted to do badly in the Christmas exams, but, while he toiled away at his bedroom desk on Monday and Tuesday evenings, he yearned for her presence.

He had not told his parents about Saturday night and being back with her, but if they asked, he wouldn't hide it either. Meanwhile, his father barely acknowledged him and his parents' verbal duelling continued with sickening regularity, often over what seemed to him to be utter trivia. He sympathised with his mother, but wished she knew when to keep quiet and not goad his father into further flames of bad temper.

Now and again on those evenings, however, Geraint's attention wandered to Wednesday's decision. What had he to lose by saying yes? They'd given him a choice as to how active he wanted to be, how publicly he could make his membership known. After all, he would still be a civilian, a free agent, and no one outside LAW need even know he was a member. And with a satisfying love life, the tranquillity on that front made him more inclined to get involved. Life was opening up to him. New horizons, experiences, achievements.

Wednesday arrived. At afternoon registration, Geraint and Mel sat on the window sill in one of the library's book bays. They chatted, holding hands, most of the time oblivious of their surroundings and the buzz of conversation. But just before the bell went, while they sat silently, something made Geraint aware of a female voice near him. She was hidden by intervening bookshelves, but the words were clear: 'God, those two look happy.' And another voice, also female, added:

'Yeah, why not? Like father, like son.' Then he missed a few words, but picked up, '… the other day… and in a parked car, too. At his age!' Then the bell went and hubbub reigned supreme.

He looked quickly at Melanie but she obviously hadn't heard and was gazing dreamily out of the window behind them while stroking his ear. His face felt hot, his stomach sick. Could it really have been a reference to… ? No, surely not. He realised the first speaker was someone he didn't get on well with: Tina Johnson – flash, sexy in a cheap, obvious way and loud-mouthed.

In a daze he collected his books, smiled mechanically at Mel and they went their separate ways.

After school, he saw Melanie back to her house and then returned home, still turning over in his mind what the girls had said. No one was in and he munched chocolate biscuits, flopping in his father's fireside chair. He had switched on the TV and was half watching some inane puppet programme when the phone rang. Still watching the screen, he automatically went over and picked up the phone, saying hello.

A male voice. 'Geraint?'

'Yes.'

'El Ay double-u. Yes? Or no?'

'Er, yes.'

Click. Silence. And suddenly the realisation exploded. He was a member of the Liberation Army of Wales. He had expected the call later; in fact, for some reason, he had thought it would have come at about ten or eleven o'clock. He had not recognised the voice – certainly not a Scouse accent, anyway.

For a minute he leant against the sideboard, hands in pockets, grinning. Why wasn't there someone there who could congratulate him? He wanted to shout, 'I'm in! I'm in!' He wanted people to slap him on the back. He wanted 'his' Luger in his grip, he wanted to don the uniform – to hell with secrecy, he thought – and to march behind the *Draig Goch* whipped by the wind, the drum beat hypnotic, the crowds lining the pavement, adoring (especially the girls), the teenage lads jealous.

He wondered about going to see Llŷr but remembered he would still be at work and, in any case, might be annoyed at this breach of his precious security. He wandered around the house, unable to decide what to do, overawed by his own *yes*. Eventually he lay on his bed, hands under head, and stared upwards, although not really seeing the ceiling. The day melted into swirling fantasies of sex and guns until, exhausted, he sank into a deep sleep.

The next day he still felt strange – not least because he had to guard his tongue from even hinting at what had happened. As he walked towards the school entrance, he smiled as he thought how bizarre it was to be soon sitting in the library for registration and then behind a desk to listen to a teacher, while at the same time being a member of LAW, destroyer of pipelines, embryo army of a free Wales, target of savage and vitriolic attacks by Labour and Tory politicians.

After assembly, his mate Pete asked him why he was going around with a silly bloody grin on his face. He thumped Geraint on the back as they ambled towards the library, saying with a leer, 'Oh come on, Ger, you've finally done it… with Melanie?'

They squeezed through the double doors, Geraint trying to think of a suitable reply and being saved by Willoughby-Smythe coughing and hesitantly asking for attention. As they all perched on chairs, pipes and tables, he went on to tell them that he had a supply of Post Office first-day cover competition forms and leaflets. To Geraint's surprise, the deputy head asked him, in front of everyone, to distribute them and try to get younger kids to support it.

Geraint was taken aback and was instinctively going to take the proffered pile and say 'Yes Sir, three bags full Sir' when he girded his mental loins, remembered what he was now a member of, and quietly but firmly said, 'Sorry Sir, but I'd rather not get involved.'

A second's silence was followed by a 'Very good!' in Welsh from Gwenllian, the head girl, sitting at the central tables. Next to her, Catrin nodded, smiling agreement at him. Willoughby-Smythe looked at Geraint, blinking owlishly. Whatever he was thinking, it didn't show. Geraint wondered if he was going to try to force him – and what the result of his continued refusal would be. His blood seethed, his stomach churned and he sat, tense and rigid. It reminded him of that famous incident earlier in the term, the one that had set in train a chain of events he could never have envisaged. But Willoughby looked away, his gaze fell on Anna, Mel's friend, and he asked her if she would be willing. Of course Sir, yes, six bags full Sir. And Geraint's tension oozed away.

As he turned away, he saw Melanie looking at him. She slowly shook her head and said quietly, 'Oh, Ger.' Then she went away to talk to Anna. Life is not simple, thought Geraint, and he went over to join his mate Ieuan who was sitting with the diminutive Siân. They both congratulated him and his spirits lifted somewhat.

'What would you have done if Willoughby had insisted?' asked Ieuan in Welsh, perched on the central-heating pipes under the window.

Geraint shook his head. 'I just don't know. I suppose I would have insisted I was having nothing to do with it, whatever he said.'

'And then?' asked Siân.

'Who knows?' answered Geraint, shrugging his shoulders and staring over their heads out of the window. He wished he could share his secret with them and explain all about LAW.

'Wonder why he specially asked *you* to organise this?' asked Siân, slowly.

Chapter 6

THAT EVENING, CLOSETED in his bedroom, Geraint finished an A-level essay on a play by Saunders Lewis, learnt a couple of quotes from Chaucer's *Prologue* and then flopped onto the bed. Putting his hands under his head, he stared at the ceiling.

He recalled his first, nervous day as a sixth former, worried about whether he could cope with the A-level courses, whether he could conjure up the appearance of authority to boss little kids around. My God, he reflected, if that was all he had to worry about now. Suddenly he realised with satisfaction that he *was* coping with both demands – and more vast problems and issues now took possession of his head.

He would never forget that Friday, 11 October, not long before half-term. Just a simple request from his Welsh teacher, Medwyn Thomas. Geraint had been sitting quietly in the library during morning registration when Medwyn had suddenly appeared. He looked round as though seeking someone suitable, and the next thing Geraint knew was that he was to take a note to 2C's registration room and read it out. He had groaned, knowing how shy he was at having to disturb other classes, standing there with sixty or more eyes fastened on him.

He had wormed his way through a group of sixth formers blocking the doorway. Kids of various ages, also on messages, genuine or spurious, ambled along the corridor. Through the frosted glass windows of the classrooms, he was aware of distorted silhouettes of chattering pupils, enjoying the last few minutes before lesson one.

He walked past the women's tiny, crowded staff room, the head's office, his secretary's office next door, and then arrived at the geography room, 2C's registration room. He paused, swallowed nervously and opened the door of the high ceilinged room. It was one of the few that did not have old-fashioned oak desks with tip-up seats. There was a restrained hum of conversation from the thirty or so pupils.

Geraint realised that the regular teacher, Aled Price, was not there, and registering the class was Mrs Archer, a supply teacher who sometimes came in to cover for absent staff. She and her husband had not long moved to the area from London and had opened a pottery somewhere in the hills. She was in her late thirties, Geraint guessed, with long, lank brown hair and a thin-lipped air of resentment that made him slightly wary, even though he had never come into contact with her before.

As the note was in Welsh, he assumed this was why Medwyn had asked him to read it out rather than give it to her. He noticed someone standing at the back of the room and talking to two girls sitting at the corner table. Oh no, he groaned inwardly, Melanie, also a sixth former. Why does she have to be here selling her blasted raffle tickets now?

In English, Geraint said, 'Miss, Mr Thomas asked me to announce something to the class about the Urdd.'

Mrs Archer continued to write figures in spaces at the bottom of the register page, as though he were not there. 'The *what*?' she asked with asperity.

'The Urdd, Miss. Welsh League of Youth. You know, the eisteddfod, Llangrannog and all that.'

'Oh get on with it then,' she snapped, and began to rummage in her bamboo-handled shopping bag on the floor.

Geraint groaned again, hoping she would have quietened

the class for him. He hated reading out messages. He hated speaking in public. He hated having a spotlight of any kind on him. His shyness was unreasonable but powerful, and not yet shaken off, despite his being a prefect. He tried to speak out loud, 'Er...' but his voice cracked and no one seemed to listen as the buzz of conversation continued.

He waited, nonplussed. Mrs Archer suddenly looked up and raised her voice: '*Quiet* everyone. This person has a message about something.' There was just a hint of sarcastic emphasis on the last word.

Conjuring up some courage and hoping he wasn't blushing, Geraint raised his voice to try to be heard at the back and read from the piece of paper: '*Neges i bawb sy'n mynd i Langrannog y flwyddyn nesa. Wnewch chi...*' He got no further.

'Young man!' This was accompanied by the flat of Mrs Archer's hand slapping down on the table. 'What do you think you're doing?'

Geraint looked down at her, seeing her long face poking towards him angrily, the hand still flat on the table. He noticed her fingernails, cut short – no, bitten – and unvarnished. 'Er, what d'you mean, Miss?'

'What do you *think* I mean? I will not have you or anyone else coming into my registration room and jabbering something to my class in that foreign language when you *know* I don't understand it.'

Her rather sharp nose seemed to be quivering. She held the Biro she'd taken from her handbag as though it were a dart about to be thrown. Geraint felt as though he was undergoing a bad dream; her reaction was so unexpected and bizarre that he remembered the tiny calm bit of his mind assuming that she must be under some sort of emotional strain. Perhaps the pottery was going bankrupt.

He was conscious of the hushed class, faces staring at the welcome drama during the normally boring session before lesson one. He felt his face colouring and growing hot. He looked again at the note he held, a page torn from an exercise book, with Medwyn's familiar curly writing. 'But, Miss, the note is in Welsh and Mr Thomas Welsh asked me to read it out.' He shifted feet and looked at Mrs Archer, whose knuckles had gone white – as had the end of her nose.

'If you don't have the common courtesy to speak English in front of me, I'm sure I can ask the headmaster to knock some... some *politeness*, some *decency*, into you. Because your parents have certainly failed.'

Geraint remained silent, thoughts swirling, anger mixed with embarrassment and uncertainty as to what to do. Before he could resolve the struggle, he was suddenly aware of someone coming up and standing on his left. Melanie. Someone else with a posh English accent. Was she going to *add* to his crisis? His heart sinking, his spirit drooping, Geraint cleared his throat. Oh well. 'Er, will all members of the Urdd... '

'Stop, Geraint!'

He halted, shocked. It was Melanie, not the teacher, who spoke, her voice firm and confident. He continued to look at his precious piece of paper – at least his hands had something to do.

'Read it in Welsh. You've every *right*.' That refined English voice, just like the teacher's – but was she *defending* him? Melanie?

'I *beg* your pardon?' demanded an astounded Mrs Archer, scraping back her chair and standing up, placing her hands on her bony hips. 'Who do you think you are?' She wore a long smock-like brown dress with two large front pockets.

'Sorry Miss, but Geraint should read it in Welsh.' Melanie's voice was clear, firm, without a quaver. Geraint wondered how she could be so confident and controlled. '2C is a class of Welsh speakers and the notice *is* in Welsh.'

Geraint stole a look at her. She stood near him, a determined look in her brown eyes. His shyness was displaced by bafflement: Why is *she* defending me? They hadn't got on since her first day in school, just over a month ago. Since then, Geraint had avoided her, even though she occasionally spoke to him. He had always assumed that whatever she'd said was a mere prelude to something scathing, so he'd shied away. Oh no, he thought, feeling a sudden hot flush. Surely she's not trying to set me up to get me into even worse trouble; some sort of twisted humour? And then suddenly anger took over as he realised she was saying what *he* should have said, what deep down inside he had *wanted* to say.

He suddenly remembered something else about Mrs Archer, something he'd not bothered about at the time. He had been standing near two little kids waiting to go into her classroom. One had told the other – in Welsh – not to speak Welsh to him in the classroom 'or Miss'll go mad – she won't let us talk Welsh to each other in her lessons.' He felt hot as the adrenaline flowed, his mind made up.

'You… you arrogant little madam!' burst from Mrs Archer's lips. 'Go and see the headmaster at once!'

'If you want, Miss. But there was no need to insult Geraint either. He was just asked to read the note to the class.' She looked at Geraint and said quietly, almost intimately, 'Go on then. Read it out.'

'How dare you!' Mrs Archer slapped the Biro down on the desk and took a step towards Melanie. Geraint thought she was going to hit her.

'Melanie is right,' he said quietly. He began to read loud

and clear: '*Neges i holl aelodau'r Urdd — pawb sy'n mynd i Langrannog y flwyddyn nesa — bydd cyfarfod heddiw yn…* '

'Out! The pair of you!' shouted an incredulous Mrs Archer with a gasp of rage and a threatening gesture, her small breasts trying to heave with emotion beneath her loose smock. 'The headmaster,' she gasped, and pointed at the door.

Geraint looked at the rows of gaping second years' faces, some smiling with glee, others startled and scared.

'Right, come on, Geraint, let's go,' said Melanie, turning towards the door, anger at last vibrating in her voice.

Geraint stood still. The paper shook slightly in his grasp. He stared at it, and with a tremor in his voice, said quietly but audibly in the deathly hush: '*Bydd cyfarfod yn ystafell pedwar.*' He finished the message then followed Melanie out.

Something had happened that had aroused him more than anything ever had. He felt a turmoil of emotions but above all, elation; a sense of triumph and wonder at his own daring, his conquest of nerves and shyness, rather than his usual withdrawal from confrontation. Even much later, he wondered what had galvanised him to rebel so completely. He scarcely heard the clanging of the bell for the beginning of first lesson.

They took but seconds to reach the headmaster's door which opened out directly onto the assembly hall. Geraint felt isolated somehow, almost unaware of his surroundings, the criss-crossing streams of book and bag-laden pupils heading for their first lessons. He vaguely saw Melanie knock on the head's door. His hands were still shaking and he knew he could not speak without a tremor in his voice.

'Come in.'

Melanie opened the door and they squeezed into the small, cramped office.

'Yes?' The head looked up from a pile of opened letters next to the ripped envelopes.

Melanie stood slightly in front of Geraint, who felt he ought to be doing the talking but couldn't now conjure up the courage. He glanced almost surreptitiously at the head's face. Mr Caradog Talbot Jones was glaring, his lined face expressing annoyance at being interrupted at mail time. That morning, he was obviously in a worse temper than usual.

'Er, excuse me, Sir, but Mrs Archer sent us to you.' Melanie paused and turned to look at Geraint, at which he found himself moving to stand closer to her.

'Yes, well, go on.'

Speaking in English for Melanie's sake, he said, 'Sir, Mr Medwyn Thomas asked me to read a message to 2C about the Urdd, and Mrs Archer, who was registering them, told me I had to read it in English.' Geraint knew he was sweating. He stared at a flattened letter on top of a pile in front of the head, trying to read the printed heading. Looking up, he noticed the impatient, puzzled expression on the head's face, and added lamely: 'But I wouldn't.'

Before the head could speak, Melanie added, 'It was my idea, Sir. You see, Mrs Archer was quite insulting to Geraint, and I told him he had the right to read a Welsh message in Welsh.' Her initial firm confidence seemed to have dwindled as she tailed off rather quietly and weakly.

Mr Talbot Jones planted a large Stephens' ink bottle in the middle of his pile of letters. 'Let me get this straight.' His eyes bored into Geraint's, the voice sharp, the words clipped and arrow-headed. 'Mrs Archer told you to read a notice in English. You refused. This young lady,' he paused as though seeking appropriate words, 'this young lady, who has always struck me as being just that, a polite young lady, in the short time she has been with us, aided and abetted this open rebellion. Am I correct?' He glared from one to the other.

'Well,' Melanie said, her voice soft yet determined and firm, 'I wouldn't call it rebellion, Sir, it was… '

'Oh wouldn't you? What would you call it when a sixth former disobeys a direct order from a teacher, inspired or provoked or goaded by another?'

'But she insulted his parents.'

Feeling a growing calmness and almost eerie confidence, Geraint went on before the head could speak: 'Sir, Mrs Archer is only a supply teacher and all the Urdd business, well, except for learners, is done in Welsh.'

'*Only* a supply teacher?! Get this straight, young man. Either you go back to Mrs Archer and apologise, and read the notice in English – I assume you are able to translate it – or… or you are here and now suspended, and the governors can hear all about it.'

Too late, Mr Talbot Jones realised the registration class would have departed and, more importantly, the governing body was not what it had been in those simple years just after the war. 'And you, madam,' he rasped, looking at Melanie, who stood erect and unabashed, 'can apologise also – or you too can join this rebel under suspension until both sets of parents pay us a visit to resolve the matter.'

Silence. Only a few feet behind Geraint and Melanie, children swirled and chattered their way to lessons.

'I'm afraid I can't do what you want – Sir.' Geraint heard himself speak as though listening to a stranger.

'Nor me, Sir.'

The head looked from one to the other, as though in disbelief. 'Very well.' He picked up the top letter and, looking at it, went on: 'You will both go to the library and remain there until I send for you. You will then go home, taking a letter for your parents. And you will remain away from school until further notice.' Mr Talbot Jones, even less enchanted with this Friday morning, pushed his spectacles up his nose and rustled his mail. Too late again, he remembered it was half-term holiday next week.

The two left. Geraint couldn't bring himself to look at Melanie so he turned a corner and headed for the boys' toilets. He locked himself in a cubicle and sat on the seat, his head in his hands. Even seated, he could feel his legs shaking. He brushed away a solitary tear. These things just don't happen to me, he thought bitterly. Other boys were in trouble occasionally, but not me. A lifetime of obedience and deference and conformity, now up the spout. Then, feeling cold and numb and with a knotted stomach, he headed for the library.

Medwyn Thomas had found out by then, of course. He had come blazing into the library to see Geraint, asked him for his version and then told him he was proud of him and would do what he could. This made Geraint feel a little easier. One vital ally. Willoughby-Smythe, deputy head and their form teacher, merely seemed baffled by what he and Melanie had got involved in, and walked off, shaking his head in disbelief.

Geraint had spent a miserable and disconcerting afternoon at home. His mother was out on something to do with one of her many committees and his father was at their shop. It must have been about three when the phone rang. Expecting someone to ask for his mother, he picked it up and was surprised to hear a man ask if he was Geraint Rees. After a stammered yes, he heard the other voice add: 'It's the *Liverpool*

Daily Post here. We understand you have been suspended for speaking Welsh. Is that right?'

'Well, yes, in a way.'

'Can you explain what happened.'

Geraint did his best to relate the details. Eventually it was over and he cursed, recalling things he should have said, details he'd forgotten, a better way he should have explained. Then the implications sank in: not just anyone had asked him what had happened, but a newspaper, and one read by a large percentage of people in the county. And the following morning, it would plop through their own letter box.

He went back into his bedroom and flung himself down. As if it wasn't bad enough being infamous in school. No doubt, he reflected bitterly, they would have been tipped off by that nosey old councillor who lived in the High Street. He acted as local contact and occasionally wrote little articles for not only the *Post* but also the local weekly paper.

He lay there, cursing life and dreading the arrival of his parents, especially his father. Neither of them was particularly political; they were a Welsh-speaking family but his parents did not approve of either Plaid Cymru or Cymdeithas yr Iaith, the Language Society, and his father followed the tradition of being an independent member of the town council and was very conscious of his dignity. As far as he could work out from occasional comments, at election time his mother would vote Liberal and his father Labour. As for Plaid Cymru, they seemed to regard them as being in the same league as the IRA, the Vietcong and Yasser Arafat's Palestine Liberation Organisation.

His mother came in first. He groaned as she asked before even closing the back door: 'Geraint, love, what's this I hear? Mrs Roberts Adfa says she was told you've been suspended, or expelled, I'm not sure which, for insulting teachers who don't speak Welsh, swearing and causing a fuss, refusing to apologise and some sixth-form girls are mixed up in it too. And this just doesn't sound like you.'

He tried his best to explain while she emptied shopping bags in the kitchen and clucked around him, asking worried questions that proved to him she was only half taking in what he was saying. He didn't mention the *Daily Post* or the subsequent phone calls from BBC Cymru and Harlech Television. Eventually he shocked her by losing his temper and yelling, 'Mam, will you shut up and sit down and listen!'

In sheer surprise, she obeyed, and, feeling even more guilty for shouting at her when he noticed how tired she looked, he explained and she read the letter suspending him until the governors met to consider the matter. He pointed out that at least they had now broken up for a week's half-term holiday, so that it might be sorted out ready for school re-opening.

His mother sighed, and patted her permed, brown hair. 'Well, love, I don't know what your father will say. I can't imagine he'll be overjoyed, I mean he does have a position in the town as councillor. He has to work with all the councillors and go to County Hall and he and the headmaster are both in the Rotary and then there's the Chamber of Trade, I mean you ought to think of these things before you go off being silly about the language.'

'Mam, I… '

'I mean the next thing you'll be daubing road signs and getting arrested with Cymdeithas yr Iaith and then where will your studies be? And you hoping to go to university and me having to face the other women on the WI county committee, to say nothing of the hospital League of Friends.'

By the time his father came home, he had heard it as a brief item on the Welsh television news. There was nothing said by his father, but his face was sufficient warning of impending typhoons. They had pecked at their meal, a restrained affair accompanied by sparse and brittle small talk, and Geraint assumed his father had warned his mother to 'leave it to him'.

When his mother had cleared the table and disappeared to the kitchen, the storm began with a gentle but ominous gust, just enough to scatter torn bits of newspaper and send inn signs creaking. His father had enthroned himself in his armchair by the fire, newspaper on lap, and listened impassively to his halting explanation. As always, they were speaking in Welsh. When he finished, his father said harshly, 'But if all you had to do was read a notice in English – and it would have been easy to translate – why didn't you do it, and then everyone would have been happy? I mean it's so simple.'

Geraint gripped the top of the settee and looked at his father's annoyed, baffled face. 'But in a way, Dad, it's not so simple. She insulted my upbringing and, anyway, what right does she have to *force* everyone, well me, to read it in English, and them to listen to it? It was a teacher's note, and about the Urdd.'

His father slapped the paper against his knee and thundered, 'I've met Mrs Archer, and I don't believe she would insult anyone; it seems to have been the other way round.' He glared at Geraint. 'And it doesn't matter *what* the note was about! You are there to do what teachers tell you, to learn obedience. Mrs Archer *is* a teacher. I mean you *can* speak English and the class *can* understand it, so what's the problem?'

'Jesus!' Geraint hadn't meant to say it, and his father got up and faced him.

'Don't you indulge in profane language in this house! How dare you!'

Geraint fought back the instinct to apologise, to grovel and retreat in the way that he normally did when assailed by paternal wrath. Straightening his back, he noticed how he was now a half inch or so taller than his father. He even managed to meet his severe gaze without flinching, and noticed how his hair seemed greyer than it used to be and receding further. 'Sorry,' Geraint conceded, more because he felt sorry that his father was so blind to the truth, the implications. 'You just don't understand.'

His father turned away and stood with his back to the fire. 'Someone put you up to this. It's not the sort of thing *you* would do on your own. I never bring politics into the home and it shouldn't be brought into school either.' Though he still sounded angry, he seemed to Geraint to have lost a little of the sharpness and aggression, as though for the first time he realised his son was not going to be cowed by the usual tactics.

Geraint came from behind the settee and sat on the edge of the table. '*No* one put me up to it,' he said with exasperation. 'I *was* going to read it in English, until Melanie made me realise. Or because I'd been too shy, too chicken, to stick up for my rights.'

'Oh yes,' put in his father, hands deep in pockets, 'there's a girl in this too. What part does *she* play in all this?'

His mother came in from the kitchen and silently began to tidy things on top of the sideboard.

'All she did was have the guts to speak up for me and, well, somehow I felt I wasn't going to give in to some old English woman who'd just moved here and thought she could order us to speak English.'

His father frowned and looked as though he was going to issue another blast on respect for teachers. However, in a quieter tone, he asked, 'Who is this Melanie, anyway?'

'Melanie Wilson. She's in the sixth form doing English with me. They live in one of those big houses on the Aberdyfi road the opposite side to the hospital. You probably know her father. Accountant in town.'

His father looked surprised and his mother stopped fiddling and looked at Geraint, obviously realising whom he meant.

'Yes. Clive Wilson,' said his father thoughtfully. 'But they're English! They've only lived here for five or six years. He's in the Rotary with me.'

His mother rearranged the apples in the fruit bowl and said fussily, 'Well, Geraint, I think you ought to write a letter of apology to this teacher and to the headmaster and your father can see the head and try and smooth things over.'

'No!' Geraint moved away from the table and put his hands deep in his jeans pockets. 'There's nothing to apologise *for*! If anyone should apologise, it's *her*! Even Medwyn, Mr Thomas, just said to me afterwards, "Well done lad."'

His father snorted and picked up the *Daily Post*. 'Well, I didn't think *he* was one of the Welsh nash teachers. I mean I know some of the teachers, and far too many are Welsh nash and bring politics into school, and go off to these Plaid Cymru meetings and then use their position, a position of trust, to influence pupils to join. It's… it's *scandalous*!'

Geraint walked over to the door. 'You don't know what you're talking about.'

'Now love,' said his mother as she went over to him to pat him on the shoulder.

Geraint wriggled away. 'Look, I've had enough of this. I made a stand for the language, *our* language, and all you two can do is behave like a couple of... a couple of peasants!'

'Now that is enough!' His father wagged a finger at him. 'We'll discuss this later.'

His mother patted her hair and said, 'Oh, Geraint dear, you always used to respect authority. They always said how well behaved you were in school reports.'

Geraint gripped the door handle tightly. His father looked at his watch.

'I've got to be at a planning sub-committee soon. I never thought the day would come that my own son would be mixed up in a scandal like this. I mean, yes, we speak Welsh. As we're doing now. But we have to be courteous to the English who live here. This *is* Britain, after all. And we're only a little part of it. We *depend* on the visitors, remember, round here. Not least in our shop, which pays for your clothes and everything, and don't you forget it lad!'

'Yes, dear,' put in his mother, 'and remember your father has a *position* in the town.'

Geraint could stand no more. He went out into the hall, slamming the lounge door. He opened the front door and, outside, stood for a few moments, breathing in the clean, sharp night air. Then he walked. Without realising why he had gone there and oblivious to the last few minutes, Geraint found himself in the High Street. Stopping, he frowned and felt nervous about the fact that he could not remember walking that way.

'Geraint!'

He looked across the road and saw Ieuan crossing over to him. Not really in the mood for company, he just emitted a 'Hi' and the two walked on.

'Fancy going to the caff?' asked Ieuan.

Reluctantly he acquiesced, thinking he ought to make an

effort to overcome his mood. Having acknowledged greetings from some of their school colleagues, they took a corner table and sipped from bottles of Coke.

'So, congratulations!' said Ieuan, blinking behind his specs.

Geraint looked at him, realising what he must mean. 'Oh yeah, though all I've done is make life one huge complication.'

'Never mind. You did what was right, what was needed. It's about time we put people like her in her place and stood up for our rights.'

'Hey, Ger lad!' The speaker was his other best friend, Pete, broad-shouldered, with a mop of fair hair and football-mad. He plonked himself down next to Geraint. Slapping him on the back, Pete went on: 'Ger, man, what you playing at today, eh? I never put you down as Welsh nash, like Ieuan here.'

Geraint groaned. 'Neither did I,' he muttered. And then he felt a tinge of shame, remembered Melanie's bravery, and said, 'But I suppose I was right.'

'Of course you were,' said Ieuan. With Pete's arrival, they had switched from Welsh to English, even though they both knew Pete could speak the language – if he made the effort.

Pete shook his head, saying, 'So she asked you to read it in English – what does it matter? We understand both languages.'

Ieuan pushed his spectacles up his nose and his dark hair out of his eyes. Geraint knew that the intellectual, wiry, not-very-sporty Ieuan still had the capacity to argue and to breathe fire.

'Well, if *we* don't stand up for it, who will? It's *our* language and it's about time we had the right to use it, to see it on road signs and so on.'

Pete leant against the padded back of the seat. 'Yah, you're just saying that because you and your family are all Welsh nash!'

Geraint listened, not sure what to say, but found himself sympathising with Ieuan's stance for the first time. Ieuan retorted: 'No, it's the wrong way round. We're members of Plaid Cymru *because* we speak Welsh and are proud of it. And why should it be illegal to have forms in Welsh, road signs in Welsh, and why should other countries have a parliament, and not Wales?'

Pete just looked down and shook his head, muttering, 'You'll never get a parliament, you'll never get another MP. And Welsh is a dying language.' He looked up. 'Which I suppose is a pity, but that's life.' He got to his feet. 'You coming, Ger?'

Geraint felt torn between the two. But, glancing up at Pete, he merely said, 'Er, not yet. See you later.'

After he'd gone, Geraint said, 'It's funny. I used to think the same way as him but, well, somehow, not now.'

Ieuan grinned. 'Conversion. St Paul.'

As Geraint looked mystified, Ieuan explained, after which Geraint couldn't help saying, 'Yeah OK, Reverend, just because your dad is a minister!'

Smiling, Ieuan said, 'Sorry. But more important, what about coming to a Plaid Cymru rally next month in Llanegryn. Plaid's president, Gwynfor Evans, is speaking. You won't regret it – he's a great speaker.'

Automatically, Geraint said, 'Oh I dunno. I'm not a member.'

'That doesn't matter – it's open to the public.'

'Yeah but... I'm not into politics.'

'Politics! This isn't *politics*! It's... it's your country, our language, fighting for our rights – within the law of course.'

Geraint weakened. 'Well, I suppose there's no harm in going to hear him. How will I get there?'

Smiling, Ieuan said, 'Oh don't worry, you can squeeze in with us. Dad won't mind.'

Beginning to feel more relaxed, Geraint asked, 'You said, fighting for our rights *within the law*. So does that mean you don't agree with the Welsh Language Society smashing English-only road signs, and those who blow up water pipelines?'

Ieuan looked thoughtful. 'Well, I don't agree with violence – at all. The end does not justify the means. I think the Language Society ought to march, yes, organise petitions, refuse to fill in English-only forms et cetera, but not smash public property or throw green paint everywhere.'

'And the bombs?'

'No. Definitely not. Plaid Cymru is right. We campaign by constitutional methods, the ballot box. This is what Gwynfor says and I agree.'

Geraint realised how much at home Ieuan was with such language, and how unfamiliar he was with it. Smiling, he looked at Ieuan's serious face and said, 'Well, just don't tell my parents I'm going to a Plaid Cymru meeting!'

Chapter 7

'I PROMISE TO dedicate my life to the cause of liberating my country from foreign domination and that I will uphold the discipline and honour of the Liberation Army of Wales. I will honour the sovereignty and rights of my country, people and flag, its language, tradition and culture. I solemnly swear in the name of God and all our dead patriots that I shall never reveal any secrets of our organisation, even if I am captured and tortured. If I betray this faith, I shall deserve the punishment of death as a traitor and may eternal contempt cover me.'

There was a brief silence after Geraint finished reading. Guto Evans held the double-edged dagger under his throat for a few more seconds before removing it, and Geraint let go of the corner of the Welsh flag.

'Congratulations!' said Llŷr from behind him, and others joined in, patting him on the back or shaking his hand.

The commandant, Marcus Ifan ab Owain, smiled and said, 'Well done. Now remember this: the current password is the question, "What is the way to Abaty Cwm Hir?" followed by the answer, "Llywelyn rest in peace." All right?'

Geraint nodded and hoped that amid all that was happening to him, he would remember. Looking back on the day later, he recalled a blur of events, fragments that came back to him at different times, rather than an ordered sequence. They had gone to a barn near Borth. That he did remember. And he handed back to the commandant the duplicated sheaf of papers he had received from Llŷr the previous night and hidden in his bedroom after studying everything. The first page was headed:

BYDDIN RHYDDID CYMRU,
the Liberation Army of Wales:
NATIONAL MILITARY ORGANISATION OF WALES

Object: to organise, train, discipline and equip the manhood of Wales into a voluntary Military Organisation as a basis of a National Army of Free Wales, with sole allegiance to the Welsh nation and people…

It also declared, to his approval:

The Army does not stand for terrorism or domination but for a policy of restraint unless the liberties of Wales and the Welsh people are threatened, as at Tryweryn…

After he had digested it all, he filled in his name after the word *I*, so that it read:

I, Geraint Rees, have read the objects and aims of the Army and agree with them, and desire to be enlisted for service in Wales…

'Don't worry about your uniform,' said Llŷr. 'We've agreed we won't expect you to pay for your own, and if we go out into the country for weapons practice, we'll organise whatever you need.'

'Fine,' said Geraint. 'And no one minds my keeping membership secret, because of my parents and all that?'

'Course not,' said Llŷr, patting his arm and then blowing cigarette smoke all over him. 'Everyone understands. They're just glad to see a keen youngster joining, especially someone who has stood up for the language as you did.'

There were more people there than he'd expected, presumably, thought Geraint, because there was a contingent from the south with Marcus. He had been looking forward to meeting the bossman, glimpsed occasionally on the news and seen in newspaper photographs. Before the ceremony, Llŷr had introduced them and Geraint had an impression of nervous energy, a frank, open manner and a touch of impatience, as though he wouldn't suffer fools gladly. He was tall, slim, in his 30s, guessed Geraint, and wearing black trousers and fawn shirt with a black tie, a black leather belt and a peaked cap with a dragon badge. Geraint remembered part of what he had said, about being on their way to 'awakening the Welsh people from their serf-like mentality', and then he had wished him good luck. After a firm handshake, he had disappeared to join another group, itself blotted out by a cloud of smoke pouring forth from Pedr's pipe. At this rate, thought Geraint, Mam will begin to think I'm smoking every time I go home from a LAW meeting.

He was disappointed not to see any weapons, though he reflected that they would have been out of place at such a meeting perhaps. Mair was there, somewhat at a loss, he thought, without Scouse to cast adoring glances at. And there was Carl in animated conversation about 'the bloody Investiture' and the price of lambs in his usual turned-down wellies and cloth cap with the peak almost over one ear. Guto was boasting to someone Geraint didn't know about some woman he'd recently met and who... And he missed the rest.

Llŷr told him that in the morning meeting, before Geraint arrived, Marcus had confirmed Scouse as the Commander of the Western Wales Brigade – now also his own group, Geraint was proud to think – and that he was engaged on 'something important'.

Later, Carl gave Geraint a lift to Borth station. Llŷr said he was staying on for a while and then going to the Skinners in Aberystwyth for a night's drinking with some mates.

When he got out of the train after the short journey to Dyfi Junction, Geraint longed to be able to share his experiences with Melanie.

Chapter 8

Sitting in Dyfi Junction waiting-room, Geraint stretched out his legs, feeling lonely and isolated in the dusty, cobwebbed silence. He stared unseeingly, the bizarrely immense room seeming even more vast than usual. The main road was some distance away, reached by a long, winding, muddy path, and the only sounds were of the wind swishing through long grass and reeds, and the croak and scream of birds.

He felt a strange mixture of exultation and nervousness. He, Geraint Rees, a soldier in the Liberation Army of Wales. In secret, maybe, but a soldier nonetheless. Would it impress Melanie? And again he realised: she must not know.

He closed his eyes, thinking about that strange night, the night they had met by chance. It was half-term, when the suspension had been lifted, and he had dutifully worked on an appreciation essay of Auden's *Musée des Beaux Arts* until he could bear the claustrophobia of his bedroom no longer. Avoiding his parents, he had gone straight out, deciding he needed air.

It was a peaceful, almost wind-free evening with a full moon and a brittle coldness as though winter was warning them of its approach. He headed for the south end of the promenade and the long beach with its acres of sandhills, his favourite spot when lonely or churned up emotionally.

Not in the mood even to see Pete or Ieuan, he was soon plodding through soft sand. The tide was out, and he walked slowly in the Aberdyfi direction. He was wearing his beloved, old, battered, brown leather, fur-lined jacket that he had bought in a second-hand shop in Liverpool when on a visit with Pete. He pushed the zip up a bit and then thrust his hands deep into the pockets.

From somewhere to the right came a low, rhythmic surr-surr of the flood tide breakers, beyond the satin-ribbon strips of water stranded in hollows along the beach. On the seaward side, the silver-grey moonlight glinted on the waters of Cardigan Bay. And above, the stars. Untold millions, thought Geraint as he pondered the immensity. Could there really be other worlds out there? Ahead of him, slightly to his right, pin-prick jewels of light marked Borth, and further on was the solid yellow blur of Aberystwyth, town of the university college and intended temporary home of Prince Charles.

Geraint ambled along, becoming less aware of his surroundings, embracing the friendly darkness, the freedom from people and all their demands. Somewhere ahead, a dog barked. Again, nearer. Suddenly it was lolloping towards him. It was playful, vigorous, bouncy and unthreatening, revelling in the freedom of open space. It nudged him, the wet nose seeking his hand. Geraint instinctively bent over to stroke its head and then knelt to play with an ear and stroke its back. Honey-coloured. A labrador perhaps.

'Hello.'

The voice expressed surprise and maybe pleasure. A girl's: a familiar voice. Geraint stood up, one hand on the dog's head. Walking slowly towards him was Melanie.

'Oh hello.' He didn't feel embarrassed for once. Nor any of the usual mixture of animosity and alarm. 'Your dog?'

'Yes. Pankhurst.'

'Pankhurst?'

'Not my choice of name, though I don't dislike it. Mum

chose it. Sort of into women's rights, et cetera.'

'It's different.'

'True.'

Melanie was breathing deeply as though she'd been running. For a moment neither spoke. Geraint felt shy, a touch of the old embarrassment returning, but somehow in a different way from the past when he'd been near her. He remembered Pete once saying with a grin, 'I reckon, me old son, that that Melanie has her eye on you. She fancies you!' Geraint had told him he was talking rubbish, but had wondered if he was blushing. The next day, however, she had been standing in front of them in the café. Without at first realising it, he had found himself admiring her slim legs, the swirling mini-skirt and the definite shape of breasts under the white blouse. He saw in the moonlight she was now wearing tight jeans and a high-necked sweater.

'Where are you going, down here then?' she asked, running a hand through her soft hair. Pankhurst was rubbing against his legs, seeking attention.

'Oh, just walking. I wanted to get out of the house, felt sort of hemmed in. Thought I'd wander along this way for a bit.'

'I like it here too.'

She turned to look out to sea, the moonlight bathing her face, enabling Geraint to see more clearly her profile, the firm, full jaw, the straight, well-formed nose. He realised how he liked even her lips, the appealing, slightly thick curve, the lower lip projecting just a little beyond the upper, seeming both sexy and indicating strength of character.

'Mind if I tag along?'

The request took Geraint by surprise. 'Er, well it's a bit cold now. I reckon I'll head back.' Damn, that's not what I wanted to say, his inner voice declared.

Pankhurst, tired of trying to regain Geraint's affection, turned to Melanie and began leaping up as though attempting to lick her face.

'Pankhurst, down! Well, I'll tell you what. Why don't you come back to my house? My parents are out. We can have a chat, perhaps talk about the head and tomorrow – and what's happened while I've been away over half term. You seem to be a celebrity.'

Geraint felt his head pounding. 'Yes, OK – if you're sure your parents don't mind.' He turned to head back, feeling that she must have noticed his flushed face even in the dark – and the tremor in his voice. Why was he feeling like this? All he was doing was going to a mate's house. But That Girl's? And he realised how unfair that was; after all, she had helped him discover self-confidence, priorities.

It was a detached house, solidly massive and imposing, if in need of some exterior paint. He knew it was her home, having noticed her going in and out on his way to and from school. Cil Enlli was the name on the slate plaque on the brick gatepost. The house was set back from the road, beyond a lay-by, the surviving portion of a bend after the road was straightened out. At the front was a high wall over-shadowed by dark, gloomy evergreens. A short, sloping drive led down to a pillared porch.

Melanie opened the door with her key, Pankhurst pushing past and heading automatically for the kitchen. 'Come on, we'll go up to my room,' she said, taking off her duffle coat. Geraint took in the wide hall, expensive-looking carpet, gilt mirror and a watercolour depicting a country scene. Grinning at him, she beckoned and ran up the stairs, followed by a slower, shy Geraint, nonetheless admiring her rear view.

'Wow!' he said. 'This makes my bedroom look like a cupboard.' He noted the long wardrobe with sliding mirror doors and an atmosphere of bedroom-cum-den-cum-study-cum lounge. 'Dead smart! All this room, your desk, books, loads-a-space.' Then he felt a pang of guilt, as though being disloyal to his parents.

'Yes, I like it. I persuaded Mummy and Daddy to let me have it. This one has the best view, especially at sunset.'

Geraint couldn't stop gazing at everything, the bright colours, the posters of pop stars juxtaposed with Che Guevara, Marx and the 'Welsh Labour Party Rally, Wrexham'.

'Perhaps I should become an accountant.'

Melanie gave a short laugh, and said, 'Oh, it's not *that* profitable! Mummy has money on her side of the family. They had some sort of engineering firm in Coventry – but her father sold it to one of the big companies, car components or something boring. Then he died and she inherited. And as they used to come here on holiday when they were courting, they decided to move here. Come on, sit down.' She flopped onto a huge, round, flowery cushion by the bed.

Geraint got down and lay back on the carpet, raising himself on one elbow. She pushed back her hair and said, 'Come on then, tell me what happened during half-term. I've seen the *Cardigan News* article. A bit emotional, though you'd expect that; a bit biased against you.'

Geraint began, slowly at first, to relate what had happened. By that Friday evening, it was a brief item on the Welsh radio and TV news. He told her about reporters ringing the house and that after his father had returned from the shop, he had forbidden him to answer the phone. On the Saturday just gone, quite a big piece had appeared in the local paper, plus letters from 'Outraged' and 'Patriot' (both varieties), the majority of correspondents condemning him.

'What about your parents?' he asked.

She smiled wistfully. 'I must admit they didn't exactly applaud what I did. They seemed more baffled than anything. Dad said he couldn't believe how something so... so trivial, could be so newsworthy. I tried to explain that with the Welsh Language Society active, the language being, well, sort of a political hot potato these days, it wasn't surprising.' She gazed thoughtfully at the bearded Marx on the wall. 'I tried also to explain that I said what I did, supporting you, out of principle. But all they could say was that I was in danger of being brainwashed into Welsh nationalism now that I'm in that school. "If only you could have stayed at Dr Williams'," was Dad's comment.'

'Because?'

'Oh, I was a weekly boarder there, you know where it is, don't you?'

Geraint nodded. 'Oh yes, we've all heard of the famous Dr Williams' School in Dolgellau.'

'Exactly! Where nice young ladies could be brought up in an oasis (as some parents thought of it), insulated from the Welsh language and culture.' Melanie smiled as though feeling guilty. 'But the school was facing financial problems and before the sixth form was formally closed down, my parents persuaded me to move to Tywyn after my O-levels.' Melanie suddenly got up and went over to Geraint. She looked down at him and then joined him on the carpet. Putting her hand on his knee, she said, 'Oh, Ger, you have been through it, haven't you?'

'That's the first time,' he said quietly, smiling at her.

'Eh? First time for what?'

'First time you've called me Ger. I like it. I mean I like it when *you* call me it.'

She laughed, and took her hand away. 'I'll have to watch it. I'll be turning Welsh nash if I'm not careful.' She slid across to the bed and sat against it, putting her hands up behind her head, and stretching out her legs so her feet were almost touching him.

'Don't call it "Welsh nash".' Geraint said this instinctively and was surprised at himself.

'Why not?'

He was conscious of her keen eyes on him. 'Well, I'm not sure. It just sounds derogatory. Hey, that's a good word, eh?' He laughed, a little embarrassed again.

'Oh, reading the dictionary are we?'

'No, but you know. It's really only those who are against it that call it that.'

'Well, what should I say? And I *am* against it, remember.'

Geraint was silent, thinking. 'Well, maybe just nationalist, or Plaid Cymru, or pro-Welsh.'

'Yes,' Melanie put in, 'but I *am* pro-Welsh – in some things. I mean I'm pro living here, I like most of Wales, especially this coast. Though I haven't seen much of south Wales. But I could never be Welsh na… I mean,' she laughed, 'never be a nationalist or support Plaid Cymru.'

'Well, at least you pronounce it right,' Geraint said, moving a little so that he could touch her foot with one of his. 'Anyway, why couldn't you?'

'Oh, come on, I'm not Welsh!'

'So what? You live here.'

'I don't speak Welsh, Geraint.'

'But there are people who don't and are in Plaid Cymru.'

Melanie looked at Geraint with a half smile and quizzical expression. He returned her gaze, puzzled.

'Anyone would think you were,' she said.

'Were what?' asked Geraint defensively.

'In Plaid Cymru.'

Geraint looked down. Yes, he realised why she had said that. A little disconcerted, he looked at her. 'Well, you have to stick up for your country. I mean, I don't really know much about Plaid Cymru and I've never got involved with them, but at least they stand up for Wales and the language which is more than… '

'… the other parties do!' Melanie interrupted. They both laughed. Melanie pressed hard against the sole of his foot. 'Anyway, you! Why were you always so horrible to me, avoiding me and scowling at me? And me helping you in English and so on?'

Geraint looked straight at her and said forcefully, 'Hey, that's not my fault! *You* were the one that was nasty to *me*! Remember your first day in school and me helping you to pick up your books when they fell out of your bag?'

She looked down, saying, 'Mmm, think I remember.' And then smiled mischievously at him.

'Well, then! Who was a Miss hoity-toity and didn't like people speaking "that bloody language" to them?'

Melanie went red, which, he thought, made her look even more attractive. 'Ah, yes.'

'See?'

'Yes, but – well, I'm sorry, Ger. It was a bad time. I hadn't wanted to leave Dr Williams', but, you know, they were eventually going to phase out the sixth form and it seemed better to move at the end of the fifth year, sort of logical time. I missed my friends and hated the idea of going to the local comprehensive.'

'OK, truce, and I'll let you off.'

'Wow, thanks! But I'm still not going to be a nationalist!'

'Hell, who said *I* was?' Kneeling in front of her, he became conscious of how inviting her breasts looked. 'All I've said is that I stick up for Wales and the language.'

'Well that's Plaid Cymru,' retorted Melanie, throwing a small teddy bear at him. Geraint caught it and, flinging it back, added: 'I don't know about that, but perhaps we do need our own parliament to protect us from the Mrs Archers who come here – and doubting English females who won't learn Welsh!' He felt guilty as he took a quick gaze at her thighs in the straining, skin-tight blue denim of her jeans.

'That hit me on the ear, brute!' Melanie looked mock-offended and flung the bear back at him, hitting him on the stomach. Geraint hugged the teddy bear, wondering if sexual thoughts were displacing political ones in his head. Part of him was baffled as to how he suddenly found so attractive someone he had, until That Day, previously loathed.

'Anyway, socialism knows no borders or boundaries. The workers need to break down national barriers to unite against capitalist exploitation!'

'You what?' Geraint whistled and looked at her in amazement. 'Well, who's going to be an MP one day?'

Melanie looked down at the carpet. 'Oh, that's what someone said in a Labour Party meeting I went to. Neil someone, can't remember his other name. He was going on about "narrow nationalism" and "parochialism".'

'Oh.' These were concepts Geraint had never thought of and understood nothing about. He was impressed, though. '*You* go to these meetings?'

'Sometimes. Mummy and Daddy are keen that I should not neglect my political education.' Melanie had put on a different voice and smiled, mimicking, he assumed, her mother.

'But aren't they boring?'

'Mmmm, sometimes. Not always. Sometimes there's a visiting speaker. Like the one I mentioned. I know! Kinnock – that was his other name. He's really good – very fiery and left-wing. *And* your friend Mrs Archer goes, usually with her husband. He's bearded and *very* serious about everything.' Melanie sighed and folded her arms, squeezing her breasts. 'Anyway, I'm usually with Anna, you know, Anna Hughes in the sixth.'

'Her? To Labour Party meetings?' Geraint wondered why he was surprised. Obviously lots of Welsh people supported Labour, or why would Meirionnydd be a Labour seat?

'Why not?' asked Melanie, pouting in mock annoyance. 'Geraint, you ought to take an interest in politics. It won't be long before you can register to vote.'

'Ah. I'm not interested. It's boring. I mean you need to get really involved to understand politics. They're all liars, anyway.'

There was silence; each looked down, as though deciding what to do next. Melanie pushed his foot again, saying, 'Oh come on, Ger, cheer up! We're young and life's all before us, and you'll see sense one day and help me set up a branch of the Young Socialists.'

'Rubbish!' Geraint smiled and flung the teddy at her, hitting her on the nose. 'Hey sorry, Mel – didn't mean to do that.'

Melanie looked at him, her big brown eyes serious but not offended. For two seconds, neither moved. Either Geraint could ignore the power of the moment that suddenly electrified him or react to the feeling. Melanie it was who moved first, and her face was almost touching his. Geraint bridged the gap and they kissed, tenderly, and then looked into each other's eyes.

'Melanie,' he said softly. He pulled her against him, crushing her anti-apartheid T-shirt against her breasts. A little clumsily, they kissed again, exploring the taste of each other's lips, the softness, warmth, the sensual cavity beyond, their tongues probing and seeking new delights.

After a while, their lips almost sore, they sat up and he said, 'Melanie, I never thought – I mean, you and me! I always thought you hated me.'

'Oh, Ger, you are a bit blind, even thick!'

'What do you mean?'

'I've fancied you for quite a while now.'

'But what do you see in me? I mean, you're so attractive and I'm, well, not exactly dead handsome.' Geraint wondered whether it was wise to utter such thoughts – but too late.

Melanie smiled and shook her head. 'Ger, you *are* attractive! And I like the way you're not big-headed. You're not always going on about females and sex and stuff like Pete and some of the other lads.' She went on: 'Anyway, sometimes I couldn't help feeling sorry for you, wanting to hug you, you looked so embarrassed or scared and so on.'

'Gee, thanks!' Geraint felt embarrassed now.

Melanie put down her drink and put a hand on each of his cheeks, saying softly, 'You know your trouble – you have no confidence in yourself. You're not bad looking at all. You're good at A-level English – except when Eleri asks you your opinion, and I presume you're good at Welsh and geog.'

Geraint grasped her hands and lowered them to his chest. 'OK, my psychologist! How come *you're* so confident and good at speaking out. What's the secret?'

She moved back and leant against the bed. 'Well, being an only child is important, I suppose. But then so are you. Oh,

Mummy and Daddy have always involved me in discussions, encouraged me to give my opinion and argue my case. And I get on with them, well, until recently.'

So did I with mine – until recently, he thought. But then he reflected: yes, they decide, and I acquiesce. Until recently. He smiled at her and said, 'What would they have said if they could have seen us a few minutes ago?'

She laughed. 'Oh I suppose they wouldn't have gone mad, more a bit embarrassed. They wouldn't like to see it – but would be forced to admit it's natural. I mean they know how old I am and we once had an "adult" chat about Boys and What They Are Capable Of and so on. They sort of trust me, I suppose.' She suddenly felt impelled to move over to him and gave him a kiss on the cheek, squatting next to him. 'But,' she added, 'if they knew I'd been seduced by a violent Welsh nationalist who refuses to speak English in school… well, Daddy would get his shotgun to you.'

Geraint laughed and kissed her cheek. But a part of his mind worried just what they *would* think when the relationship became known. At least, he thought, if this *is* to be a relationship. And I hope to God it is.

Chapter 9

H E WAS ON his way to the kitchen when the doorbell rang. It was Ieuan. 'Ready, Ger?'

Geraint looked at him, puzzled, before suddenly remembering. 'Er, yeah. I'll just get my jacket.' He had almost forgotten it was the night of the Plaid Cymru branch meeting, his second since joining, and the last one before Christmas.

As they walked down towards the drill hall at the other end of town, Ieuan asked, 'What's up? You lost the old enthusiasm already?'

And again Geraint felt the burden of his secret, his other allegiance. 'Course not,' he said, trying to sound positive. 'It's just, well, the last meeting was a bit sort of boring, compared to listening to Gwynfor.'

Ieuan laughed. 'Yes, I know what you mean. But the general election is less than two years away and we have to be ready. That means money in the bank, knocking at doors to find out where our voters are... you know.'

Geraint nodded, acknowledging the truth of this, but thinking how already LAW had pushed Plaid Cymru somewhat into the background.

The folding wooden chairs were hard and uncomfortable, thought Geraint as he sat with Ieuan near the back. The sudden whiff of stale tobacco smoke presaged the appearance of Llŷr who sat next to them.

'Right everyone, let's get started – it's gone half-past seven.' The speaker, one of the teachers at Geraint's school, sat facing them, along with the branch secretary and treasurer.

The dozen or so other members were scattered around the rows of chairs. Geraint sighed, and consoled himself with the thought that he was doing this for Wales, and anyway, Llŷr was also there. And sliding into the end chair was Mike Barraclough who nodded at Geraint.

He looked round, depressed by the dusty wooden floor, torn, dust-laden curtains and all the atmosphere of a run-down village hall, contrasting it with the cosy, welcoming farm kitchen of his first LAW meeting.

'So,' said the chairman, 'any apologies for absence?' Two names were offered up and noted. 'Minutes of the last meeting. Anyone propose they're accurate?'

Alwyn, the young chap who worked at the bank, said, 'Well, item 4a should read "might be a good idea", not "would be a good idea". There is a difference, and I don't want to be misquoted.'

Buddug, the flame-haired PE teacher and their branch secretary, looked up from her notes, saying, 'Well, Alwyn, I don't have it that way here. But I'll alter it. Sorry.'

'Anything else?' asked the chairman. 'Minutes correct, thank you. Now, matters arising.'

Geraint could not help a loud sigh, and then smiled guiltily as Ieuan looked at him.

'Patience,' muttered Llŷr, also grinning, adding, 'you know why we're here.' Geraint nodded and told himself to be more positive.

They ground their way through the agenda, with secretary's report and treasurer's report and press secretary's report. During the latter, Geraint at least managed a smile. Ieuan interrupted, highly incensed at what he called the bias and anti-Plaid Cymru smear campaign of the local weekly paper. To lots of nodding and 'hear-hears' from those around, he said: 'I think we must make an official protest to the editor and the proprietor. I mean, a front-page photograph of Dafydd Wigley, our general election candidate with the headline right over it: "Manure on road." Of course their excuse will be that the headline refers to another article, on the left of the photo, but I reckon it was deliberate.' They agreed to protest.

Wow, reflected Geraint, from blowing up pipelines to moaning about a headline…

Then there was an involved discussion on who would look after which stall in the Christmas fair and how much money they could spare to boost the constituency's election fund, and someone gave a rambling report on the last constituency committee meeting and someone gave another on the national council meeting in Aberystwyth. There was an item on canvassing, and the chairman, looking over at Mike, said, 'Mike, have you understood everything up to now?'

Mike coughed and answered in English, 'Oh yes, most of it. I'm working hard on my Welsh but I understand it more than I can speak it. And my Yorkshire accent keeps getting in the way.'

To laughter, the chairman said, 'Well, I'm sure everyone admires your efforts and dedication. So how did your first canvassing go?'

Mike smiled. 'Well, Griff and I thought we'd do Aberdyfi – so many English there, we thought having an Englishman knocking on doors for Plaid Cymru might be a good idea. And whenever we had the inevitable "But I'm English, not Welsh", I was able to point out that I had moved from England but I recognised that Wales was a different country, with its own language and history, and, well, there were not just three main parties… Oh, sorry, you know the reasons! Anyway, apart from all the hills and steps – phew, was it tough going! – Griff did most of the talking and I learned a lot. Let's just say we sowed seeds and left leaflets.'

'Well, we have to keep trying. Sometimes they open their minds to us! Thank you, Mike.' The chairman looked at Geraint. 'And welcome again to our newest member. As Llew can't be here tonight, Geraint, how did you get on with him?'

Feeling a little self-conscious with all eyes on him, Geraint summoned up some self-assurance. 'Er, yes, we went to Bryncrug. And like Mike said, it was pretty tough.' He thought of leaving it at that, but couldn't resist going on: 'I must admit I was surprised – and depressed. Not just that we couldn't persuade people. I mean you don't mind a discussion on self-government or London rule, but they seemed so daft, in fact plain stupid.' Ignoring a nudge from Ieuan, he continued: 'There was this woman. We said we were calling to see if she would vote for Plaid Cymru, and all she could say was, "Oh I leave all that sort of thing to my husband to decide." Another woman, English I think, kept asking, "But are you Labour or Conservative?" Then there was some idiot who said we were paid to split the Labour vote and another bloke, too big to argue with, who said we had better move away fast because he didn't like people who blew things up!' He couldn't help noticing the broad grin on Llŷr's face.

The chairman looked at him sympathetically. 'Well, thank you for going. And don't be disheartened. Everywhere starts off like that. I must admit our best area is still Llanegryn.'

Finally, under any other business, Llŷr took the cigarette out of his mouth and spoke loudly: 'Mr Chairman… '

There was a rather unenthusiastic sounding 'Yes?'

'Last meeting I was told we had no time to discuss the

Investiture of Prince Charles. This time I want us to address the issue. After all, it is supposed to take place in less than eight months.'

Buddug, the red-haired secretary, interrupted him. 'Come on, Llŷr, we all know your views and you know ours. As people said in the conference last year, we all know it's a trap set by the government. Just leave it.'

The chairman felt constrained to say, 'Well, we'll let him have his say, briefly.'

Llŷr stood up, something no other speaker had done. 'This whole business is a challenge to Plaid Cymru. The Crown, the English establishment, aided by the Welsh quislings and hangers-on, the OBE-seekers and so on, are using this, this pseudo-historical event to try to smash Plaid Cymru and halt the growing sense of national consciousness. I know it, you know it. But what are we doing about it? Sod all!'

'Er, language, Llŷr.'

'Well, I feel strongly. If we claim to be a national party, where is our clear opposition to this event? Why can we not at least make clear the party, united, opposes the Investiture?'

One of the farmers spoke up. 'But you know the problem. Where royalty is concerned, we can't be united. There are people who are members and go "Ah!" every time they see the Queen or Charles on TV. "Oh, isn't he a nice young man?" you hear. And if we attack him, well, we'll lose votes, even members.'

Geraint heard a 'Hear, hear!' somewhere near the front and a 'Rubbish!' from Llŷr, who added: 'We don't attack *him*, Charles the bloke, we attack the event, the office of prince, the idea of a prince of Wales!' He gripped the back of the chair in front. 'Yes, some people go weak-kneed at even the name Charles, but remember the *Western Mail* survey last year? Fifty-three per cent of the 21–34 age group think the Investiture is a waste of money!'

The chairman was gathering up and tidying his pieces of paper as though anxious to escape. He said, looking anywhere but at Llŷr, 'Party policy is to try to ignore it, carry on and hope that afterwards, we won't have lost support.'

'Cowardice and treachery!' shouted Llŷr. And then, as though making an effort to control himself, he went on more quietly: 'Mr Chairman, I propose a motion. That this branch of Plaid Cymru expresses its outright opposition to the proposed Investiture of Prince Charles and calls on the Welsh people to do all it can to have the event called off as it is an insult to the nation.'

He sat down to silence. Even the top table had stopped shuffling their papers. Mike coughed and pointed out in heavily Yorkshire-accented Welsh that a motion was on the table.

'Yes,' said the chairman, sounding unsure. He gazed around. 'Anyone second it?'

'I do.' The words were out almost before Geraint realised he had said them. If anyone was surprised at his action, no one showed it.

'Well,' said the chairman, 'anyone want to speak before we vote on it?'

'Oh, put it to the vote; it's getting late and I want to go to the Corbett before last orders!'

Geraint was looking down but thought the speaker was Roy, a young chap who worked at the agricultural merchant's by the railway sidings.

'All those in favour of Llŷr's motion, please show. Thank you.' The chairman coughed nervously. 'All those against?' Geraint looked around. 'Well, the motion has clearly fallen, two in favour and twelve against.' And against a background of scraping chairs and loud voices, he added, 'The meeting is closed – thank you for coming. And see you all at the Christmas Fair.'

Outside, in the frosty night air, Geraint thrust his hands deep into the pockets of his leather jacket. Llŷr patted him on the back, saying, 'Thanks, Ger – you see what we're up against.'

Ieuan looked hesitantly at them, asking, 'You coming, Ger?'

Before he could answer, Llŷr said, 'Come on, Ger, we'll get one in at the Corbett before they finish.' And then, seeing Geraint's look, added: 'Oh, yeah, you're too young.'

'And even if *you* bought them, Dad would soon hear!' said Geraint.

'Well, come back to my place for a quick chat.'

'OK. See you tomorrow, Ieuan.' He sensed Ieuan's disapproval.

Llŷr lived in the flat over where he worked, the gas showroom near the garage at the station end of the High Street. As Geraint sank into a battered, scratched leather armchair, he couldn't help saying, 'Wow! I've never seen so many books in one room, apart from a library!'

Llŷr laughed, saying, 'Here, get this down you.' He handed Geraint a chilled can of Blue Bass. 'Just because I work in Jones and Williams' gas showroom doesn't mean I don't like books – mainly political, history, et cetera.' He sat in the armchair opposite and switched on the log-effect gas fire.

Geraint felt emboldened enough to ask directly: 'Llŷr, how old are you?'

'Twenty, why?'

'Just wondered. You know so much, you know what you

want. And then all these books. Did you never want to go to university?'

Smiling, Llŷr replied, 'OK, the short autobiography of me. Sixteen years of nothing notable, three weeks of A-levels in Porthmadog before I walked out and said no, not for me. Parents went mad. I did odd jobs and then, sort of got this job. It's not bad. Rent is low as I work for them and can keep an eye on it when it's closed. Intellectually deadening, but then it leaves me time and energy to read, think... and LAW et cetera.' Looking thoughtful, he took a drag on his cigarette and added, 'Oh, I suppose one day I might try for A-levels, or Coleg Harlech and then university. But as a mature student.'

Geraint drank some beer before asking, 'Do you think we, in LAW I mean, will eventually get involved in something sort of direct, trying to do something about the Investiture?'

Llŷr smiled at him. 'Well, are you still glad I invited you to that first LAW meeting, remember, when I introduced myself to you the night of Gwynfor's visit?'

Geraint laughed. 'Yes, I remember. There I was standing in the gents when you started talking to me!'

'Well, no one else was there. And it was a great night!'

Geraint frowned. 'What I can remember, yes! After Gwynfor's speech, hurtling through those dark lanes to the Railway in Abergynolwyn, more beer than I've ever drunk – and all that great singing!'

Llŷr nodded. 'Oh yes. We're very good at singing patriotic songs, aren't we? Oh, don't get me wrong – we all get carried away, even me. But once we've left the pub – or the rugby match – how much are we prepared to actually *do* for poor old Wales?'

'Well we've just been to a meeting tonight,' said Geraint. 'We go round trying to persuade people to vote for us. And

Gwynfor did win Carmarthen in '66, our first-ever MP.'

'And what did tonight's meeting achieve? And how many of Gwynfor's votes were real nationalist, rather than votes for a nice guy, a local guy, a way of stopping Labour winning? And more important, is it going to get independence for Wales?'

'Mmm.' Geraint took a swig and went on: 'But Harold Wilson has just said he'll set up a committee or something to look at the UK constitution. So maybe we're beginning to make an impression, Plaid Cymru *and* LAW.'

Llŷr shook his head vigorously. 'Ger, the prime minister just wants to make us feel happy, to make us think something worthwhile could happen so that we stop putting pressure on them. The "Commission on the Constitution" as he calls it, is just a sop by a wily old Labour politician.'

'Yeah, I suppose you're right. Ieuan said the other day that once Plaid Cymru wins all thirty-six seats in Wales, or even the majority, they will be forced to lower the Union Jack at midnight and hand over power to a Welsh prime minister.' Geraint frowned and as Llŷr smiled, went on: 'But after canvassing round here, I can't see that ever happening.'

Llŷr was nodding. 'Exactly. Ger, you know how that business in school was the key, the key to making you see things clearly? Well, that's what the Welsh people need – an event, a shock, something to destroy their complacency and shatter the crust of unthinking Britishness, equals Englishness. Like what happened in Ireland after the executions of the Easter Uprising leaders, or even the way flooding Capel Celyn, Tryweryn, changed many people here, and the trial of the three in the 1930s, after burning the RAF bombing school buildings at Penyberth.'

Geraint emptied his can and said, 'But so far, what LAW

has done, blowing up water pipes and so on, it just loses votes for Plaid Cymru.'

Llŷr looked up and blew a smoke ring. 'Stage one, Ger. Look at the Language Society, occupying post offices, smashing road signs, daubing green paint. It shocks and offends the polite lace-curtain middle classes. And as for the working class, they just dismiss them as idiots. But I'll bet you that *one* day, they'll win. One day we shall get bilingual road signs and forms and TV licences and so on. And then, when the dust has died down, people will accept it and wonder why we never had such things before. And we'll have taken a step forward.'

Geraint nodded enthusiastically. 'Yeah, I see what you mean. They might not agree with blowing things up, but if we win, what? Water controlled in Wales, sold to England rather than just taken… '

'Oh, and a lot more than that.'

'Then the need for the violence will have gone, the aims will be achieved.'

Llŷr leant forward. 'Yes and no. LAW aims to do more than solve the burning question of Welsh water. It's *one* problem. We really need to go deeper and change the whole outlook of our compatriots, to make them *Welsh* – whatever their language. *Think* as Welshmen and women. See?'

'Plaid Cymru would agree with that!'

'Yes, but not with the *how*!'

Geraint thought for a few seconds before asking, 'What do I say to Ieuan when he says violence is never justified?'

'Ah,' said Llŷr, inhaling deeply then blowing a twin smoke-stream from his nostrils, 'violence, destruction, can – paradoxically, perhaps to you and others – can be a creative act. Violence is man recreating himself. As I said, we can't expect the masses to suddenly see the truth, reject their *Daily Mirror*, their *Sun* or *Daily Post*, their telly and bingo.' Geraint felt that Llŷr was speaking to someone he could not see, or merely thinking aloud. 'When the revolutionary kills, a tyrant dies and a free man emerges.' Suddenly he focused on Geraint and went on: 'Ger, if your mother or, what's this girlfriend of yours called?'

'Melanie.'

'Well if one of them had cancer, or gangrene, and could only be cured by cutting off a limb or taking out an organ – that is, violence against the body – wouldn't you be happy if it meant they became healthy again?'

Geraint nodded. 'Oh, Mel,' he said quietly.

Llŷr laughed. 'I don't know, Geraint Rees. No Welsh girl good enough for you?'

A little defensively, he retorted, 'It's not that. It just happened. And remember she stood up for me, pushed me, that time.'

Llŷr smiled. 'The English sense of fair play. One day it just might enable them to give us sovereignty, just as they have been doing in their other colonies.' He tapped his cigarette on the ashtray rim. 'Doesn't it lead to arguments though, her being English?'

'Dead right!' said Geraint. 'She'll agree up to a point, and then – wham! I can't make her see sense.'

'So it's not just that you fancy her. It's love!'

'Of course.'

'And she feels the same about you?'

'Yes.'

'Does she know about LAW?'

'Hell, no! I get flak about Plaid Cymru now and again but LAW... you're the only one round here who knows.'

They sat silently for a few seconds, before Geraint asked, 'Llŷr, you know Scouse, how did you say he became the leader of the group?'

Llŷr blew smoke and then said, 'Well, as Pedr told you, he hasn't been with us all that long. Sort of turned up with one of Marcus' friends from the south. He sort of vouched for him and said Marcus had appointed him to get things going. You know the rest: post-grad student, ex-Foreign Legion, knows about weapons and explosives, and we hope that this will lead to something soon.'

Brow furrowed, Geraint said, 'Isn't it, well, odd – an Englishman leading us?'

'I thought that,' said Llŷr slowly. 'But he explains it away by saying he's actually a Liverpool Welshman, you know, loads of Welsh families moved to Merseyside for work in the Thirties... and even earlier, in the 19th century.'

'Yeah, and there's Mike.'

'What?'

'Mike Barraclough. Yorkshireman. He's seen the light, knows that if he moves to live in Wales, well... '

Llŷr looked thoughtful. 'I've often wondered about him.'

'Mike?' Geraint asked, puzzled.

'Yes, jolly, cuddly Mike. How do we know he's genuine? Not someone sent in by, I dunno, MI5, Special Branch, to keep an eye on us. Or worse?'

Geraint tried to grasp this but failed. 'He seems genuine.'

'He would have to, wouldn't he? Oh, I'm probably up the wrong tree. It's LAW we have to be careful about. That's why I go on to you about security and not being seen together too much out of Plaid Cymru meetings.'

Geraint looked at his watch. 'I'd better get back. Mam will be wondering again. She's a real worrier.'

They stood up. 'Hey I've enjoyed the chat,' said Llŷr. 'It's good to be able to open up to someone without having to justify yourself. Call again, any time.'

Chapter 10

THE SECOND DAY of 1969 – year of the Investiture of Prince Charles as so-called 'Prince of Wales'. Geraint stared nervously out of the train window as it gathered speed, heading south past the Tywyn goods sidings and under the bridge. It was his first LAW meeting since his initiation. Llŷr had phoned him with the details and here they both were again, sitting in separate carriages at Llŷr's insistence, as though, thought Geraint with amusement, police spies were watching every train and would draw conclusions from their sitting together.

More importantly, he thought, maybe it *was* Scouse who had blown up the water pipes recently, temporarily disrupting supplies to Birmingham. He read in the papers that, as usual, LAW or Plaid Cymru fanatics, or both, were to blame for 'this appalling near-tragedy and one day someone will be killed and constitutional methods' – blah blah.

At least that day Melanie had relatives visiting so they could not have met anyway. Ah well, he thought happily, we're still going out together even if things at home aren't any better. True, Christmas Day itself had been peaceful if not over-jolly. Boxing Day had begun well, but the night ended with an almighty slanging match that had been going on for some time before he came home from seeing Melanie. Mercifully it subsided after he came in and his mother went to bed early while his father drove off in the car; presumably, he thought, to calm down or just get away.

Still, Christmas had cast its gentle, romantic aura over

Melanie and himself, and they were close, relaxed, together. He had bought her a Celtic cross on a silver chain to wear round her neck, and he had been very impressed by the snazzy pair of Chelsea boots with Cuban heels she had presented to him. He puzzled for some time as to how she had got his size right, but Melanie refused to divulge her secret, smiling enigmatically. She had spent quite a bit more on him than he had on her. Thank heaven, he reflected, he had managed to get a few days' work at Amaethwyr Dysynni, the agricultural merchant's by the railway. Despite his good Christmas exam results, his dad had not restored his regular pocket money – stopped after he had refused not to join Plaid Cymru.

The meeting took place in the farm just outside Machynlleth, the one Geraint went to on his introduction to LAW. This time, not only was Scouse there but he was the centre of attention more than usual.

Again they sat round the ponderous scrubbed table in the stone-slabbed kitchen, warmed by the Aga, supping tea from capacious white mugs. Scouse sat with his back to the stove; he was dressed in dark brown corduroy trousers and a thick, dark, polo-necked sweater that made his wide, powerful shoulders seem even more massive. With his sharp, restless and piercing eyes, he impressed Geraint as a man of mental as well as physical strength. To Geraint, the thick beard and Scouse accent somehow added to the underlying aura of controlled aggression. It was comforting, he reflected, and a sign of our strength, that a man of such skill, background and character was on *our* side.

It had been a solo job. All eyes were on him as Scouse related details of his mission. 'We'd found out that the pipelines carrying Welsh water to Birmingham were exposed above ground at West Hagley, two miles from Stourbridge. So this was where I caused the explosion. It tore a five-foot gash in one 42-inch pipe and fractured a second. The result? Water to Birmingham cut by half, a serious matter when 90 per cent of their supplies come from the Elan Valley in Wales.'

In the awed hush that followed Scouse's account, Carl asked, 'And what did you use, I mean how did you set it off?' And why didn't he take one or two of us with him? wondered Geraint, feeling jealous.

Scouse took a long draught of tea and replied, 'Well, I'm not going into all the technical details; the fewer that know, the better. The simplest part of it was the trigger device – nothing more than the mechanism of an ordinary, cheap alarm clock.'

Sitting next to Scouse was Mair, whose eyes bespoke adoration and fascination. In her Anglesey accent, she said, looking round the table, 'Did you see the *Western Mail*? "Obviously the work of experts... not a large amount of explosive – just enough."'

Scouse laughed. 'Presumably a tribute from bomb disposal. Much appreciated, I'm sure.'

'And as usual,' said Pedr quietly, 'Plaid Cymru comes in for a lot of criticism.'

'No sign of police or guards when you were there?' asked Guto.

'No,' Scouse answered. 'Obviously I sussed out the site well beforehand. Isolated, nothing there. That's why it was chosen.'

Pedr was tapping his fingers with a pencil. 'I wonder how many more times we have to teach them that they can't just march into Wales and flood any valley they want. Or take our water at dirt-cheap prices.'

Guto shook his head. 'There will have to be a lot more of

this sort of thing before they're forced to give us our rights and respect our land.'

There was muttered agreement and then Geraint spoke up, curious. 'How do you, I mean, we, decide on missions, targets? Who makes the decision?'

Scouse placed his podgy hands palm down on the table and looked at Geraint. 'Well, something of this importance is decided at the top and on a need-to-know basis. I mean, this was something I worked out with Marcus Owain, our commandant.'

'Where do the explosives and so on come from? How do we get them?'

In answer, Scouse tapped one side of his nose with a forefinger. 'No questions, Ger lad, and you'll be told no lies; no knowledge, no blabbing, know warra mean like?' Geraint nodded, still curious. Scouse went on: 'We have friends, we have supporters who help us financially.'

Llŷr, next to Geraint, coughed and stubbed out his cigarette. 'I have to say that we have scored a major success in last month's explosion.' His angular face wore an expression of intense seriousness. 'And I also have to say, not for the first time here, that I think we are wasting our time holding public parades, strutting around in make-believe uniforms and so on. This is more like what we need: hitting them hard. We must be more aggressive towards England. You don't see Vietcong saboteurs parading through Saigon in uniform, do you?'

A 'Hear, hear' from Guto was followed by Scouse shaking his head. 'I can't say I agree, mate. We can do both. When Guto, Mair and others march through the streets in uniform, carrying the flag, we let the people know that we exist, that LAW is parading to show them the nation is not asleep, to rally them, to awaken them.'

Llŷr fumbled with his cigarette packet and interrupted impatiently. 'The best way to awaken them is by blowing up pipelines – and other symbols of colonial oppression.'

'Yes, but we can do both, surely?' put in Scouse.

'Too dangerous, too dangerous,' said Llŷr. 'We've talked about security leaks before – the explosives in the lake, and worries nearer here. But I won't go into that now. Let's operate *out* of the limelight, underground.'

Mair touched Scouse's arm and said, 'Well, I agree with Arthur. We can do both. It's important to *inspire* people. I mean we need to go on marching, and to get more people who can play drums and even try to get a sort of band, more flags.'

Llŷr blew a cloud of smoke across the table, muttering angrily, 'Kids' stuff.'

Mair still looked annoyed. 'Of course, Llŷr, if you haven't got the courage to march in public to show your loyalty to Cymru… '

'Courage!' He took his cigarette out of his mouth and looked derisively at her. 'Where's the courage in taking part in a circus parade?'

'Well it takes courage to be seen to be standing up in public for your country,' said Mair angrily, leaning towards Llŷr opposite her. 'Not everyone in the street just watches, you know. Remember? There are those who spit, who shout insults. And in any case, Arthur is the only one so far who has risked himself on a real mission, so I don't know that you're entitled to think yourself so aggressive!'

'Well, as he has always told us, he's the only one with military experience and explosives know-how – and none of us has been asked to do anything.'

'OK, OK,' said Scouse firmly. 'Let's stay cool, eh? The

policy of LAW is to parade as well as to initiate direct action; that's how it is for now and we have to accept it. And talking of the Investiture brings me to future action – whereby you *will* be invited to do something.'

He stopped and looked round the table. Carl, still wearing his cap, leant over and scratched the ear of the black cat curled up near the Aga. The light outside had faded; dark clouds rolled across the sky and a single light illuminated the barn doors across the yard.

'About time,' muttered Llŷr, pulling the wrapping off another packet of ciggies.

Scouse went on: 'In view of our recent successful operation, and following detailed discussions with Marcus Owain and the other central committee members, we have the honour to come up with a realistic plan to... well, *do* something about the Investiture. When I was with Marcus in Carmarthenshire we talked about all sorts of possibilities, but in the end, it was decided *we* should come up with ideas, and if they meet with approval down south – bingo, we're on!'

The only sound was the rasp of a striking match as Llŷr lit up. Everyone else looked intently at Scouse who stared at the table and then let his eyes roam the room, gazing intently at all those present. Geraint had thought of asking when they could have weapons practice, but what Scouse said put that out of his mind.

From the end of the long table, Pedr spoke, stroking his chin slowly for a second or two. He was the only one wearing a suit, though it was crumpled and obviously old. 'You mean we are actually going to get cracking on a real joint mission – not just marching in public, not just skulking in farmhouses and barns and packing and unpacking weapons to look at them?'

Scouse looked up at the ceiling through the gathering haze of tobacco smoke. 'You've got it mate.' He stood up, scraping back his chair and manoeuvred his bulk along the gap between chairs and the wall. While he refilled his mug from the pot on the Aga, no one spoke. 'And we'd better have one thing crystal,' he said, leaning back on the Aga rail, 'if anyone doesn't have the guts to be involved in this, if anyone wants to be excused and wait for the next marching exercise, fine – off you go. But remember your oath of secrecy and loyalty. However, if yerra true Welsh patriot and you want to make the rest of our comatose compatriots wake up, if you want to hit the English establishment where it hurts… OK, stay and let's come up with a plan, right?' He went back to his seat.

There was silence. 'Shoot him! Let's keep it simple.'

'Eh?' asked Carl.

'Charlie,' said Llŷr simply.

'Subtle, Llŷr – as always.'

'Volunteering, are you then?' Geraint detected sarcasm in Mair's voice as she looked at Llŷr.

'Any time, lovely, any time,' said Llŷr slowly. 'On my own if I have to.'

'Well, there's one idea,' said Scouse, pushing his chair back so that it groaned and creaked under his weight. His tone and expression suggested his lack of enthusiasm.

Geraint shivered, despite the warmth of the room. He wanted to speak but couldn't conjure up any sound. Pedr, however, articulated what he felt. 'Well, I for one don't agree with that. Blowing up a pipeline is one thing, a bloody good thing. Marching is OK. I could maybe even see that it we ever faced troops, shooting back and killing one of them would be necessary. But killing a civilian, even him, well, that's something else. It would be cold-blooded and, well, I just couldn't take any part in it.' He spoke calmly and slowly and then sat back, his hands clasping his empty mug.

Llŷr cursed in Welsh and then said angrily, 'Well what the bloody hell's the point of being in the Liberation *Army* of Wales if we're not willing to strike a blow that will help at least liberate people's minds from a serf-like attitude?'

'I don't see how such a killing *would*, and anyway, there's a difference between killing in combat, in war, and murder,' said Pedr.

'We *are* at war. England is using every weapon at its disposal to weaken and wipe out the Welsh nation. The Investiture is just another weapon – and Charles Windsor is the tool. We must awaken the masses and get the people out onto the streets.' Llŷr spoke quickly, vibrantly, and Geraint noticed a fleck of white at the corner of his mouth.

'Oh, I see,' put in Pedr, still calm. 'Killing Charlie will achieve this? For God's sake man, the masses, as you call them, are the most conservative people around. The women will stand for hours just to glimpse someone royal and wave a flag at them.'

Guto, on Geraint's left, said, 'He's right. My mother's like that. She'll vote for the Blaid – but boy, you criticise the Royal Family... And Lowri, the girlfriend, is the same. She... '

Scouse intervened, holding up his hands as a gesture for silence. 'OK, Guto, what we have to decide is what exactly we want to achieve. Is it to *stop* the ceremony from taking place? To disrupt it when it's actually on? Or to somehow put ourselves in a position of strength, to give ourselves bargaining power – and maybe not injure anyone?'

'That's right!' came from Mair, nodding, though what she was actually agreeing with, Geraint wasn't sure.

He glanced sideways at Llŷr, who puffed away, merely

regarding Scouse with what may or may not have been agreement. The phrase 'bargaining power' stuck in Geraint's mind. Almost without realising he was speaking aloud, he said, 'Like kidnapping him?'

Someone snorted, as though in derision. Maybe Carl. Geraint felt as though things were somehow unreal. The room was growing more and more smoky; the darkness outside seemed to have isolated them all from the world of normal people, from the mundaneness of everyday activities, from the boring rituals of school, parents, shopping, keeping your room tidy. And even from the ecstasies and challenges of the opposite sex. An intense frost gripped the still, skeletal trees and spiky grass, creating intricate silver patterns on the roofs of the cars parked outside.

And yet, thought Geraint, it was almost like an A-level discussion group and the possibility of killing, causing death, of attacking the heir to the English throne, seemed a mere intellectual exercise, an academic theory such as they tried to unravel when probing the minds of poets and dramatists and novelists in Welsh and English, before going away to write an essay. He was suddenly aware that Scouse was speaking.

'Our youngest and newest member has made a suggestion – an interesting one, if I may comment.'

Llŷr turned towards him, ash dropping onto the table. 'Come on, Ger lad. What do you expect? We just walk up to Buckingham Palace, knock at the door and then grab him? Escape in a taxi?'

Geraint was silent; it was just an idea, not a master plan he had developed. Mair spoke up. 'Of course not. But he *is* coming nearer to us soon, isn't he? Remember, Llŷr? Student in Aber?'

A 'Huh!' was all this elicited from Llŷr, but Geraint added

gratefully, 'Yes, and we could do something then.'

There was a brief silence before Scouse said, 'Well, anyone else want to comment? I mean right now all we have to do is decide *what* we want to do – as long as it's feasible, of course – and then later work out the MO.'

Pedr said through his pipe smoke, 'It's a more intelligent suggestion than the previous one. Just think of the impact, the publicity. The effects would be fantastic.'

'Yes and we could demand – oh, I don't know, something really great!'

Well, thought Geraint, that's Guto showing some enthusiasm, too.

Carl nodded, and in his awkward, heavily accented English, said, 'Indeed it is true. We could keep him kidnapped until they give in to us.'

'On what?' demanded Llŷr scornfully. 'A withdrawal of England from Wales? A seat in the UN? Let's blow him up and then they'll *really* panic.'

'But are you saying that kidnapping *won't* make them panic?' asked Mair warmly.

'In the first place,' said Llŷr, 'more difficult to kidnap than blow up or use a high-powered rifle. Remember Kennedy. Secondly, where the hell would we hide him? And thirdly, they killed our last Welsh prince, Llywelyn – so it's only revenge. And I'm not suggesting we treat his body they way they did Llywelyn's.'

Pedr shook his head and said, 'No. If we kill him, that's it. We've nothing left. Just a manhunt to end all manhunts, arrest and being despised by most people. If we survive, of course. But with kidnapping we can issue a list of demands, like reasonable ones, such as Welsh to have legal status as a language… and the Dulas Valley not to be drowned for yet another reservoir, the setting up of a Welsh Water Board to control water and charge the English, a democratically elected parliament. Oh, I don't know, we could come up with lots of good, serious demands, ones that would strike outsiders, people in other countries, as completely reasonable.' He leant forward, put his pipe down and joined his hands as though in prayer. 'And there must be plenty of places where we could hide him.'

'I think we're on the right lines,' said Scouse. 'We combine action with publicity and political demands.'

'And no one gets killed,' added Pedr.

'But you're overlooking one small thing.' Llŷr paused and then went on. 'If they are to take us seriously, we have to make our demands – with an "or else".'

There was silence. 'What d'you mean?' asked Mair.

'Don't be naïve: we say we want this and this or we… what? Kill the prince.'

Scouse shifted in his chair, making it creak. 'Yes, you have a point. But I don't think it's an insuperable problem. We can phrase the threat in some way that will give us a let-out but still make them fear the worst. And if our demands are reasonable, we'll not have the dilemma.'

'But if we do?' asked Guto.

'What?'

'Have the dilemma?'

'Then we act on a majority decision. OK? Anyway, I'm not suggesting to you that we actually murder Charlie. In any case, I doubt if it would be okayed down south. Marcus and co would have been quite happy with some plan to blow up part of Caernarfon Castle, or anything to disrupt, even stop the proceedings. But I'm more than happy with the current idea. In fact, if it works, we could be onto a winner whatever happens, short of shooting him.'

'What d'you mean?' asked Pedr.

No one spoke. Scouse smiled as though the strategy was becoming clearer in his mind. Carl got up and drew some heavy curtains over the windows that looked onto the farmyard. As he went back to his seat, he said, more cautious than normal, 'Yes, we could just kidnap him for a while – and let him go.'

'Oh yes, brilliant,' remarked Llŷr, throwing his hands up in the air.

Carl seemed embarrassed by everyone's gaze. His accent became more noticeable, as he went on: 'Well, *hogia*, to keep him kidnapped for a lot of time, like, it would be very difficult. Why don't we just take him and, well, let him go after a few hours?'

'But what on earth is the point of that?' asked Mair.

Carl didn't answer, but Pedr said slowly, 'You may have a good point there, Carl. We don't want to commit a sort of mass suicide and end up in prison for decades, as whatever we do, there will be risks, and the more drastic and complicated, the more dangerous for us.' He looked round at everyone, but no one spoke. 'If we kidnap him and keep him locked up for some time, that would pose a hell of a problem. Where would we hide him? How would we guard him? What if our demands are not met? And so on. This way, we could, well, issue a warning, make a real impact, or even try to persuade him.'

Scouse was smiling benevolently as he gazed round at everyone with pride, like a university lecturer at a tutorial, happy at the way a theory was being developed without his intervention.

'Persuade him what?' snapped Llŷr, seeming slightly more interested than before.

'Well, to see things from our point of view – to sign an agreement perhaps.'

Again, there was silence. Geraint wondered why Scouse was saying nothing. He merely looked at whoever spoke, occasionally nodding. Geraint was beginning to like Carl's idea. It seemed more practical and less dangerous. A gesture, true, but one with less of a moral problem.

Mair asked, 'If we keep him for only a few hours, how does anyone even *know* he's been kidnapped? I mean, anyone apart from the police and Queen and so on.'

'Yes, good point,' said Scouse. Mair turned to give him a treacly smile.

'Take a reporter – with a camera.' Pedr again.

'Eh?' asked Carl.

'We've done this sort of thing before. Or rather Marcus has. Remember last year, that American reporter came over, wanted to do a feature on LAW. Marcus took him by car, blindfolded him, drove all round the place to disguise the route and place, et cetera. And then showed him some of the lads practising with their weapons.'

'That's it, eh, Scouse?' said Carl.

'Yeah, I suppose it could be done.'

'So what do we do with him while we've got him?' asked Mair.

'Well,' said Pedr, 'we could make him listen. Talk to him. Tell him *why* we're against the Investiture, that it's not personal, against him. Tell him what we want to happen to Wales.'

'He has no *power* though,' said Llŷr.

'Yes, but he at least could understand how we feel. I mean, it's probably unlikely but he could even back out of being made Prince of Wales. Anyway, the least we get is one helluva lot of publicity – and LAW will become much more powerful. They'll begin to *have* to take us seriously, maybe negotiate with us. Let's face it, we'll be making *world* headlines!'

'Who says they don't already take LAW seriously?' Scouse asked this so quietly that Geraint heard him with difficulty. Then, at normal volume, he added: 'And if we wear balaclavas, we have a chance of disappearing afterwards and not being caught. After all, we'll know the land intimately, know which routes to get home as quickly and unobtrusively as possible.'

They talked on, discussing more how such time as they held him could be used and less on whether it should be done. Scouse was definitely keen on the idea, and Geraint felt that it was a good escape route from the problems posed by the original kidnapping strategy.

Llŷr alone retained doubts, if not hostility. 'I still think we should keep him. Demand something worthwhile and tell them that if we don't get what we want… ' And he drew his forefinger across his throat. Mair shook her head authoritatively, and looked sideways at Scouse who merely sat impassively. 'OK, if you're squeamish,' Llŷr went on, 'why not grab him and hide him away till they agree to call off the whole sodding pantomime. Or at least until after July. That way, they'd all look pretty silly.'

'No,' said Pedr. 'We'd never do it. Wales will disappear under a blanket of helicopters and blue uniforms within an hour of us taking him. I reckon twenty-four hours is the most we could manage,'

'You're right,' said Scouse. Llŷr appeared to be scowling at his overflowing ashtray and said nothing. 'Right then,' said Scouse decisively, 'let's vote. All those in favour of this plan to kidnap the prince for a short period, and to let him go after publicity and so on.'

Geraint raised his right hand, and then without trying to show it, looked round at the others. Pedr's hand was up. Carl merely stared ahead unseeingly and then slowly raised the fingers of one hand. Guto's hand was up, high above his head. Mair's too. 'And those against?' Llŷr raised a hand, held it there for a second and then lowered it. 'Abstentions none. Carried.'

'What about your vote?' asked Llŷr.

'Arthur is the chairman,' snapped Mair defensively.

Scouse went on as though neither had spoken. 'Right, we have a democratic decision. I shall take this back to Marcus and the central committee. I don't reckon they'll go against it. The hard part comes now. You all know the prince is due to spend two terms at Aber. This is the only reason the idea is feasible. What we want is intelligence — that is, information. Where he will be, where he will go.'

'And how do we get this information?' asked Carl.

'Some of it surprisingly easily,' answered Scouse. 'The newspapers will carry news of his engagements, where he'll be going. What's the use of royalty without publicity, going around the country and getting flags waved? A secret prince would be as much point as a secret whore. And in any case, Wales is a small incestuous country, everyone gets to know everything. So keep your ears and eyes open. And finally, with Mair and me being in Aberystwyth, we've a good chance of finding out things because that's where he himself will be staying, of course.'

When the Land Rover dropped them in Machynlleth, Llŷr and Geraint ambled slowly towards the station. 'Ger,' said Llŷr, tentatively, 'I hope you didn't mind me speaking against you. Nothing personal, just, well, you know my views.'

Geraint shook his head, wondering at the same time if his companion had abandoned his security precautions. 'I don't mind, but, well, this time I don't agree with you.'

'Well, congrats on coming up with the kidnap idea. Pretty good for someone who's only just joined us!'

Later, sitting together on the train, Llŷr said, 'By the way, if we were going to assassinate Charlie, I would have insisted that you were not directly involved. It wouldn't be fair for someone your age.'

'Thanks,' said Geraint quietly, looking over his shoulder to make sure no one was sitting near them.

Chapter 11

THERE HAD BEEN no snowfalls in Tywyn that Wednesday the arrests were made. A few miles inland, however, Cader Idris wore a white mantle, and the slate-grey houses and grey slate tips of Corris and Aberllefenni had received merely a dusting of white fluff, much to the children's disappointment, as the Tywyn school bus had no trouble negotiating the sharp, steep bends.

Geraint was in the bathroom when he heard his mother shout, 'We're off, love – don't be late for school!' She was driving his father to a meeting at the county council headquarters in Dolgellau and then going on to a WI meeting in Bala before picking up his father later, on the return journey. This had been a source of bickering the night before, over whether they could afford another car. Mair would be looking after the shop in the morning and it would close, as normal, for the afternoon.

Geraint still felt sleepy. He had been awake late, trying to master Welsh poetry quotations for a test after break. He dried his face and hands, unlocked the bathroom door and ambled through to his bedroom. In the kitchen, a radio voice burbled and then gave way to the graver, measured tones of a news reader. As Geraint buttoned his shirt, he heard something that made him freeze.

Fragments of the bulletin hit him like iced darts: ...*pre-dawn arrests this morning... nine people... Liberation Army of Wales... Carmarthen police station... charged with... A police spokesman said that... no confirmation yet that... series of bomb blasts that have rocked Wales and border areas since…*

And then news of a murder in Splott, Cardiff. Geraint sank onto the edge of his bed, his hands dropping to his bare knees. No names had been given in the bulletin, and he wondered about Llŷr, Scouse – and himself. Why, how, had he escaped? Too unimportant? Or would he be arrested in an imminent trawl of members? Would there be a ring of the doorbell any moment? 'For God's sake,' he told himself, 'I haven't done anything yet.'

If only Mel were here. Yet even if she were, what could he tell her? Should he ring Llŷr? He didn't know his number, though he assumed he could find the shop one in the book. But what if *he* had been arrested? Maybe a policeman would answer the phone.

Geraint sat there, shivering from fear and cold; a growing nausea forced him to get up and stagger to the bathroom. He lay over the sink, shaking. He felt even worse than the day Mrs Archer threw that wobbly. Something that had been exciting, stimulating, had suddenly turned frightening. He looked up into the mirror. Pull yourself together, Ger lad. Nothing has happened to you. If they were going to arrest you, wouldn't they have done so by now?

He suddenly found himself walking mechanically, half-buttoned shirt flapping round his bare thighs, to the kitchen. He switched off the radio and headed for the lounge. Without really thinking, he dialled Melanie's number.

'Hello?' A miracle – her.

'Mel?' he croaked.

'Hello? Geraint?'

He paused, finding it difficult even to get out the single word, 'Yes.'

Silence. 'Ger, what's the matter?'

'Mel, can you come round here? I'm on my own.'

'Why? You mean, now?'

'Yes. I have to see you, please.'

'But I'll see you on the way to school... or there.'

He rested his elbow on the sideboard. Oh God! Why didn't she just say yes? 'No, here! I won't be in school. Mel, just please come here as quick as you can, right? Number fifteen.'

After a short pause, she answered tetchily, 'I know which house. OK, see you there.'

'Thanks.' He put the phone down, remaining hunched over the sideboard, leaning on both elbows, eyes shut. Forcing himself to stand up, he went back to the bedroom and made his mind up. He took off his school shirt and rummaged in the wardrobe for an old check one. Jeans on, sweater, and into the kitchen. He thought about breakfast, but even the idea seemed sickening. He sipped some cold water and went back into the lounge.

He saw the morning paper on the table and brought it over to his chair, but of course, the arrests would have been too late for it. He tried to combat his nervousness and impatience by concentrating on the print. Opening it at random, he came upon the editorial where something caught his eye:

The pageantry of the procession and of the ceremony itself to the subsequent royal tour through Wales seem certain to inspire in all but the most churlish keen interest and excitement... The Investiture emphasises the nationhood of Wales... a welcome touch of colour and gaiety... the rewards for tourism... It offers all Welsh men and women an opportunity of uniting in the service of their country...

Sighing, he looked away and read on the opposite page:

British Railways yesterday defended a plan for constructing a £2,000 station at Caernarfon for the royal train... said that the town's existing station was too near the castle… British Railways said that the whole line from Bangor to Caernarfon will be closed permanently a few weeks later…

The whole page seems to be on it, thought Geraint, even though there are five months to go. What will it be like nearer the time? Trying desperately to divert his thoughts, he glanced at the letters page, but there was no escape. The British Legion chairman declared that he hoped 'the Legion throughout the principality will do its utmost to prove to some of our misguided people that, though we may be Welsh, we are still British… '

Where the hell are you, Mel? He flung the paper on the floor with disgust and impatience. His stomach was all churned up and his hands felt hot and sweaty.

And then there was a faint knock on the front door. He rushed through and opened it. 'Come in,' he panted, drinking her in with his eyes and feeling a surge of love, relief and, to his surprise, almost confidence. They stood uncertainly in front of the lounge fire. Melanie put her school briefcase on an armchair. 'Ger, what is it? Why aren't you coming to school?'

Geraint didn't answer at first but put out his arms to her. He hugged her tight, his eyes shut, breathing her fragrance, enjoying the lessening of tension deep within him.

'Ger, you're trembling. Have you got a fever?' She tried to release herself to look at his face better, but Geraint held her too tight. She relaxed into him again and whispered, 'Hey, come on. It's me. What's up?'

Geraint let go of her and shook his head. He was afraid that if he spoke he would burst into tears and that, he thought, would not do. Eventually he whispered, 'Let's sit down.'

Melanie guided him to sit on the settee. 'Now come on Geraint Rees, this is your old Mel here – as requested. I want

to know what the problem is. Your parents? Has your father…
I mean… ' She stopped, confused, and took his hands in hers.
'Tell me,' she said.

Geraint looked down. Outside, he heard two small yelping
children skipping along on their way to school. A tractor
towing a livestock trailer rumbled past beyond the narrow
garden sloping down to the front of the bungalow. 'Mel,' he
stammered. 'It's just that, well, I got a bit scared… and just
had to see you.'

'Scared about what?'

Geraint looked almost unseeingly at her bare knees and
lower thighs beneath the short school skirt. 'Mel, please trust
me, but I can't tell you. It's just that… well, I couldn't face
school today and I want you to stay with me.' He felt that
what he was saying must sound ridiculously inadequate and
unconvincing and even silly.

'So it must be important, Ger. Can't you tell me?'

He shook his head. 'Not yet.'

Melanie looked round the room, and Geraint reflected
bitterly that at last he had got her in his own house. Ironic, he
thought: how he had planned and schemed and imagined the
two of them alone here, indulging not just all the pleasures
of the flesh but the more intimate and innocent moments
of togetherness. Now, irony again, he just wanted the two
of them to escape, to get far away. The room, the whole
house, had suddenly become claustrophobic. He felt trapped
and vulnerable. 'Let's go somewhere.' He stood up and spoke
with an energy he hadn't felt up to now. 'Mel, I've got some
money – let's get the train and go for walk.'

She hesitated. 'Why do we have to get the train?'

'Oh, it's just that, well, where I want to go, we'll have
to.'

She looked down and then straight at him. 'I still think you're being unreasonable not telling me what's the matter. Still, OK, I'll have to go home and change. Just as well Daddy's at work and Mummy's gone to Aber for the day.' She could foresee problems if she wasn't home before her mother, but another look at Geraint's face made her feel that that was something she would worry about later.

'I'll come with you,' said Geraint, almost panicking at the thought of her suddenly leaving him.

'No, Ger. It's better if you don't.' She seemed embarrassed. 'Just that the neighbours might see and, well, you know what people are like.'

Geraint sighed. 'Don't I just,' he muttered. 'OK, well, I'll walk very slowly up to the main road and then along to the Talyllyn – you can catch me up there. Anyway, it won't take you long to change.' He conjured up a smile. 'Never mind about the mascara and eye-shadow.'

'OK, OK, just plain, unadorned me.' She smiled and shook her head at him, before kissing him on the cheek and leaving. For a few seconds, he stood there, immobile, hating the absolute stillness and emptiness, the non-Melanie-ness as it hit him. His mind was swirling with fears and plans and doubts; he went into his bedroom and gathered some loose change scattered across the desk. In the top drawer he found two pound notes and a ten-shilling note, and stuffed them into the back pocket of his jeans. He put the front door key in another pocket and pulled on his leather jacket. 'Mel,' he murmured to the air, and went out, slamming the door.

He walked up the road, trying not to hurry. Although no one was about, he seemed to be conscious of eyes peering at him from behind lace curtains. The sky was dark grey, the icy fingers of the wind nipping his face and neck. As he walked down towards the Talyllyn station, he kept looking behind but no one passed him on the pavement. There were just a few cars and lorries on the road, and the first of the day's three Crosville single-decker buses for Machynlleth trundled past towards Aberdyfi. He turned left and left again, down the Talyllyn slope, remembering the tense wait for her the last time they had met there.

He cursed and fretted, walking up and down in front of the display window with increasing nervousness. Unable to bear it, he hurried back up to the main road and saw her, just yards away, hair blown by the wind, panting with exertion. She wore her blue jeans and a thick, floppy white sweater under her fawn duffle coat. They hugged as she got back her breath. 'Now what?' she asked.

'We've missed the ten-to-nine and it's too early for the next train,' he said.

'Well we don't want to walk past school, do we? So let's go the long way round to the station.' She pulled his hand and led him along Neptune Road and then down Warwick Road towards the beach. After a long silence, Melanie asked him again what the matter was but Geraint shook his head, and when she persisted, muttered, 'Maybe later.'

An oppressive grey sky glowered over them and, as they stood on the promenade looking out over the ranks of advancing, wind-whipped rollers of the flood tide, a few flakes of snow swirled and fluttered. They walked slowly along towards the Beacon Hill end and down the concrete ramp onto the beach, watching the breakers pounding in towards their feet before exhausting their fury and hissing back with an angry rattle of pebbles. Their heads patterned white by slowly melting snowflakes, they turned round and headed for the station.

They walked silently under the railway bridge and entered

the station yard. To Geraint, the town seemed so normal, so ordinary. Over to the left, in the weed-tufted railway sidings, past the dilapidated wooden warehouse, he could see Gwyn and his dad shovelling coal from a railway wagon onto their lorry backed up against it. And just past them, it looked like Sulwyn humping blue plastic bags from a covered railway wagon onto the farm merchant's lorry, the peak of his battered cap down over his left ear as usual. And on their right, a green Crosville single-decker, destination Dolgellau, the driver scanning the *Daily Mirror* spread across the steering wheel. And not far away, classrooms full of children.

It was nothing out of the ordinary, of course, reflected Geraint. But that was the point: he suddenly saw the attractiveness of the mundane, the everyday, the rituals and trivia of safe, daily life.

Through the booking-office window, Geraint recognised Archie, in his 50s, stout and slow-moving, but friendly and good-humoured. He was shifting a stack of parcels and stopped when he saw them. He greeted Geraint in Welsh and added, 'Not in school today, then?'

'No,' he answered, trying to think of something. 'Doing a geography field trip,' he said, blessing the subject for its necessity for occasional wanderings around the county.

'Well, you've chosen a cold day for it,' said Archie, mopping his brow from the exertions of parcel shifting. He peered through the opening at them. 'Where you going then?'

Geraint paid for two day-returns to Barmouth. There was the familiar clunka-clunka as Archie pushed the tickets into the dating machine. In the hope of avoiding further conversation, Geraint turned away and walked back out to the platform. They crossed over to the other side.

And then an icicle thought pierced his reverie: was there somewhere a policeman with orders to pick up Geraint Rees?

Chapter 12

THEY WALKED TO the small white shelter, Geraint sitting on the old, sun-bleached bench outside, Melanie standing by him, shivering. 'Oh come on, Ger, let's go inside.' They leant against the wall, hugging each other, Geraint trying not to think of what he had enjoyed with Bethan in exactly the same spot. 'Did you have any breakfast?' asked Melanie.

'Er, no.'

'I didn't have much myself. Getting hungry already. Can we get something in Barmouth or I'll faint.'

'Yes, OK.'

Disentangling herself, Melanie moved away and stared at him. 'Ger, exactly why are we doing this? Why do we have to leave Tywyn? Why not go to school?'

Geraint seemed to be studying the tarmac. He glanced up at her, wishing she would just silently hug him again. 'I'll try to explain later. It's just that, well, I couldn't stand being imprisoned in school. And I need to escape, to get away from here. And think.' She was silent, but he sensed her dissatisfaction with his answer. 'And, Mel, I need *you*.'

Melanie shook her head as though baffled, but neither of them pursued the matter and he appreciated her moving back to hold his hand.

Once they were on the train and it had moved off with the usual snarling and rattling roar, Geraint felt an immediate lessening of tension, whether from the warmth or the fact that they were leaving the town, he wasn't sure. As it trundled north, passing the seemingly chaotic collection of gigantic sea-defence boulders and then on the other side, the regimented but deserted avenues of wooden huts, once a Royal Artillery camp, Geraint wrestled with the problem of whether to disclose to Melanie some, all or nothing of what had caused him to panic. Fragments of what he had sworn floated through his mind: *shall never reveal any secrets of our organisation... shall never reveal... shall never reveal... never... never...*

But, he reasoned, the fact that I am involved with them *doesn't* have to be a secret. After all, that was *my own* decision. And he suddenly felt relieved. Yes, he told himself, I can go some of the way. Needn't tell her of The Plan, needn't disclose the oath – well, not what it says, nor the password, not that I've ever used it – nor who's in the group.

Eventually the train siren blasted him back to awareness of his whereabouts as the two-coach diesel unit slowed, passing the Fairbourne narrow-gauge railway sheds, then crossed the road and stopped in the small station. 'We'll get off next stop,' he said to Melanie.

She looked quizzically at him. 'But that's not Barmouth, it's the one after.'

'I know. But we can walk the rest of the way. I said I wanted, needed to walk. This is part of it.' He squeezed her knee and tried to smile. 'Somehow, walking in the open air always makes me feel better.'

She nodded and held his hand. 'Well, this sure is a funny old day.'

The engine revved beneath them, making further talk almost impossible. As the train moved off, the sickly smell of diesel fumes infiltrated the coach. It trundled slowly along and before it could gain more speed, pulled up. Geraint jumped down onto the platform and turned as Melanie followed, virtually falling into his arms – such was the gap between the coach step and the low platform. Doors slammed and the train roared off, curving to the left, the sound soon dying away. No one else had alighted.

'I've been through here before,' said Melanie, breaking the silence and looking at the wooden sign proclaiming Morfa Mawddach in peeling paint. 'I've never got off, though. It's in the middle of nowhere – nearly as bad as Dyfi Junction.'

'Worse,' said Geraint. 'Here you can't even change trains.'

They stood just under the canopy of the station building, a large, brick edifice with a slate roof and boarded-up doors and windows. They looked over towards the viaduct crossing the Mawddach river and could just see the train reaching the other side. The wind moaned in the wires and bent the long grass on the other side of the track. The sky no longer had that threatening grey, but was a smudged, dirty dishwater colour. And for a few seconds, Geraint was a small, five-year-old boy again, remembering the sights and sounds of Manor locomotives waiting at the platform, the hissing steam, smoke curling up, doors slamming, the whistle blowing. 'All gone now,' he said quietly.

'What?' asked Melanie, shivering.

Geraint shrugged. 'Oh, just thinking of the steam trains – when you used to change here for Dolgellau, Ruabon. My grandad was a station master.'

'Well, they were dirty, those old steam trains. And anyway, it's progress, Ger boy.' She tried to jar him out of his melancholy. '"The old must pass away… " Remember when we read that Keats poem in English a couple of weeks ago? "Hyperion"? The old gods kicked out by the new. You can't hold up change.'

Geraint sighed again. 'Come on, let's make tracks.' And he managed another smile.

He led her down off the platform, along the cindery trackside and through a little wooden gate which led to a sandy path. After a few yards, the path widened enough for Melanie to walk alongside him. Sounding worried, she asked, 'We're not going to *walk* over the viaduct?'

'Why ever not?'

'Well... ' Melanie stopped, not sure how to explain her reluctance. 'It's, well, it's all high up, over the water. Just planks from what I've seen from the train.'

Geraint stopped and looked at her, amused. 'You're not scared, are you, Miss self-assured Melanie Wilson?' He put his hands on her shoulders and grinned. 'Hang on to your Uncle Ger and you'll be fine.'

Melanie looked unconvinced, but took his hand and they set off past sand dunes and pools. As they neared the viaduct, Geraint said with enthusiasm, 'It's a beautiful place, just look around.' She followed his gaze, admitting the truth of what he said. Behind them, rocks and crags, and further back, the hills, spotted with green clumps of bushes and twisted and stunted trees, and even higher, the mountains presided over by the majestic Cader Idris.

They were soon on the viaduct, and Geraint suddenly realised that the walking, the effort of fighting the wind and Melanie's presence had all dulled the gnawing fear deep within him. He stopped and turned, amused by her hesitation. 'It's pretty strong you know! Got to be to take the weight of trains and stand up to all the gales.'

'Maybe,' she said, advancing to take his hand. 'It's just that I don't like looking down – those gaps in the planks and the water swirling madly along.'

Geraint squeezed her hand and they walked briskly on, a sense of exhilaration slowly filling him. He had done the walk only twice before, but each time in the summer. He had always wanted to try it in the winter, with no one else about. And the wind roaring, the tide racing. They walked a little further and then Geraint stopped and they leant on the wooden rail, looking upriver. Behind them, the single, raised railway track, and alongside it, the pedestrians' path they stood on.

Melanie moved away from the rail, the icy easterly wind blowing back her hair and reddening her cheeks. As though to reassure her, Geraint clutched her hand and shouted, 'The view's even better from the middle – but even here, isn't the estuary fantastic?'

Melanie nodded, wishing she could enjoy it from a warm, comfortable train seat, even if diesel fumes sometimes swirled around them. Still, she reflected, he's right. The broad estuary, crossed here by the 800-yard viaduct, its 500 wooden piles straining against the increasing pull of the ebb tide, was impressive, whatever the season of the year. 'Shall we go on?' she asked hopefully.

Geraint looked at her and realised she was serious. 'OK, sorry. Let's go!'

They plodded on, hand in hand, buffeted by gusts of wind, cheeks glowing with effort and cold, the raging rain and snow-fed river tumultuous beneath the planks they trod. Geraint breathed deeply and felt, if not calm, at least more relaxed, despite the physical effort and the weather. He glanced from time to time up the estuary, appreciating the view of dark, inexorable water, the bare hills, the way the estuary narrowed in the distance, becoming ghostly and indistinct, and the large, riverside house on the far bank, built on rocks projecting into the water. What a place to live, he thought, especially to write or paint. I was right to get out of the house today. No, I won't think about it all yet. And he drove away intruding thoughts of what had happened.

As he strode on, slowing or stopping occasionally to gaze upstream, he also felt elated, exalted, by the fact that this beauty was part of Wales, *his* country. All this rugged grandeur, he thought, it's *my* land, and not just Wales but my county of Meirionnydd, my bit of coast. Can't have changed much since the days of the Welsh princes, since Llywelyn, Owain Glyndwr and others, marching to battle or just relaxing in peaceful summers. He desperately wanted Melanie to appreciate both the beauty *and* the fact it was Wales, not England.

Melanie held his hand, and, despite her longing for warmth, sensed some of what Geraint felt, aware that to him, the only beauty that mattered at the moment was that of the scene around them. She appreciated the beauty, saw the potential for a painting, but if she tried to analyse and compare her thoughts about it with those of Geraint, she would have merely regarded it as an impressive part of Britain, or of a region of Britain – which of course it was. But there was a great gulf between her perception of it as a nice part of 'the country', of that area of Britain where she lived, and Geraint's more proprietorial vision of it as Wales rather than England – a Wales worth fighting for.

Soon they reached the shelter of the little toll booth on the far side. He peered in but could see no one. 'Come on – free walk today.'

The Meirion Milk Bar was crowded and steamy and the plate-glass windows ran with condensation, distorting the dark shapes of passers-by. Locals, no tourists at this time of year.

Mostly speaking English, the whine of the English Midlands notable here and there.

Sitting side by side on the soft seat, they ate; Melanie with as much gusto as upbringing and boarding-school refinement would allow; Geraint, slowly, a chip at a time, picking it up with his fingers, feeling it thoughtfully and eating almost reluctantly.

They were sitting near the counter, within earshot of a crackly transistor radio blaring music, the sound mixing with the chatter and hubbub, the clattering of plates and the jingling of cutlery and hissing of steam. Melanie licked her lips demurely, and said with satisfaction, 'That's better.' She looked at her own empty plate and said, 'Hey, come on, Ger, you've got to eat.'

He didn't answer, but pursed his lips in a vague sort of acknowledging smile. Suddenly, the radio music stopped, an announcer wittered briefly and then was silent as the pips pipped. *Twelve o'clock and the news today is that...* Neither of them paid much attention – until Geraint picked up the word *Wales.* He put his hand on Melanie's leg and gripped her knee. She looked at him, noticed his alert, worried look and realised he was listening to the news. *With only two months to go before the Investiture of Prince Charles as Prince of Wales, police in Wales have arrested nine people in a pre-dawn swoop. All are allegedly members of the so-called Liberation Army of Wales and are being held...* It gave brief details and another item followed quickly.

Geraint closed his eyes for a second, rubbing them with his hand. He relaxed his hold on Melanie's knee and something made him look at her. She was staring at him strangely; he looked away, as though guilty.

'Ger – that report. It wouldn't be anything to do with

you being in a panic, us here today and so on? Would it?' He stared ahead unseeingly at the backs of the heads of people at the near table. 'Well, is it?' She spoke more sharply this time. 'Geraint, tell me! Are you mixed up in all that?'

His silence, his look, confirmed it to her. He looked at her, putting his hand gently on her knee. 'I'll tell you later, Mel. Let's get outta here. It's stifling.'

She stayed sitting as Geraint slid out and stood up. 'Ger, you've evaded every question I've asked you since you phoned me. I've a right to know. I came round when you asked. I've skived school.' He stood there, shoulders sagging, looking weary. 'Now come *on*.'

'Mel, I promise I'll explain. But not here. I need air.' He extended his hand but she followed him without accepting it.

The sky was a darker grey, and the cold nipped and picked at their faces and hands after the warm fug of the café. The street seemed as grey as the sky, as slaty and cold. It took them from the steel-grey sea and deserted beach, over the railway lines at the level crossing, and up to the main shopping street with its grey buildings, so that even the shop lights seemed murky and subdued. Behind the shops and cafés, steep hills glowered down on them.

Leading Melanie by the hand, he crossed over and turned right into a short side street. He felt a little less tense when her warm, soft hand squeezed his. They headed up a narrow, short road, so that they were soon level with the flat roofs of shops, the shabby, pipe-festooned, peeling paint, back–yarded face of commercial brightness and colour. Then past a four-storey boarding house, massive, with pillared windows but an air of gentle decay as though slowly sinking into the re-claiming rock. They turned left and plodded, bent forward, heads down, up an even steeper section. Already the railway station below seemed a carefully constructed model layout.

He led her right, off the tarmac and onto a grassy path which turned back so that they were soon rising and level with the weathercock of the mini-steeple atop the church tower. Both were soon breathing heavily. Melanie stopped, panting, and Geraint went behind her and, putting his hands on her jeaned rear, he puffed, 'Push you up, then, weakling.'

She turned quickly and, unsmiling, slapped his hands away, saying sharply, 'No thanks. I'm fitter than you are any day, mate.' She set off again, Geraint following, admiring the view, despite his dark mood. They struggled on, silent but for their panting, Geraint in front, with a determined energy that he didn't know he had, as though the climb was leading to some definite objective, some purpose, some important place which he had to reach.

They gingerly tiptoed and manoeuvred their way through occasional patches of water and mud, past tangles of brambles and bushes and what seemed to Melanie to be the narrow opening to a cave from which came the echoing, amplified sound of falling water. At last, Geraint stopped and turned round to look at Melanie, only a few paces behind him. 'Let's have a break.'

Melanie nodded, relieved. She looked round and moved over to the dry stone wall. The ground was almost level and free of gorse. She sat down on the soft, short grass and leaned back against the wall, glad to be out of the wind. Geraint sat next to her, drawing his knees up.

They were silent for a few minutes, Geraint concentrating apparently on the grey sky. Melanie spoke. 'That news report on the radio... you had, have, something to do with it.'

Geraint turned to look at her, realising how much he loved

her, admiring her face even with its current severe expression. Her hair was blown straggly by the wind and she pushed a hand through it. 'Yes,' he said.

Pause. 'Well, go on. How? Why? What on earth are *you* doing mixed up with *that* lot?'

Geraint wished she hadn't spoken the last two words with such derision. 'It was last year. I knew someone who turned out to be a member of LAW and he thought I might be interested, and they invited me to a meeting. In Machynlleth – that day I saw you at Dyfi Junction.'

'Ah, Machynlleth. I thought so.'

He noticed irrelevantly that she still hadn't mastered the pronunciation of the name. 'What do you mean, you thought so?'

'Ger, I'm not a fool. Some of your trips. Oh, go on.'

'Well,' he said, looking at his shoes, 'I was getting a bit fed up with Plaid Cymru, well, not fed up, just that it was a bit boring in branch meetings, and going round door-knocking, well, people can be so stupid.'

'If they don't agree with you, you mean?'

'Yes, well, no, I don't mean just if they don't agree.' He looked at Melanie, wishing he had not implied what he had about her. 'You know, you argue, and they don't argue back, they just say what they believe, and their minds are so closed, so blinkered. Half of them don't know why they vote the way they do. It's because their parents voted that way, or other daft reasons.'

'So what's this to do with LAW?'

'Well, they don't just talk about things, they… ' He paused, realising the need to be careful.

'Yes, Geraint, they what?'

He sighed. 'Well, some of them march in public, in

uniform, to try to arouse people, make them proud to be Welsh, to show the flag, that there is a Welsh army being formed. And others, well, campaigning in various ways.' He ended lamely, unable to explain further.

'*What* various ways?'

'I... they... ' he fumbled, speaking quietly, looking at her face, willing her to meet his gaze and take his hands. 'I took an oath when I joined. It's not a secret that I'm a member – just that I didn't want anyone to know, because of Mum and Dad.'

She looked at him, seeming astonished, and snapped, 'An *oath*?'

He felt nervous, feeling her eyes on him. 'To keep our activities secret.'

Suddenly she pushed his hands away and got up. She shook her head as though puzzled. 'Geraint, they are *extremists*, they blow up things! You can't be mixed up in that! You must be mad! I mean, you're only sixteen for one thing.'

'Nearly seventeen.' Geraint heaved himself to his feet and faced her. 'Melanie, please don't rant and rave. It's not as awful as you think.'

'Ger, don't be naïve! They're lunatics!'

'No they're not – there's some very intelligent people in it.'

'Like who?' He shook his head silently. 'I can understand, I suppose, you being in Plaid Cymru, but *this*... I mean, are they going to arrest you?'

'Hope not,' he said, attempting to smile, feeling weak in the knees.

Melanie gripped him by the shoulders. He looked down and then forced himself to meet her searching eyes, radiating a mixture of concern and condemnation. 'Ger, have you had anything to do with bombings, you know, water pipelines and stuff like that?'

Geraint noticed the perfect neat curve of her eyebrows, the long lashes, the fierce glint in the piercing brown eyes. The mouth he knew so well was now not so much inviting as set grimly, the lower lip jutting so slightly and firmly. She shook his shoulders and repeated with exasperation, '*Have* you?'

He said firmly, 'No I haven't.'

'And you won't ever, will you?'

Geraint was silent and averted his gaze. I can't bear lying to her, he thought desperately. He looked up but remained silent.

'Ger!' Then she let go of him and walked over to the wall which ran alongside the path. She sat on it and swung her legs over, feet dangling. She stared out across the sea. The daylight had faded a little and the clouds had thickened sufficiently to blot out any hint of the sun. She hugged herself as though cold and then turned, angry, eyes flashing. 'Oh, this is ridiculous! Geraint, what the hell are we doing here? I just don't believe you're into… We've got A-levels to get through for heaven's sake!' Geraint stood behind her, thrusting his hands into the pockets of his leather jacket. 'C'mon, Geraint. Just pack them in – resign. Promise me: tell them you're no longer a member and maybe you'll be safe. Even if the police do question you, you can say you've not been involved in anything and in any case you've resigned.' She paused, before adding, 'It can't be against the law just to be a member.'

He sighed. 'It's not as simple as that.'

'Why?'

'Because… ' He put his hands gently round her neck but she wriggled free. 'Mel.' His arms hung limply. 'Mel, I'm glad you came round today. I was so scared this morning. I still am. But there's nothing I can do to alter what's happened. Just let's leave it at that. I can't tell you more about LAW because, well, it's the rules.'

'Oh bother the rules!'

Geraint stared at the back of her head. She folded her arms and went on, quieter, more controlled: 'You're being so childish, so stupid about this. And unfair to me, to *us*.'

'What d'you mean?'

'You asked me to help you, to come to you. Now I have, you won't tell me everything I want to know, and you won't help yourself by getting out of the organisation. How the hell can we have a relationship with all this going on?'

'Well, you're involved in Labour Party stuff.'

'That's not the same and you know it.'

'No it isn't. What the government is doing to Wales is harming the country, the language, and Plaid Cymru is fighting back.' He began to feel a little more certain of his ground. 'No one listens to polite argument – it's only when something like LAW does things that the government sits up and takes notice. And Cymdeithas yr Iaith.'

'Who?'

'The Welsh Language Society. It's only when they organise direct action that we get changes, justice.'

'Sitting in the road or smashing road signs is not the same as blowing people up.'

'No one's been blown up by LAW.'

'Well they soon will be – it's bound to happen.'

'Now you don't know what you're talking about. All they hit is *things*, like pipelines.'

'So far. I just cannot accept it. I can't see how you can justify violence for political reasons.'

Both fell silent, avoiding each other's eyes.

'Anyway,' he muttered, 'you can talk. With your dog.'

'What's that supposed to mean?'

'Pankhurst. The suffragettes didn't exactly go round asking politely for votes for women. Bloody window smashing, acid attacks, handcuffing themselves to railings...'

'They didn't blow things up. And anyway, if men hadn't been so stupid and pig-headed... It was a real injustice they were fighting.'

'Oh, and LAW isn't? Wales is well treated and everything's fine here, is it?'

'For heaven's sake, look at all the problems in the Third World, people dying from lack of food and safe water and decent homes.' She stared at him, incomprehension mixed with anger, her eyes piercing into him. He thought he had not seen her look so angry since she had defended him against Mrs Archer. She was nearly shouting when she said: 'I mean, I wanted to go to London last month to join in that massive demo outside the American embassy in London, you know, telling them to get out of Vietnam. You know, Ger, Vietnam? A *real* problem. Then there's apartheid in South Africa, another genuine, *real* problem – and you lot are bleating about Welsh road signs and you can't have our water as it's ours so there, yah-boo!'

Geraint felt a rage surging up within him. 'Well the Third World is millions of miles away and I can't solve their problems here. This is Wales and I live here and I'm Welsh. And centuries of English rule is killing our language and culture. A real *Welsh* problem!'

'Oh to hell with the Welsh!' She shook her head and swung her legs back over onto the path. She walked back down, Geraint silently following, despairing, brushing away a tear with his hand.

Well, sod off then, he thought, anger mixing with panic

and sudden desperation not to lose her. Despite this, pride and anger kept him from speaking. What do I do now? he wondered. Stay with her – but can I calm her down, make her see sense? He kicked a stone as hard as he could, watching it soar away and out into space until it fell silently into the dead brown heather far below.

They retraced their steps and when they came to a softer grass path leading away in another direction, along rather than down, Geraint called to her, 'Mel – hang on. Don't let's go down yet. Let's walk this way.'

He stopped but she merely kept on walking and shook her head. For a moment, he thought of following – but then felt angry enough to hold back. He watched her disappear and then went along the other route which led south, towards the estuary, and he soon had a panoramic view that normally would have impressed him. Now, everything seemed colourless, flat, empty, devoid of life. He sat on a rock. No summer sounds of pounding disco music from the dodgems, no snaking little train puffing away towards Fairbourne, having met the ferry from Barmouth. He stared glumly out to sea. For what seemed like hours, he sat there as though sculpted, chin in hands. Eventually the penetrating wind made him conscious of time and he looked at his watch.

I suppose I'll have to go down, he thought. The train service was infrequent enough even in summer, and in the winter, if he didn't catch the school train, the next one wouldn't get him home till pretty late. He looked at his watch again and realised he must have missed it. Instinctively looking towards the viaduct, he saw the two-coach train becoming smaller and smaller as it approached Morfa Mawddach. Ah well, he thought, just have to wander for a bit. If I'm late, so what? What is there to go back to?

He clambered carefully down the steep hillside to a well worn path that led to the main street and people, chattering women with pushchairs, idling pensioners and all the boring ordinariness that he craved. He mooched into Woolworths and bought a bar of chocolate, all the time tense in case he spotted Melanie. Is she going to wait for the next train? he wondered. Or phone Daddy for a magic carpet? Surely she'll get the train, he thought, it's such a long way to expect him to drive. And how could she explain being here?

Eventually he reached the station. The train was waiting, the level crossing gates still closed. He walked over the line between the two sets of ponderous gates and turned left for the station entrance. A few people were hanging around or going through to the train – but no Melanie. He ambled along, looking through carriage windows, desperately aching to see her and, if not heal the breach, at least be able to chat.

She was sitting at the rear, on the far side. He gingerly approached and sat next to her, close, as it was a two rather than three-person seat. She merely glanced quickly to see who it was and then turned her head away. Neither spoke for a minute. The train's engine clattered and roared into life. A door slammed. He could see the level crossing gates beginning to swing open, slowly, then faster. A shout from the platform, a double buzz from the guard to the driver, and they began to trundle out of the station.

'Mel.' No response. 'Mel.' Geraint leant forward and put his hands on the top of the seat in front. 'Hey.'

Suddenly she turned. 'Geraint, are going to promise me you'll resign from this... this *outfit* and have nothing more to do with them?'

'Mel, why? Why is it so important to you? I mean, why does it have to affect our relationship?'

'God, you can be so stubborn. And naïve!' She looked away, out of the window, through the quick rhythmic pattern of criss-crossing steel girders as they crossed the swing bridge, the near part of the viaduct. 'Can't you see? I'm trying to save you from yourself. Oh, you think it's so noble and patriotic to be a member of this "army", but you won't feel so noble and elevated when you're responsible for someone getting killed or maimed or... And what if you're arrested? I didn't start going out with you just to see you clapped in prison or some sort of Borstal or whatever they'll put you in.' She looked through the window again, into the darkness.

'Mel, I love you. Surely that's all that matters? And I'm not going to maim or kill anyone. I don't want to. I love you, but I also, oh it sounds so corny and daft, I love Wales. I want to *do* something.'

How could he really explain? How could he get over the feeling of being Welsh, that complicated tissue of nationality within what so many people, including Melanie, thought of only in terms of the United Kingdom? The name implied a one-nation island of Britain with regions containing those also known as Scots, Welsh, Yorkshiremen, Cornishmen and Midlanders, all not that different from those in the Home Counties, the heart of Englishness, Britishness. We're British, yes, aren't we all? But as long as British equals English, so, thought Geraint, Wales will need its LAW.

'Geraint, if you're in Plaid Cymru, I can live with it. I don't agree with it but, OK, *be* a member. But LAW, God no! If you don't give me your word you're getting out of it... '

'What?'

'That's it.'

Chapter 13

THE JOURNEY WAS completed in silence, with each hoping that the other would yield. Geraint wanted to put his arm round Melanie despite his anger at her unreasonableness, but he didn't. Melanie wanted to put her arms round Geraint despite his unreasonable pig-headedness, but she didn't.

They parted, still not having spoken again. Half hoping that she would relent, Geraint followed her up Brynhyfryd Road, but when she headed for her own house, he crossed over, slowly, heavily, dragging his feet.

Only his mother was in. She was sitting at the table and greeted him in a distracted sort of way and went on poring over papers to do with the WI. He had expected a major interrogation, and couldn't believe his luck when she merely added, 'Geraint, love, you're late for tea. It's in the oven.'

Standing in the doorway to the kitchen, he asked, 'Where's Dad?'

'He told me he had to go to a meeting in Aberystwyth. And not to wait up.'

Geraint was puzzled, perhaps because she'd said, 'He told me,' whereas he was sure she would normally say, 'He's gone to a meeting.' It unsettled him slightly, nagged at him, because he couldn't account for the feeling. He shook his head and went into the kitchen. As quietly as possible, he slid the chop, potatoes and peas into the bin and crumpled some kitchen paper over it. He took a couple of Penguins from the tin and shouted, 'Anyone, er, call for me or phone?'

'What's that?'

He repeated the question, feeling tension returning to his stomach. He had half expected to see a police car outside the house.

'No love, no one.'

He was torn between trying to contact Llŷr to see if he'd been arrested – and if not, asking him what they ought to do – or staying in, hoping Melanie would ring. Finally he called out, 'Er, Mam, I'm going out. See you later.'

'All right, don't be late.'

He went into the darkness and decided to visit Llŷr. Nothing suspicious in his going there. After all, they were both members of the local branch of Plaid Cymru. He rang the bell by the side door and could hear a faint ring far off. The door had no window so he was unsure anyone was coming until it opened.

'Ger, come in lad!'

'I didn't know if you'd be here or… '

'In the nick?' asked Llŷr, going upstairs ahead of Geraint. They went into the lounge, its two windows overlooking the High Street. 'Hang on,' said Llŷr, lifting a pile of books from the armchair next to the gas fire. 'I tried to ring earlier.'

'Yeah, I went out this morning, skived school, and came back only an hour or so ago.'

'When did you hear?'

'The radio, breakfast time. Panicked a bit and went off somewhere by train, walked, thought.' He felt calmer already, realising that at last he could talk about LAW and Wales without arguing or trying to justify everything.

'Christ,' said Llŷr, shaking his head. 'I don't know how I got through this morning's work. Thank God for early closing.'

'The others?' asked Geraint.

'I don't think any of our lot have been arrested. Odd, isn't it? Especially when we, that is, Scouse, has not long ago been so active.' He took a cigarette from a packet lying in the hearth. 'On the TV news tonight, the names were all people from other areas, including of course Marcus himself. No mention of Scouse or Mair. And I spoke to Pedr and he's all right.'

'What about Scouse?' asked Geraint. 'Can we contact him?'

'I don't know how to,' said Llŷr, blowing smoke towards the ceiling. 'Nor does Pedr. He always rings us – or Mair does. Certainly keeps himself to himself. But I suppose that's good security. Carl might know where he lives, but there was no answer when I phoned him – several times. Suppose he could just be out, at a sale, or on the hills.'

'Why *did* they arrest just those in the south?'

Llŷr looked at the glowing imitation logs of the fire, his brow furrowed. 'Dunno. Maybe they could get definite evidence of some kind against them only. Or maybe they've just been chosen as sort of specimens – to frighten us all from doing anything.' He looked up at Geraint. 'And yet what they said about charges, "quasi-military organisation", could be used against all of us, though we're a bit short on the weapons front.'

'Who looks after ours?'

'I think it's Scouse, or possibly Carl. I've only ever seen them at Carl's farmhouse and the one time we went up into the hills near Llandrindod to practise with them.'

Geraint stared at the fire and then said, 'So what do we do now?' He felt a little easier in his mind, less tense, now there seemed no immediate danger of arrest. It also helped to be sitting there, warm, cosy and talking to Llŷr whom he trusted, despite some of what Geraint thought were his extreme solutions to Welsh problems.

Llŷr lay back in his chair and stretched out his feet towards the fire. He was wearing no slippers and Geraint noticed holes in his socks. 'Nothing – for the moment. We'll wait – and I'll try to find out more about what's happened.' He stood up. 'Ger, *bach*, I reckon we need a beer.' And he went out, returning with two cans of chilled Blue Bass.

They drank deeply and Geraint welcomed the beginning of an alcoholic buzz, not least as anaesthetic for the emotional strains of the afternoon. He asked, 'What d'you reckon will happen to Marcus and the others?'

'Those bastard English!' spat Llŷr with a venom that startled Geraint. 'Ah, I suppose it had to happen some time, if I'm honest with myself. The bloody establishment will let us go just so far, and then... depends on whether they've been found in possession of weapons or explosives, et cetera. I reckon they'll be kept locked up and denied bail. They'll delay a trial for ages. They'll ask for more time "to pursue their inquiries".'

Geraint couldn't help wondering again what would have happened had he been arrested. He thought of his parents having to visit him locked up, what his father would say, and he could hear his voice, the actual words. Worst of all, Melanie. Would she simply have abandoned him, rejecting him as a crazy political extremist – as she seemed already to have done? He drank more beer and tried not to see her face, feel her soft hands, hear her voice or experience the effect of her smile.

Neither of them spoke for a while. Llŷr went out and came back with more cans. 'Your parents still don't know any of this, of your involvement?'

'No. I don't want them to!'

'Melanie?'

'No.' He said it without thinking, and then willed himself to quickly slam shut his mind's doors on the tornado of emotions that had threatened to shipwreck their relationship.

'Well,' said Llŷr, 'if we are left alone, and if we are still going ahead with the plan to take Charlie, I reckon we should make sure that everything is planned round the table by all of us – no fait accompli or Scouse-action we have not agreed together.'

Geraint wasn't entirely convinced by the last idea, but diplomatically stayed silent. They talked about the members of the group, about Plaid Cymru's dilemma of whether to oppose the Investiture, of this, that and the other, lubricated by more and more cans of beer.

When Geraint realised his eyes were open only with a great effort, and that he'd been drinking on an almost empty stomach, he said, trying to enunciate his words clearly, 'Hey, I'd better have no more. Time to go. Thanks for everything – beer, the chat, and I feel easier in my mind.'

Llŷr stood up. 'OK, Ger. I'll let you know as soon as I know anything.'

Outside, the keen night air helped. Geraint stood on the kerb, waiting for a green van to head past on the other side. But as he was about to step off, it slowed and stopped. The window quickly went down and a Yorkshire voice said, 'Hello, Geraint. Off home?'

There was no other traffic about so Geraint walked over. 'Oh, hello, Mike. Been working late?'

'Yes, long day, doing a survey ready for new planting at Ynysymaengwyn.' He paused. 'Hey, strange news today, wasn't it?'

Geraint assumed he was referring to the arrests, but merely

asked, 'Er, what news?'

'The arrest of our Liberation Army soldiers. In the south.'

Geraint tried to sound nonchalant, if not downright uninterested. 'Oh yes.'

Mike shook his head. 'Just as well you're not mixed up with them, eh? Or me!' He laughed. 'Right, too cold to sit here with the window down. See you then.'

'Yes. Goodbye, Mike.' As Geraint headed up the road, he wondered first why Mike had not offered him a lift as far as his turn-off by the hospital, and then why he had mentioned the arrests. He felt so tired that he merely muttered to himself: 'Ah, I'm getting paranoid.'

His mother was watching television without the lights on, which surprised the last remaining sober compartment of his brain. His father was still not back. He managed to shout, 'Night, Mam!' before visiting the toilet and collapsing on his bed.

Chapter 14

THE NEXT DAY, Geraint was late for school – a rare occurrence. He had not really woken up properly when his mother called him, and by the time he surfaced after a series of increasingly strident *Get up*s, it was gone 8.30. His instinct was to panic and rush out without any breakfast, but he calmed himself by thinking, well, what can they do to me? Anyway, I can sneak in after assembly. Not the attitude I once had, he reflected.

Feeling he ought to try to eat something, despite the surface of his tongue being like a coir mat and a couple of hammers occasionally playing rock'n'roll in his cranium, he managed to get down some Weetabix. His mother told him she was off to a one-day Help the Aged conference in Newtown. In answer to his terse enquiry, she said his father had 'come back late' and had already left for the shop.

He found the morning paper and scanned the front-page story on the arrests, learning nothing new, but getting confirmation that none of his own group was in custody. The previous day seemed like a bad dream; he felt drained emotionally, even numb, as though nothing else could shock or panic him, and the alcoholic haze that ended the day merely intensified the impression. Then a sudden awful nagging – Melanie. What could he do? No answer lit up the dark recesses of his mind.

As he headed for school, looking at his watch to time his arrival for the chaotic few minutes between the end of assembly and settling down for registration, he was tempted to skive again, to go home knowing his parents would be out all day. After all, he could get any English notes from Pete, and for Cymraeg, from Ieuan. No, he thought, better go. 'Life must go on, and I don't want to risk anything with these exams… if I'm still a free man by June next year,' he muttered to himself.

He used the back entrance by Trefeddyg, where the few girl boarders lived. It was easy to mix with the crowds heading in all directions in the corridors, and slip into the library before the tall, thin, absent-minded Willoughby fluttered in to register them.

Geraint headed for his customary book bay and sat on the radiator with his back to the window. He'd already glimpsed Mel on the far side of the room, but she didn't appear to have seen him.

'Oh yeah, and where were you yesterday?' asked Pete, who appeared round the book shelves and joined him on the radiator.

'Oh, felt like a skive,' said Geraint, trying to sound nonchalant, and answering in English, the language Pete had used.

'*You*, skive? What is the world coming to?' asked Pete, shifting his bum on the hot pipe.

Sighing, Geraint decided to get his English books ready and, as he got up, glanced across the room to see Melanie walking towards the door. Their eyes met for a moment and he saw her lips close tightly and her look harden, before she moved out of sight.

Willoughby was still sitting near the door, completing the register, something he did by merely looking around and putting down marks for all those he saw. As Geraint passed him, he remarked, 'Ah, Geraint, you were away yesterday?'

'Er, yes, Sir. I wasn't very well.' Which was true, he thought. Willoughby merely nodded, reminded him he needed a note and marked him present.

English was a penance, or a purgatory, or simply a pain in the arse, thought Geraint. At first, he sat on his own at the back, until Pete turned round and gestured with a smile that he should join him. Melanie was on the far side with Anna. Happy at this sign of their still being mates, Geraint shoved in next to him. Pete whispered, 'Now what the hell's up with you two?' He gestured towards Mel. 'And she was away yesterday too. Come on, what's going on?'

Geraint forced a smile. 'Ah, women!' he said, trying to appear wise in their ways. 'Just a little row.'

Pete stared suspiciously but Geraint avoided his gaze. 'Oh well, if you're not gonna tell your Uncle Pete... ' He delved into his bag on the floor and took out his file. 'Did you hear the one about the young couple out shopping? They came out of the shop and the bloke started pushing the pram left outside the door. "But Henry, this isn't our baby!" protested the woman. "Shut up!" he answered. "It's a better pram."'

Geraint couldn't even conjure up a faint smile. Pete looked quizzically at him and before he could dredge up any more wit, Eleri Jones English roused herself from her book which she shut with a bang and, with legs crossed and bony knees protruding from her wooden throne, said, 'Right, dearly beloved elite of the sixth form, let us take a hard look at these prose appreciation essays I've marked.'

By the final bell, there weren't many sixth formers left in the library. Like many others living locally, Geraint had slipped out early and utilised another useful escape route down the field, past the old stables and along a narrow path by Bryntirion, a large, detached house facing the High Street.

He decided it was safe to visit Llŷr in the shop if no one else was there. Geraint's voice shook as he asked if he'd heard anything.

'No,' answered Llŷr, 'but it's a bit early yet, I suppose. Rather than my ringing you and maybe getting your parents, why don't you drop by tomorrow? I might have had a call by then.' He laughed and asked, 'Any trouble getting up this morning?'

For Geraint, the school eisteddfod was something of a blur. His attention tended to waver from the events being staged to wondering why Melanie was nowhere in sight, to thoughts of LAW, prison cells and Prince Charles.

Saturday brought some consolation, however. Bethan; the fifth-year girl with not only beautiful contours but a warm personality as well. The Plaid Cymru branch had organised an informal *noson lawen*, or social get-together, at Ty Llwyd, an old, stone-built converted farmhouse in Bryncrug where one of the primary school staff lived. People sat where they could and Geraint found himself on the carpet, wedged between the side of an armchair and Bethan – who squeezed next to him seconds after he'd sat down.

One firm, white T-shirted breast often caressed him and after a couple of cans of beer, Geraint felt relaxed and glad of her company – and smiles and leg-rubbing. They both enjoyed the traditional evening, organised as a fund-raiser. A huge hearth and rough stone fireplace complete with blackened oak beam, soft corner lights and the inevitable Salem painting on the wall, formed a warm backdrop as everyone joined in the singing, told jokes and relaxed. No one had to worry about offending anyone with 'other' views on sensitive matters. There was a pungence of burning pine logs with their red glow, and an occasional cascade of sparks as someone threw more wood on.

After Bethan came back from a toilet visit, she sat down and whispered in Welsh, 'Hey, what's on your mind?'

He shook his head and smiled. 'Is it that obvious? It's nothing really.'

She snuggled closer, if that were possible, and kissed his cheek. 'Come on, is it... you know?'

He knew whom she meant and he knew she knew he knew. 'Sorry Beth, it's just that... we get on fine for a while and then, well, something blows up.' Could've put that better, he reflected.

She was quiet and then said, 'If you want to talk about it, it's fine with me.' She brushed his cheek with her hand.

Geraint suddenly thought, God, if I didn't love Mel so much, tonight could be the start of something big. And then he smiled at the pun, glad the lights were low.

They joined in the song that had just begun: '*Mi fûm yn crwydro hyd lwybrau unig...* ' He gripped her hand. '*Mae'r wlad hon yn eiddo i ti a mi.*' Home-made wine circulated, beer bottles were snapped open and Geraint suddenly realised Mike Barraclough was there too. Their eyes met across the room and if Mike was surprised at the substitution of Bethan for Melanie, he showed no sign of it. Someone shouted in English, 'Come on Mike, your turn. Give us a song!' After cheers and shouts of encouragement, Mike responded with a full version of 'Ilkley Moor', teaching them the chorus. 'The national anthem of the independent republic of Yorkshire!' he announced at the end.

Any fantasies or longings involving Bethan were soon dissipated when Geraint realised her mum was driving them home, though he enjoyed being close to her on the back seat for a few minutes.

★ ★ ★

He made himself go to the next Plaid branch meeting, reminding himself that he was still a member and it was a duty, even if the proceedings were tedious. After some discussion, and on a proposal actually seconded by Geraint, they decided to send £30 towards the branch quota of the party's annual St David's Day Fund. They also discussed how to get more people involved in the voluntary work rebuilding and redecorating Tŷ Gwril, an old shop being converted into a constituency office and headquarters. He acknowledged the enthusiasm of the members, the dedication that could coax twenty people out on a cold evening. He heard them talk about the forthcoming general election and the chances of getting Dafydd Wigley elected. A realistic hope, many asserted. Geraint said nothing but wondered how this would happen with so many dim thickos when you went round canvassing. All rather different from LAW meetings, he thought ruefully.

Llŷr was there. He had come in late, sitting next to Geraint who had gone there with Ieuan as usual. Before they went their separate ways, Llŷr had muttered to Geraint, 'Nothing yet. Keep in touch.'

The following day in school, Geraint was looking for a book in the library when he turned into a book bay only to see Melanie sitting on the radiator in the window, reading. She looked up and blushed. He stood still and mumbled, 'Oh, er, hi.'

'So how are you these days, Ger?'

It was said in such a way that Geraint felt his knees go weak. And the fact that she said 'Ger', he thought, and in that tone. He put one hand on a nearby bookshelf and said, 'Er, fine, busy.' Oh sod it, he thought, out with it: 'But missing you.'

She said nothing, looked at his face and then down at her book. He noticed how strands of brown hair fell forward over one side of her face. She brushed them back but they fell down immediately. She looked up. 'I hear you've been consoling yourself with someone, though.'

How the hell? 'Come off it. We were both at a Plaid Cymru evening. And her mum drove us home.'

'Oh.'

'Mel.' Now he was living dangerously. 'You're the one who matters to me, you know that. So come on, let's go to the caff or for a walk. Tonight?'

She looked down and turned the page of her book. I've blown it, he thought, cursing inwardly.

'Great,' she said.

What? But then she looked at him and added quietly, 'Don't get too... I mean, if things haven't changed. You know what I mean, well, don't expect too much.'

He said nothing.

'So what time then?' she asked.

'Hospital corner? Say half seven?'

'Sure, OK.' And she did actually smile, a little one, a faint re-shaping of the lips and hint of sparkle in those brown eyes. Feeling embarrassed, he mumbled, 'See you then,' and went off to work at one of the central tables, forgetting he hadn't found the book he had wanted.

Evening at last. He arrived early and skulked in the shadows of the hospital wall and pine trees, trying to watch for her crossing the road. It was nearly twenty to when he saw her. He ran over, shouting her name. A little awkwardly, they fell into step side by side, neither reaching for the other's hand.

'Yeah, lot of reading up for an art essay that looks as if it'll be late.'

'What?' Geraint looked at her in astonishment.

'I thought you were going to ask about my homework.'

He shook his head in disbelief. 'How the hell? Yes, I was.'

She grinned. 'Must be love. If we can mind-read.' They walked on in silence until near the Talyllyn station. 'So where are we going?'

Geraint thought quickly. His house was out of the question – though if things had been right between them, he would have braved any fury and taken her there. Her house? No, no. Trixies caff was not a good idea, either, not least because there'd be interruptions from people they knew. 'Shall we walk a bit?'

He expected her to complain about the cold. However, she agreed. They walked slowly along Neptune Road towards the sea.

'Oh yes,' she said quietly as they passed the school playing-fields on the left, 'congrats on the story competition in the eisteddfod. You even beat *me*!'

He'd been surprised he had found the energy to compete. He sensed she was smiling in the dark.

'And you did well – you came first in the painting?'

'Yes.' Her voice sounded alive again, vibrant. 'I was really pleased – I thought Mairwen would beat me. You know, I saw her picture and she spent ages on it, and she's very good at watercolours. But, somehow, well, I was dead chuffed!' Another one for the folio.'

Relieved to hear how cheerful she was, he stuck out his left hand and quickly found hers, gloved. He held it, and she didn't resist. He wanted to take off her glove and feel the warm softness, but thought that might be pushing his luck. Soon they stood at the edge of the beach and stared at the horizon, a blur of dark sea and heavy black cloud.

'Mel?'

'Yes?'

'You believe me, I have missed you?'

He looked at her. They still held hands. In the moonlight, he saw her nod, and felt again the thrill of love for that profile and all she meant. She sighed. 'Yes, Ger, I believe you. And I've missed you. You don't think I wanted to end things?'

He moved closer and she drew towards him, leaning her head against him. He put one arm round her waist and thought about opening her duffle coat to put his arm round her, but decided that might come later. 'Well, then,' he said, feeling a surge of confidence, 'let's stop messing around and see each other properly.'

She said nothing for a while. 'Have you decided to... to do what I asked you to, then, about being involved with, you know?'

Diawl, thought Geraint. 'Well, I haven't been to any meetings or anything since.'

'Maybe, but that doesn't mean you won't.' She paused. 'Ger? Does it?'

'Oh come on, Mel. That's a bit unfair. I mean, you'd think I was going out almost every night on bloody army manoeuvres and setting off bombs on water pipes.'

'If you're a member, how do you know you won't at some time? And that's why I want you to pack it all in. Keep your Plaid Cymru, but pack that lot in!'

She moved away from him and thrust her hands into her coat pockets, staring at the distant, almost inaudible ebbing sea. Geraint thought. How much do I want her? Enough to?

'Listen, Mel.' He moved round so that he could face her. 'Eventually. But at the moment, there's something I want to see through – one way or the other.'

She sounded almost as though she was too tired to go on arguing. 'Oh Ger, they're *using* you, just using you – can't you see it?'

He put his hands on her shoulders. She looked down. He cupped her chin and gently raised her face. In the moonlight, she looked so beautiful, delicate, feminine, desirable. The brown eyes lacked their usual fire, though, and Geraint wished he could find the courage or desperation to renounce everything but her. If she could only leave it for a while, stop trying to force me, he thought. And he couldn't understand what she meant by 'using' him.

'Mel, just be patient. And in the meantime, can't we still see each other?'

She leant forward and kissed him on the cheek. She spoke slowly, quietly. 'Geraint, OK, we'll be friends. But not, sort of, going out with each other. Not until you do what I want.'

'But *why*?' Geraint shouted, feeling a sickening despair.

'Because, because, you stubborn, great, short-sighted Welsh nit-wit, you still mean a lot to me and I'm trying to… to… '

'… save me from myself, I know,' he added bitterly, at the same time moved by her virtual reaffirmation of love for him.

'Oh come on, Ger,' she said, sounding more relaxed. 'It's cold. Let's go back. I'm going home as I have loads to do. Look, I'll see you in school, we can talk to each other, and we can even sit next to each other in English. If you want to.'

'If I want to?' He laughed.

They held hands. She had taken off a glove and was looking at his dark face, his head silhouetted by the street lamp on the other side of the road.

'Yes, Ger.' She moved close and held him. Then she kissed him on the lips, not with passion, but with gentle love and feeling. She broke away and walked off, calling, 'Night, Ger. See you tomorrow.'

Things could be worse, he thought, crossing over, things could be worse.

Chapter 15

O<small>N</small> T<small>UESDAY</small>, <small>THE</small> last day of the holidays, Geraint got home too late to see *Wales Today* and, as they didn't watch *Heddiw*, the Welsh language news, it wasn't until he arrived in school and saw the library copies of the papers that he found out about Cardiff's new police headquarters. Its shape had been altered by a bomb – only a small alteration, at about 4pm the previous day. No one had been hurt, three windows had been broken, the lost property office and a boundary wall damaged. It was thought one stick of gelignite had been used and the remains of a pocket watch and battery were found. No one claimed responsibility but the usual ritual condemnations appeared, with LAW – despite the arrests – presumed responsible and Plaid Cymru subtly linked in one way and another.

At least Mel can't make faces at me, he thought. That afternoon he had shouted to her as she had walked past the railway sidings where he'd been helping Sulwyn hump bags of basic slag for Amaethwyr Dysynni, the farmers' company that occasionally gave him the chance to earn some valuable part-time income. Still, he reflected bitterly, I'll probably be damned by association.

He had just arrived home when the phone rang. He knew somehow it would be Llŷr. No one else was in, so it didn't matter who heard his half of the conversation. However, Llŷr was brief, merely informing him that Scouse had been in touch and there was a meeting in Machynlleth that Saturday at 2pm. It would be in a private room at the Cambrian Hotel and their cover was the Montgomeryshire Ornithological

Society. Geraint asked why on earth they didn't meet in the usual place, and Llŷr said that Scouse thought it better to vary the venue at short notice, just in case.

When the day arrived, at least he didn't have complicated explanations to make at home. His father had left earlier than usual for the shop, his mother was going to be busy with a jumble sale. Before she went out just after breakfast, she asked Geraint to get her a few things at the shops, saying she wouldn't have much time herself.

He left at ten to nine and had just come out of Baldwin's emporium and started walking back towards the post office, when he saw two figures ahead of him: Melanie and her mum, the former in jeans, her usual curvaceous, desirable self, her mother the same height as Melanie, in a long, dark coat with fur collar and perfectly permed hair. He kept pace with them as they crossed over and when her mother turned into the baker's, he hissed, 'Mel!'

She turned and they moved out of sight of the shop window. Her face lit up with a smile as she said apologetically, 'Ger, I can't talk now. See you this afternoon?'

He groaned inwardly – she seemed so pleased to see him, and possibly ready for a reconciliation. Then he thought, no, not quite that. But ready for something. 'Er, no, Mel, sorry. Going to Mach.' Then he wished he had just said 'out' or 'canvassing'.

'Machynlleth?' she asked, still, he noted, pronouncing the 'll' as 'cl'. He nodded. She compressed her lips the way she did when annoyed. 'I see.' And she turned and joined her mother in the shop.

Damn, he thought, and walked on, feeling sick and angry with himself. In a daze, he finished his shopping and went home. He left everything in the kitchen and lay on his bed for long enough almost to fall asleep. Eventually he looked at his watch. He couldn't just not go. Anyway, the present feeling would pass. He was committed.

Llŷr was already at the station when he arrived. He bought his ticket and joined him on the platform.

'Nearly phoned you again last night,' said Llŷr. 'Thought I wouldn't be able to make it. Neither of them could stand in for me, though I managed to persuade them in the end.' He looked round. Four or five people were waiting, a few on the other platform. 'Better split up,' Llŷr said. 'Just to be on the safe side. See you in the Cambrian Hotel.'

Geraint couldn't understand the need for such drama but didn't argue and went to the other end of the platform where he leant on the rail and looked along the High Street to see if he knew anyone.

He knew the Cambrian Hotel – at least he knew where it was. The Cambrian was a solid and substantial, old-fashioned hotel in the centre of Machynlleth, just across from the Victorian clock tower. He let Llŷr walk on ahead and ambled along behind until he saw him disappear inside through the double doors. He followed, feeling nervous about going into such a prominent building. He had never walked into any hotel on his own before.

Standing in the small lobby, he looked around, taking in the desk with heavy ledger, the rack of tourist leaflets and the glass doors leading to the bar. There was no one in sight to ask, but then he saw a black notice board proclaiming: 'Private meeting, Montgomeryshire Ornithological Society, Wynnstay Room.'

He found the door along a corridor, knocked and opened it cautiously.

156

'Come in, come in!' Pedr's voice. And there were the others standing round a long table. Llŷr was talking to Carl who was dressed in his customary turned-down wellies and sideways cap. A new fashion for bird-watchers, reflected Geraint.

'And how are you?' asked Pedr, his normal, avuncular self. Before Geraint could reply, the nasal accents of Scouse asked them all to sit.

In the Wynnstay Room they were soon silent, expectant, nervous. Scouse, with a loyal, adoring Mair as close as possible, dwelt briefly on the arrests. He wasn't sure why no one else had been arrested, but assumed they had chosen what they thought of as the most prominent members, the leadership and praetorian guard, and were going to indulge in a show trial – which, indeed, had already begun. He himself had lain low for a while; he had concentrated on his studies, he said, without explaining what they were, and lived the quiet life of a mature student.

'However,' he said, and paused, looking through the thickening clouds of tobacco smoke at the attentive faces, 'I have managed to send a message to Marcus, and received one back.' No explanations as to how; the fewer who knew the better, as usual. They were to operate as they saw fit, especially as regards the Charles operation. Or 'Operation Scene Change', as Scouse said they could call it for security purposes.

'And don't forget we are all ornithologists, which reminds me. Before we go, please put some money in the dish at the end of the table towards the cost of tea and biscuits. It would be odd if we had refused them. As for the room charge, I'll take care of that.'

'What about the recent explosions? Anyone we know?' asked Llŷr.

Scouse nodded slowly, but perhaps not as an affirmative. 'In view of what we are possibly going to do, everything else is irrelevant – never mind about that sort of thing. I'd rather make no comment except to say that the heart of true Welshness still beats and will not be stopped by a few arrests.'

There was a brief, if slightly puzzled, silence until Pedr said, 'Well at least it proves one thing.'

'What's that?' asked Mair.

'As Scouse said, locking up Marcus and the others hasn't put a stop to direct action.'

'Yeah, bloody right!' said Guto, raising a clenched fist triumphantly. Nor did Guto strike Geraint as interested in the feathered varieties of birds. He looked his usual labouring self – muscular, tattooed arms, shirt sleeves rolled up, loose jeans.

'And *because* we are still free,' put in Scouse, 'we must be even more security-conscious. Be alert. As far as I know, we are not under surveillance, but obviously Marcus and co were before they were arrested. I don't want to scare you, but just be sensible, right?' He looked at Geraint. 'No problems as far as you're concerned? Parents? Anyone?'

Geraint shook his head. 'No. They still know nothing about this.' He hoped he wasn't blushing, thinking about Melanie.

Scouse looked at him for a few moments and said, 'Right. Good.' He switched his attention to the others. 'I had a word with Pedr and Llŷr before we sat down. Unfortunately it's too late to make any plans concerning Charlie and his flying lessons. A pity – we might have been able to do something. But I'm sure we'll get another chance. I'm cultivating a source in Aber, someone who might just let me know in plenty of time.'

'The sooner the better,' said Llŷr, tapping his cigarette ash off. 'In the meantime, what worries me is this business of getting enough warning of Charlie's movements to enable us to meet *and* work out a foolproof plan.'

'Yes, I understand that,' said Scouse, his hands clasped and resting on the table as though in prayer. 'So, to business. I'll come to Llŷr's point in a moment. We agreed at the last meeting that we would hold him for a short period. That we would try to persuade him to... ' And he briskly summarised their strategy as formulated. He went on: 'This is not the time to allocate any individual duties or tasks, of course – not until we have a detailed plan.'

There was a knock at the door, but this time a white-pinnied waitress came in wheeling a trolley with the tea things. As she transferred everything to the table, Geraint admired her long, slim legs as she bent forward.

When she had gone, Scouse announced a ten-minute break. After he'd poured his tea, Geraint noticed Scouse at his side. He nodded in a friendly way and said, 'Well, young Geraint, your birthday soon, isn't it?'

Astonished at his knowledge, Geraint answered, 'Yes, next Tuesday. How did you know?'

Scouse merely smiled, adding, 'My business to know things. Seventeen isn't it?'

'Yes.'

'How are things in the Plaid Cymru branch up there? Any sign of active opposition to the Investiture?'

Geraint felt flattered at being asked. 'Well, no,' he said, 'though Llŷr did try to persuade them to come out and condemn it publicly.'

'Ah yes, we can rely on him,' said Scouse, sipping tea, quite elegantly, thought Geraint, considering his podgy hands. 'Still happy about being involved in this current operation then?

I mean, it could be dangerous.'

Geraint looked at him. 'It's OK,' he answered, 'I want to help.' He wished he could explain about Melanie, but this was neither the time nor the place.

Scouse nodded. Everyone else was chatting, though Geraint was aware of Mair a few feet away, as though keeping an eye on Scouse. The latter continued: 'I shouldn't say this, I suppose, but you mustn't feel pressured into helping us. If you feel you'd rather not be involved, I reckon I could persuade the others to agree and that you'd keep your mouth shut.'

Geraint was surprised. He looked down into his teacup. What was he getting at? Did he *want* him out? Or was he just being really fair to a 'mere' schoolboy?

'Don't you think I can manage it?' he asked, determined to know where he stood.

'Of course I know you can,' said Scouse, reassuringly. 'It's just that, that this ain't gonna be no game, wack! It's for serious. And yes, OK, if it goes all right, no one should have a problem melting away into normal life again.'

They sat down and resumed the meeting. Scouse commented briefly on the trial again and then said: 'As for our own forthcoming venture, as I've already said, nothing must prevent the success of the operation. We won't indulge in any more weekend manoeuvres or weapons training, though admittedly it's a while since we have, anyway. We do nothing to arouse suspicion, no boasting, loose talk, hints or anything – especially in pubs. Live your normal routine, OK?'

He looked round them all. Llŷr was puffing nervously at his umpteenth fag, Geraint noticed. No one else moved. All seemed aware that they were committing themselves to a degree they had not done before.

'As soon as we have the ideal combination of place and

opportunity, which includes the time we'll need to plan,' added Scouse, 'we meet and get going. There will be practical problems – mundane ones, like, how are you to disappear for a day or two. Pedr – from his library. Flu perhaps. Llŷr from his shop. Ill parents? Geraint from school and home.'

Well, thought Geraint, through a possible geog field trip and the little attention I get from two bickering parents these days, that may be easier than I originally thought.

There was silence for about twenty seconds. 'That's it for now, then,' said Scouse quietly. 'Don't hang around outside – disperse as quickly as possible. I'll be in touch.'

Scouse and Mair followed Geraint and Llŷr into the lobby. As they approached the revolving doors, Mair said to Scouse, 'Perhaps there's a way out through the back – down there, past the toilets. You know, for security.'

Scouse looked round, seeing no one else. He smiled. 'Well, darling, I have trained you well. Ah, we'll be OK – come on.' He took her by the hand and they all left by the main exit.

Chapter 16

A DISMAL AND boring Sunday, thought Geraint, sitting at his desk in the bedroom. Certainly not much sign of spring yet. The only colour seemed to be the yellow clumps of late, rather tired-looking daffodils in the garden over the road.

He was supposed to be writing an essay, but so far he had not even worked out the first paragraph. Staring at a photograph of Melanie, he remembered that his birthday was fast approaching. Could he inveigle her into his house, officially, that is, for a small birthday party? If his parents could conveniently be out? He hadn't bothered with a party for years. Normally, his mother would cook a meal of his choice, bake a birthday cake and he would go out with Pete and Ieuan at the weekend, expenses paid by his parents. Perhaps he could invite five or six others, at about 8pm. Bring a bottle? His mum would surely do sausage rolls and so on. And if he could slip Mel in as, sort of, one of a group, surely this would subjugate any parental antipathy or hostility? After all, he had been brought up always to be polite to guests.

He looked at his watch: 4pm. His dad would probably be asleep by the fire, the *Sunday Mirror* over his knees. His mum would have tidied away the meal things – why not ask her? They'd already given him money for a clothes-buying expedition. He'd asked if they would pay for driving lessons but neither had been keen, citing the possible open-ended nature of such a financial commitment.

Half an hour later, success. Yes, she said, but apologised

that she would not be able to do much to prepare any food herself as she had two very busy days ahead, though she could be back by 7.30pm. After hearing that his father would be at a council meeting and would probably go to the pub afterwards, he found the courage to suggest she might like to visit a friend. All right, she conceded with a smile, she would go round to see Mrs Jones Monfa for a few hours. But they wouldn't get drunk, would they? Or smoke and stub out cigarettes on the carpet? 'And don't forget, you have school the following morning.' Yes, Mam. Yes, Mam.

He went back to his bedroom and picked up the photograph. Would she come? And could he, should he, invite Bethan? Pete had had his eye on her for a while and kept asking Geraint if he had made up his mind. Maybe Pete had already made his move, and she would come with him. It was his dad that worried him, though. Should he mention it to him before the evening? It seemed wise, but not now, as he was asleep.

I wonder if Dad ever had problems with Mam when they were courting, he thought. How physical was their relationship before they married? Did they ever run barefoot on the beach, splashing through waves, or cuddle in the sandhills? More to the point, he reflected, tilting back his chair and eying Melanie, if we ever got married, would we end up like Mum and Dad? He regretted the thought instinctively; it seemed too depressing. But there remained a rational doubt. Why should we be any different from everyone else who marries? Yeah, we think we are. But would it end up with our just drifting along under the same roof, living separate lives, showing no real affection? Pete's parents seemed to be in love, not hiding their affectionate cuddles from him on his visits for egg and chips after he and Pete had got back from an Anfield trip on the special bus, back in the simple, uncomplicated days.

Stretched out on his bed, he enjoyed another dozen pages of Miller's *Tropic of Cancer*, a rather battered paperback he had picked up second-hand in the market and kept well hidden from his parents. Just as well she had not opened the door a minute ago, he reflected, but smiled, thinking that if his mother did see the book, she would believe him if he told her it was for his geography A-level studies.

By the end of Monday morning break, Geraint had arranged for everyone to come – except Melanie. There would be Pete, Ieuan, Siân and Bethan, who had, said Pete, been out with him on Saturday night.

Geraint had sat next to Melanie in English before break. She had been friendly enough, but he didn't ask her to come in case the request became complicated and then he couldn't discuss it in the lesson. At break, he was too busy seeing the others and before the bell went, she had already disappeared to double history. He waylaid her in the library when she came out, history file and books held against her chest, squashing her right breast. She smiled the old, warm, unrestrained smile, giving him confidence.

'Hi, Ger.'

They walked over to an empty window bay and again he felt as though the lunchtime hubbub faded away in the aura of togetherness. She sat on the pipes and smiled again. 'More dictation!' she complained. 'My hand is about to drop off.'

Her skirt had ridden well up her thighs and Geraint felt his eyes inexorably drawn to feast on them for a second, before forcing himself to look at her face. He knew she had noticed from the smile she was giving him.

'How's the art folio getting on?' he asked, playing safe.

'Oh, not bad. I reckon four items are OK for it so far.'

He hesitated, and then plunged in. 'Listen, Mel, you know it's my birthday tomorrow?'

'Yes, seventeen, you old man.'

He felt awkward standing there in front of her. He moved a little closer and put a hand on each of her shoulders, the warmth of her body electrifying him through the crisp white blouse, and the narrow straps of her bra. 'Well,' he said, wanting to put his arms round her but settling for the current excitement, 'how about coming round to the house tomorrow night? There'll be a few others there, sort of bring a bottle. Not really a party, just a drink, a few snacks, et cetera.' He noticed her upraised eyebrows and hurried on. 'There'll be Pete, Siân, Ieuan, er, Bethan – but she's going out with Pete and anyway, you know we're just friends. And as for Mam and Dad, well, I reckon they'll not be a problem.' She looked pleased, but said nothing. 'That's if you are not forbidden to come.' He sensed her resentment at this, but felt it a fair challenge after what had happened when her parents first found out about him.

'Yeah, why not? I can't say I'm madly pleased that you've invited Bethan, and the others are all your friends, but OK.' She looked down for a few seconds and then added with more warmth, 'Yes, Ger, sorry – of course I'll come.'

'Great, fantastic!' He wanted to kiss her but restrained himself. 'And would I have invited Bethan if there was really anything between us?'

Melanie smiled mischievously. 'You might want her there in case.'

'In case what?'

'In case. In case I don't go, sort of insurance policy. And then you can have her company.'

'Come off it! I told you: she'll be there with Pete. He's

been out with her.'

The euphoria was dispersed a little later when he realised he still had to face up to telling his father That Girl would be visiting. Although he had been determined to get it over with that night, somehow, he had failed. It was a question of waiting for the right moment – though he realised all moments were rapidly ticking away. But in the obviously frosty atmosphere, with sparse conversation interspersed with grunts and monosyllables, Geraint shied away from the challenge.

At ten o'clock, he breathed a curse as he flung himself into bed, shivering in the cold embrace of clean sheets, drawing his knees up to his chest and enjoying the slow build-up of warmth in his cocoon of comfort and refuge. The last night he'd go to bed aged sixteen. Do you feel any different being seventeen? he wondered. Is age just a number, or a condition, an attitude, a set of attitudes? What does Mel wear in bed? Oh yes, she told me once: a warm nightie in the winter, a short flimsy thing in summer. What did she call it? 'Baby-doll.' Nothing when it's really hot.

He looked at his watch – almost overslept again. Had his mum called him? He flung back the clothes and swung his legs out. He heard the front door bang and assumed it was Dad going off to the shop. Seventeen – he could scarcely believe it. And then he remembered: his dad still did not know that Melanie was coming. His mother shouted, 'Geraint, are you up?'

'Yes, Mam.'

'*Penblwydd hapus!*'

'Thanks, Mam.' He shuffled to the bathroom and splashed cold water on his face. Somehow, he couldn't feel it was any different from being sixteen the previous day. How do I feel?

he wondered. Tired. The same as always on a spring Tuesday, facing two double frees and English and geography.

He went through to the kitchen, where his mum kissed him on the cheek, again wishing him happy birthday. She bustled about, saying she had made him some toast and had to rush as she was meeting two women to go to a regional committee meeting of some sort. 'Have you told your dad that girl's coming tonight?'

'No.'

'Geraint, you said you'd tell him!'

'Yes I know. Just haven't got round to it.'

'Well you ought to see him in the shop in your lunch break, you know. He still feels very strongly about her and all that. Well, we both do. But I suppose if you and she feel that close, well, I dare say it's all right if she comes here on your birthday. And you have been working hard and did well in the eisteddfod.'

'OK, I'll see him today.'

'Oh,' she added, stuffing clothes into the washing machine, 'nearly forgot. Your card's by the toaster. And I hope you have a nice day, even though it's school. The sausage rolls and food, et cetera, are in the fridge. Put the sausage rolls in the oven enough time before you want to eat them.'

'Thanks, Mam.' He opened the envelope and read the card from them. Inside was another £5, from his mother, he reckoned. He hugged her and gave her a kiss on the cheek, wishing he could be as relaxed with his father.

She hugged him back saying, 'Geraint dear, you're getting quite a young man. Taller, growing up, a girlfriend. Well, your dad and I, we just want to see you happy, working hard and one day settling down with a sensible girl, having a family.' She paused and looked at him. 'We don't want to nag you, but you shouldn't be getting mixed up with Plaid Cymru and extremists. It makes your dad so angry and, well, life can be difficult enough without him getting worked up even more.'

Geraint wondered if there was more to this than she was saying. But he merely nodded and said, 'It'll be all right, Mam.'

She hesitated and then dived into her purse and extricated two crumpled ten-shilling notes. 'Towards some drinks tonight.' And she was off, muttering, 'Now, have I got my agenda and notes?'

The shop was empty, fortunately. Geraint stood there, pushing the door shut behind him with his foot. Prince Charles smiled naïvely from an array of Investiture plates on the shelves. And from commemorative mugs. And from bookmarks. And ashtrays and teaspoon handles and coasters and the backs of playing cards. Hanging fronds covering the stockroom door parted and his dad appeared, looking at him quizzically.

'Oh it's you. Don't usually see you here on a school day at this time.' He came forward and stood behind the counter as though Geraint were a customer. Behind him, gazing down from a framed black and white photograph, stood Elizabeth and Philip; next to them, a colour photograph depicting Charles Windsor.

Geraint smiled nervously, wondering how to begin. His dad seemed equally uneasy, as though a little embarrassed. 'Oh yes,' he said, with a thin smile, 'it's your birthday. Happy birthday. Seventeen. Doesn't seem so long since you were seven.'

Geraint said quietly, 'Oh, er, thanks for the money, Dad.'

'What are you going to do with it?'

'Well, I might buy some clothes, a record or two, though I could put some of it away towards driving lessons.'

'No, we've been through that. You're too young. Maybe when you're at college. I didn't learn until I was twenty-four. And if you are buying clothes, well I don't want you looking like some damned hippy. It's bad enough with that hair, as it is. And why not buy some nice grey trousers or cords, instead of jeans all the time?'

Geraint sighed and looked down. He told himself not to start an argument on two fronts, and said, 'I came round to mention that tonight, well, a few of my friends are coming round for a bite and a drink.' He stopped, trying to gauge his father's mood.

'Yes, so?'

'Well I've asked Melanie to come – Mam says it's all right and you weren't there when I asked her, Mam that is, and she thought, well, you don't mind do you?'

'That girl?' His father shook his head and breathed deeply, as though trying to rein in his mounting anger. 'The one who got you involved in that shameful business last year? Now look here, I thought I'd made it quite clear. I don't want you to have anything to do with her. Not that you've paid any attention to what I've said, seeing her behind our backs.' He gripped the edge of the oak counter and then banged a fist on the surface. 'Maybe I won't be listened to outside the house, but get one thing clear, young man. As long as you live at home, you'll do as I say in the home. And that young lady, if I can use such a description for someone so, so anti-authority even her own father is disappointed with her – that impudent hussy will not cross our doorstep. And that's the end of the matter.' Then he barked, 'And if she is there, well, you'll be for it, really for it my lad, birthday or no birthday.'

Geraint wanted to pick up the nearest Investiture mugs and smash them on the counter. But before he could say or do anything, his father rasped, 'You've just no respect any more, no respect for your parents, your appearance, and you're mixing with people who have no respect for this country, the law.'

Without hesitation, Geraint said calmly and slowly, 'Oh you are so wrong. I have great respect for the LAW.'

His father looked at him, trying to decide if he was being sarcastic. Then he added: 'Well, you just make sure that she, that girl, does not darken our doorstep!'

Rebellious anger struggled with his accustomed submission. He was seventeen, therefore nearly eighteen in a way. And what's at stake? he thought. Mel. He looked at the counter and then up at his father. Or slightly down, as his height gave him that advantage. 'Dad, Mam doesn't mind her coming. And I live there too – it's my home as well. You see your friends there and I've got a right to see mine. She's not a hussy nor impudent. And she means a lot to me.' God, it was working, he thought, he was standing up to him. 'She's coming tonight.'

His father stared at him, cheeks reddening. For a second, Geraint wondered if was going to explode with wrath and reiterate the edict – or cave in and waffle, trying to save face. The door bell ting-ed before either could speak. Two middle-aged women came in, potential customers. Geraint turned and recognised their faces, though he didn't know their names. He looked back at his father and saw the angry lines melting into the shopkeeper's obsequious affability. He marched out, leaving the door open.

Round the corner, he stopped, breathing deeply. Just have to play it by ear, he thought. If he does appear while she is there, let's hope Mam will exercise a civilising influence on him. Deep down, however, he wondered what he would do if his dad ordered her to leave the house.

By the end of the geog lesson, he felt reasonably calm again and then spent a pleasant half hour with Melanie in the library, jointly planning a seminar on Keats' *Lamia*, Geraint teasing her that she reminded him of the poem's enchantress.

Twenty minutes before the final bell, he said, 'Right, I'm going to nip home. Got to buy some drinks and get things ready. Fancy coming? There'll be no one in.' This invitation was a sudden inspiration and he almost feared her acceptance.

She shook her head and said, 'Tell you what. We'll both escape but I've got one or two things to sort at home. And I'll see you at – seven-thirty?'

'As early as you like. Bring a bottle – or two.'

She smiled, asking, 'Is that because you can't buy them yourself?'

'No! All organised. Pete's older brother is meeting me outside the off-licence, and anyway, I know the bloke who usually serves.'

'Clever,' she said, standing up.

'The direct route, I think.' He took her hand and was pleased she returned the grip.

As they crossed the almost empty library, she said, 'Now you are leading me astray.'

Geraint lifted the lower sash window, a rush of cold air embracing them and cooling his ardour. As Melanie clambered through, pleated grey mini-skirt on high, there were wolf-whistles from the two boys sitting nearby. Geraint smiled self-consciously and climbed through after her. He pulled the window shut and they headed towards the rear entrance near the girls' boarding house.

Having checked that neither of the sports teachers was on the field, they walked quickly out, turned right and heaved a sigh of relief as they headed for the crossroads.

Shall I warn her of Dad? he wondered. If I say nothing and Dad goes up the wall when he sees her, will she cope? Would she just go, and turn her back on me? Then, if I do warn her, will this scare her off coming?

They turned left onto the Aberdyfi road, passing the corner house, whose garden flaunted a large Union flag hanging limply from a tall wooden flagpole.

'So,' said Melanie, glancing at him with a smile, 'you're sure your parents don't mind me coming?' She paused, then added, 'Why the sigh?'

Geraint gritted his teeth and then said, 'Sorry. Mam's not objecting at least. Well, I think she's just nosey. Dying to meet you. The famous revolutionary – and big accountant's daughter. Her beloved son's first girlfriend and all that.' Oh well, some of that's sort of true, he thought.

She was smiling. 'First?'

'Yeah – first steady one. Proper one.' Then he added, 'Dad's the problem. Crazy really – your parents are just the sort he'd boast about being friendly with: upper-class English, wealthy and all that.'

'Hey watch it you – Welsh peasant!'

'Yes, but you know what I mean. He knows your dad from the Rotary and Chamber of Commerce. And just because he thinks you put me up to that anti-English Welsh Nationalist demo last year… well, you're damned, my girl.' He looked at her and put his arms across her shoulders. She didn't resist. 'Courage. You'll be my guest. He'll probably be OK, and you might not see him. Council meetings and all that.'

Melanie said quietly, 'So it just might be an exciting evening. And Bethan there, too.'

Geraint looked sharply at her. 'Come on – less of that!'

She moved against him and gave him one of her warm, deeply loving smiles, the sort he hadn't seen for ages, the eyes kissing him, caressing him – and then kissed him softly on the cheek before walking away and crossing over.

God, how I love her, he thought.

Chapter 17

GERAINT WENT HOME to an empty house. He looked in his wardrobe but decided to get changed later. There were four more birthday cards on the front doormat, and he arranged them on the sideboard next to the one from his parents (in his mum's handwriting, he noticed). One card contained a record token from Aunty Carys in Blaenau Ffestiniog.

After his successful excursion to meet Pete's brother, and unloading the carrier bags, he checked the sausage rolls were in the fridge. In a tin in the cupboard was a large chocolate cake his mother had baked on Sunday, and he gathered together everything he thought could be devoured later on. After cramming most of the beer cans into the fridge, he slumped into an armchair to watch the antics of Tom and Jerry.

He was almost dozing off when the doorbell rang. He looked at his watch: seven o'clock. Mel? He dashed to the door, rubbing his eyes. Holding hands, a hippy Pete and a gorgeous, flared, white-jeaned Bethan. 'Hi – come in!'

As they came in, Bethan said, 'Hope we're not early, but I called for Pete and suggested we came round to see if you needed a hand with anything.' She took a white envelope from a pocket, kissed him on the cheek and said, 'Happy birthday, Ger!'

Geraint smiled and thanked her, noting the three kisses under her name on the card, together with a record token. Pete slapped him on the back and handed him a carrier bag with a promising bulge and weight, which turned out to be a bottle of vodka. 'Come on then,' said Pete, leading the way to the lounge. 'Where's the music? Glasses, bottle opener?'

Bethan followed, saying sharply, 'Hey you, we came here to help him get things ready.'

'That's OK,' said Geraint. 'The record player's over there. Get some records from the bedroom and I'll get the sarnies and beer.'

Bethan followed Geraint into the kitchen, where she bustled around, organising and giving orders which he cheerfully obeyed, showing her where everything was. 'While I'm doing this, Geraint Rees,' she said, 'you can get me a small vodka and orange.' At which, the strains of Amen Corner's 'Bend Me, Shape Me' could be heard.

As he poured her drink, Geraint felt a twinge of guilt relishing Bethan's appearance and tried to console himself by putting it down to mere lust. Then Ieuan arrived. Then Siân, who gave him a card and a record. 'I hope you haven't bought it, Ger,' she said, after wishing him happy birthday and standing on her toes to kiss him. He ripped open the wrapping paper, uncovering a Dafydd Iwan single, 'Carlo', currently in the Welsh Top 20.

Bethan then shooed everyone into the lounge, Geraint shouting after them, 'Be careful of the bloody carpet with drinks, or Mum'll kill me!'

At the end of the record, Pete nudged Geraint and whispered, 'Where's Melanie then?'

Geraint looked at his watch. Nearly eight o'clock. Where indeed? What could have delayed her? Parental feet going down firmly? No, it couldn't be. Much application of make-up? No, she wasn't like that. Cold feet? Bethan's presence? Surely not. He shrugged, saying, 'Put another record on,' then savagely levered two holes into the top of a beer can.

He flung the opener to one side and drank deeply. Well, if she wasn't coming, nothing else for it. He wasn't going to ring this time. He looked around. Pete was now sitting in an armchair by the red-glowing gas fire, Bethan was on the rug, leaning back between his legs, and Siân sat opposite, waving around a glass to emphasise a point she was making. Ieuan, owlish in his black specs, hovered awkwardly behind the chair and Geraint wondered if he should have tried to pair him with someone. So far, he was not aware that Ieuan had dated any girl, nor even disclosed – to Geraint anyway – that he fancied anyone in particular. With his glasses and serious expression, dark, flopping hair and rather thin face, he could look studious and preoccupied, more concerned with the aesthetic and philosophical than the carnal. Which, reflected Geraint, must come from living in a manse. Rather him than me, he thought yet again.

He stood up, wishing, yearning for the doorbell to ring. Noticing Bethan smiling at him, he made an effort to look relaxed and managed a twisted smile. Siân shouted, 'Come on, Ger, sit down here!' He squeezed into the middle of the settee and asked if anyone wanted to eat. As no one answered, he sat back and closed his eyes for a second.

'Hey everyone! What do you think of the sixth form at Ysgol y Gader?' It was an animated Siân who spoke. Faced by puzzled looks, she went on: 'You mean you haven't heard? My cousin phoned me – they're having a sit-in in the school library!'

'Fed up with school dinners?' asked Pete.

'No! It's a protest against the head volunteering to send some of the sixth form as guests to represent the school at the Investiture! And without asking anyone first if they agreed.'

'Wow!' gasped Bethan. 'Hardly fair, is it?'

'They're supposed to be staying there all night,' added Siân.

'Well, good for them,' put in Ieuan. 'The ideal peaceful protest.'

'Eh, shush you lot. I like this record,' shouted Pete, and they stopped chatting. Eventually, in the silence after 'Dizzy Miss Lizzy' by the Swinging Blue Jeans, Bethan looked up at Pete and said, 'Hey, what's the matter? It must be at least five minutes since you told a joke. Losing your touch?'

Pete took a swig and smiled. 'Right pop-pickers, in response to the overwhelming wishes of my fans… '

'Boo-o-o!' interjected Siân.

'I'll ignore that. Right then,' he said and switched to English to continue. 'One day the minister stopped little Mair leading a cow along the lane. "Where are you taking the cow, Mair?" he asked. "To the bull, Reverend," she answered. "Can't your father do it?" he asked. "No, she replied, only the bull."'

Jeers and laughter while Pete smirked and waved his beer can. They listened to more music, chatting, joking, drinking. Geraint drank faster than he thought was wise, but felt a pleasing numbing of his Melanie-anxiety. However, he sensed that he was nearing the point where to drink any more would push him down that slope that could not be climbed up until the next morning.

At nine o'clock, Bethan organised the food break and Geraint knocked over his drink, the clumsiness sounding more warning bells, partly because he didn't want to make a mess and partly in case Someone suddenly turned up.

Ten minutes later, despite the noise, he heard the strident ringing. Putting down his can carefully, he went out as fast as he could, trying to walk straight. Melanie looked nervous, hesitant even, but the mere sight of her relaxed him enough to smile broadly. 'Come in, *cariad*.' He felt his lips almost involuntarily forming the silent words, What a vision of heaven. She had put her hair up and when she took off her PVC mack, he saw she was wearing a mini–length fawn dress, sleeveless and plain except for a narrow collar and an intriguing diamond opening between her breasts. With her stockings and light brown shoes, together with a subtle perfume that slowly penetrated his befuddled head, he realised that her sophisticated, adult appearance made him nervous. 'You look fabulous.' He hugged her, sensing a genuine and unexpected warmth and power as she held him.

She whispered a 'Happy birthday' in his ear, and then released herself, picking up a carrier bag she had put down earlier. 'Sorry I'm late. And here's something, well, hope you like them.'

She took two parcels from the bag and gave them to him. Telling her to follow, he led her to the bedroom, managing to walk straight and shake away something of the haze in his mind. The Beatles were *yeah-yeahing* in the lounge. She stood there, still nervous he thought, and before he ripped off the very carefully wrapped paper with its yachting motifs, noting the labels (*To Geraint, with lots of love, Melanie xxxx*), he invited her to sit down. She sat on the very edge of his bed, thighs exposed. The first parcel contained two books, Eliot's *Four Quartets* and Islwyn Ffowc Elis' *Wythnos yng Nghymru Fydd*. She said, 'I don't think you know the Eliot, but I think its great, and I hope you will. The other one is because, well, someone recommended it. A bit like *1984*.'

Geraint kissed her lips gently. 'Great, Mel, thanks.'

She smiled and said, 'Geraint Rees, you've been doing a bit of drinking before I came, haven't you? You're swaying.'

He tried to stand erect and said carefully, 'Certainly not. Well, just a bit. While I was wondering where you were.'

'Oh, I see.' She looked down for a moment. 'Sorry. Hey, open the other parcel, and there's a card somewhere in this bag.'

He ripped the paper off a small cardboard box. Inside was something he had meant to buy for himself: a wide leather belt, patterned, with a Welsh dragon buckle. And a hippy-style headband. 'Oh thanks, Mel.' He slipped on the headband and looked in the mirror. 'It's great.'

'You look pretty good, real cool, man!'

He hugged her and then held her back, devouring her with his eyes. This was not the Melanie of school, albeit attractive in her mini-skirts. Nor the Melanie of straining-seamed blue jeans. She was a woman — in aura, in subtle make-up and perfume. Meanwhile, he was almost afraid the vision would disappear like a rainbow-coloured bubble shimmering in sunlight, and then pricked into oblivion.

And then he remembered. 'Where have you been all this time? I was getting suicidal.'

'Oh don't say that, Ger. Sorry. I just couldn't get here any earlier, honest.' She grimaced and added, 'C'mon, we'd better join the others.'

They went through into the wave of music and Bethan's cigarette smoke, and Ieuan doing the twist (Ieuan dancing? he thought) with Siân. Everyone looked over and shouted, 'Hi, Mel!' and Geraint noticed with pride the admiring surprise on Pete's face as he saw her. When the record ended, he noticed Bethan looking at Mel's dress and asking, 'Oh yeah, been to Biba's again?'

'Didn't think you'd have heard of them,' Melanie answered, quietly but tartly. Was there, Geraint wondered, a bit of the old knife going in there? Surely not. He went to the kitchen to get Mel a drink, adding a slosh of Martini to the vodka and then some lemonade. He picked up the ice cubes he'd dropped all over the floor, and decided against opening another beer for himself. The other intoxication was more satisfying, he reflected.

For two hours they all enjoyed themselves; sometimes dancing, sometimes letting the music run out and chatting; drinking – though Geraint noticed Melanie sipped hers so slowly that she was only on her second an hour after she had arrived.

He danced with her. Not during fast records but tight against her during the slow ones, her slim waist encircled by his arms, his hands sometimes running gently up and down her dress, over the hollow of her back and down. She seemed a little preoccupied, didn't laugh and talk as much as he'd expected when they were sitting around the fire. He wondered if it was down to Bethan's presence, or simply that she was a little shy in a gang she didn't usually mix with.

There was another lull in the music. Geraint and Melanie were on one armchair, she on his lap; Siân opposite, Ieuan sitting on the floor between her legs; Bethan on Pete's lap on the settee. Perhaps making a special effort, Melanie was asking Bethan something about the school hockey team, when Geraint suddenly stiffened. He recognised a sound outside. It grew louder and then stopped. His father had parked the car on the drive.

Melanie, sensing his unease, looked at him questioningly. 'Your dad?' He nodded slowly and felt tense. She slid off his lap, straightened her dress and touched her hair. Geraint stood up, too. His legs felt weak, whether from alcohol or imminent confrontation, he wasn't sure. He took Melanie's hand in his and they stood there, expectant. Everyone else looked at them, aware that something was amiss. Geraint suddenly felt foolish. 'Come on,' he said to Mel, 'let's sit down.' They seated themselves side by side on the settee while he heard the front door opening. It shut – and then the lounge door opened and his father stood there.

It was quiet enough to hear the faint hum from the record-player and a gust of wind outside. Geraint felt he should get up, but overcame the urge. He looked at his father and forced himself to say with as much calm and normality as possible: 'Oh, hi, Dad.' He thought for a moment his father was going to speak to Melanie and from the expression on his face, it would not have been friendly. But he just said to him, 'Come here,' and then went back into the hall. Geraint muttered an 'Excuse me' and got up. He stood facing his father. He sensed that his father had also been drinking – more than usual. He had never seen his father drunk. A little tipsy, yes, but never noticeably.

'That person,' began his father, seeming to be making an effort to enunciate clearly and precisely, 'is, I presume, the one you were told was not to enter this house.'

Geraint breathed in and tried to feel calm and controlled. 'If you mean Melanie, yes, that's her.'

His father looked at him and Geraint felt the anger radiating from him as he spat out, 'Well, she can leave – right now. And I shall have a talk with you, young man, tomorrow. You can bid farewell to your other friends and get yourself straight to bed. Understood?' There was just a slight slurring of the last word, he noticed.

Geraint felt as though this was unreal. He had half expected such a scene but even now it seemed almost dreamlike. He didn't know what to say, feeling it would have been easier had his father shouted and cursed at him. His father, assuming silence to be acquiescence, went into the lounge and Geraint heard him say, 'Young lady, I regret you are leaving – now No, I don't regret it. Geraint had strict instructions you were not to visit this house.'

Geraint stood there, shaking, trying to think clearly. His father stood in the lounge doorway, surveying them all 'No,' Geraint whispered without looking at her, 'you're not going.'

Melanie looked from him to his father and back. 'I better,' she said quietly.

He felt a surge of desperation. He looked at his father and then at Melanie, her eyes cast down. With shaking, scarcely controlled rage, he said to his father, 'Melanie is my guest and you have no right to ask her to leave.'

'No right? No right?' His father took a step toward Geraint and for a moment he thought he was going to strike him. But he moved past to open the front door, allowing in a cold blast of air. He held it open, looking at Melanie. She nodded and walked slowly out, not even asking for her coat his father slammed the door shut. 'Now you can explain to your other guests why they'll also have to leave.'

Geraint felt disbelief. It was a nightmare and he'd wake up soon. He stood there, eyes closed for a few seconds. Then, in a quiet and shaky voice, he said, 'Good night, Dad.'

He darted through to his bedroom and grabbed Melanie' mack. His father merely stood there, swaying, impassive, as Geraint went out. With no jacket or sweater on, he felt the knifing wind. She was passing through the orange light of street lamp and he ran to catch her. Hearing his footsteps, she turned. They faced each other and she merely said as though unsurprised, 'Ger.' He hugged her, burying his face into her soft hair. 'Ger, you're shivering, you'd better get back in.'

She took the mack and slipped it on. Geraint helped her and then enfolded her in his arms. 'I'm not going back in.'

'What do you mean?'

'Just that. I'm not going in. The bastard! Mel, I'm so sorry. It's so embarrassing. And insulting, to you.'

She ruffled the hair at the back of his head. 'Not your fault, Ger. Well, what now?'

'I dunno.'

There was a pause. No one was about. Lines of trim bungalows, neat, small gardens protected by white plastic chains, and sleeping, respectable, middle-aged and elderly couples stirring in their troubled dreams and nightly surfacing fantasies.

'So come on then. Let's walk fast to warm you up.'

Geraint didn't ask what she meant, although he guessed. What alternative was there? Pete's? Might just as well stay with Melanie, what did anything else matter? All he knew was that he couldn't stand even being under the same roof as his father.

They said nothing on the way, each wrapped up in their own thoughts. If Melanie foresaw difficulties, she gave no sign. As they walked up the drive to her darkened house, Geraint gave a shaky laugh but said nothing.

She opened the door with her key and they tiptoed into the darkness. Switching on a light, she whispered, 'They'll both be in bed.' She led him down the hall and into the lounge. A corner light cast a warm glow over what seemed to Geraint to be a luxurious room, with soft carpet, polished wood, paintings, a bookcase and chairs just inviting you to sink into them. He stood there, feeling awkward and shivering.

'Sit down, Ger,' she said, and added, 'welcome!'

'What now?' asked Geraint.

She knelt by him, putting her head on his knee. 'Lord knows, and I don't really care.'

He closed his eyes and stroked her hair. 'Mel, I love you so much.' She touched his cheek, and, opening his eyes, he felt warmed by her smile.

'Melanie?' The voice came from the hall. A woman's voice, enquiring, unsure.

'Mummy,' said Melanie, getting up. 'I thought you'd have been asleep by now.'

Geraint felt exhausted and embarrassed, but found the strength to haul himself to his feet as she came in, in her cream dressing-gown and fluffy slippers. Melanie said, 'Er, Mummy, this is Geraint.'

Geraint focused on her face, wondering if he was looking at Melanie in twenty years. She had the same brown eyes, colour of hair, and a hint of severity and stubbornness in her face. He ran a hand through his hair as he managed to say, 'Oh, good evening, Mrs Wilson.'

'Almost good morning,' was the slightly frosty answer.

'Mummy, can I have a word with you?' asked Melanie.

'I think that would be a very good idea.'

The two of them went into the hall. He could hear muffled voices from behind the closed door. The tone and pitch indicated the moods of the speakers, neither sounding as if they were pleading or submitting. Then silence.

Melanie reappeared and went over to him and put her arms round his waist, whispering, 'It's all right: you can stay the night. I too can be firm.'

He leant his cheek against hers, asking, 'Separate rooms?'

'Geraint! Of course!' She laughed awkwardly.

'You're blushing!'

She looked down. 'Be quiet, you.'

He had a sudden vision of the two of them and was jerked to reality by the strident ringing of the phone in the hall.

This time of night? Melanie thought. She pecked him on the cheek and whirled off to answer it. Before she reached the door, however, it stopped ringing. She looked back at him, saying, 'The extension. One of them has answered it.' She looked questioningly at Geraint. 'Your mum?' Geraint shrugged, and Melanie went into the hall, quickly returning to tell him that her mother said it was for him. Yes, his mother, concerned, distraught.

'It's OK, Mam,' he interrupted her. 'How did you know I was here?'

'Oh, I guessed, but never mind that.'

Geraint broke in again to say, 'Mam, I'm staying here for the rest of the night. Melanie's mum says it's all right. Mam, I'm sorry, but it was so... embarrassing, so horrible the way he was.'

'I know, love, I know, it must have been. And on your birthday. And in front of all those friends of yours.'

'Where's Dad now?'

'He's in bed, snoring away. Geraint, I'm really sorry this has happened, but you know his opinion of her, and he has been more... difficult lately.'

'What do you mean, difficult?'

'Oh, just in various ways. Are you sure you're all right? And you don't have your pyjamas or toothbrush or clean underwear.'

'Hey Mam, stop worrying – I'm only about three hundred yards away! I'll call back in the morning and get changed into school clothes.'

Silence, and then, 'Well, if you're sure you're all right.

Oh, how embarrassing! What will I say to her parents?'

Geraint wished her good night and felt a sudden surge of sympathy for her. How difficult a time had she had with his father when she arrived home? He realised Melanie was holding his left hand. She pulled him back to the lounge and gently pushed him into an easy chair. 'Sorted?' she asked.

'Yes, thanks, *cariad*.'

She smiled down at him and said, 'C'mon, sleepy, I'll show you to your room. You don't mind sleeping without pyjamas?'

He undressed in a small but impeccably furnished bedroom with a soft carpet. He got into bed and lay there, thinking, leaving the small bedside lamp on. He felt sleep drifting over him and sensed someone standing by the single bed. He forced open his eyes. Melanie. In a dressing-gown. She bent down, and a perfumed mass of brown hair swept his face as she kissed him on the cheek and said good night. Almost before she had left, he was asleep.

He had a headache, that was definite, though little else seemed to make sense. Someone was not helping by saying insistently, 'Geraint, time to get up!' Through cracked eyelids he spied Melanie – dressing-gowned, hair tousled, leaning over him and grinning.

'I think it's called a self-inflicted wound, at least that's what Daddy said once. Now come on, you! It's seven-thirty, plenty of time for you to have a shower, get home and change, et cetera. There's a towel on the chair. Bathroom – remember? Turn left, first door on the left. OK? Hurry, and you'll make it before Dad takes possession.'

'Oh, right.' Geraint levered himself up onto one elbow, groaning.

She stood there, looking concerned. 'Come on. And as an incentive, when you come back there'll be some black coffee by the bed.' And away she went, too late to see him slide out of bed wearing only his underpants.

He was back within ten minutes, already feeling half-human, and sipped the coffee. She peeped round the door and he called out, 'Hey, Mel, thanks for everything. I just don't know what to say.'

She came in, saying, 'It's I who should thank you. It's not every week I have a boyfriend who makes himself homeless on my behalf.' She looked apologetic. 'Oh, Ger, I don't mean it that way. I mean you and your Dad; you'll probably make it up.'

He sat on the bed, half dressed, and said, 'God, Mel, I don't know how you can be so calm about it. He was so bloody insulting to you. I tell you one thing: I'm not speaking to him until he apologises, and even then he can go to hell.' He looked down, embarrassed by the memories. 'I suppose,' he muttered, 'I'd better go home and see what's what. And get changed for school, though that's the last place I want to go to.'

'Yes, but we'll see each other there.'

She looked even more slim and somehow vulnerable in her tightly tied dressing-gown; he wondered if she had anything on underneath. He quickly finished dressing and said, 'Right, I'd better go.'

'Do you want something to eat? Cereal?'

'No thanks, couldn't face any food.'

She led him downstairs and, as he opened the front door, he heard a door close upstairs. He kissed her on the cheek, saying, 'See you later,' and he crunched down the drive into the cold, grey morning. As he crossed the road, a thought struck him: I've slept there – in Mel's house! Maybe on my own, but in her house!

They didn't have much time together. She had games after registration and he had Welsh after break. They sat on the window ledge before the bell went for assembly. Melanie said she had endured a silent breakfast with her parents, though an evening chat was promised. She asked how he had got on.

He sighed. 'Not too bad, considering. He was still in bed, but when I let myself in, Mam was already up. So I just said you'd been marvellous, your parents were, well, sort of OK, and got changed.'

'Your head?'

'Don't remind me,' he said, grimacing.

She smiled. 'Certainly a birthday to remember.' She thought and then asked, 'What about tonight? After school? Will you be going home for tea?'

Geraint nodded. 'S'pose so. It's early closing so he might be there, unless he's gone off on council business. Hope so – then I can talk to Mam about things.'

Someone appeared in their book bay. 'Hi, Pete,' said Geraint, feeling himself going red.

Pete came over, and realising Geraint's feelings, said, 'Hey, don't worry about it. No sweat. We just said our good nights and went. Quietly, no problem. And,' he said, sitting next to Geraint, 'we agreed that none of us would say anything about what happened. You know what people are round here, big mouths and so on.'

Geraint said with a great sense of relief, 'Oh, great! Thanks. I really appreciate it.'

Melanie thanked him, too, and kissed him on his cheek.

'Well,' added Pete, 'I have to confess it wasn't my plan,

but I agreed with it of course. Siân suggested it and we all agreed after we'd left the house.' He grinned at them. 'So how did you two get on?'

Before either could begin to explain, the bell went for assembly and Geraint just said, glad of the excuse, 'Ah, tell you later.'

Six days later, on 29 April, a bomb exploded at the Central Electricity Generating Board offices in Twyn y Fedwen Road, Cardiff. It was a small, relatively unsophisticated device with a pocket watch or small clock timer and about a quarter of a pound of explosive. Little damage was caused.

Chapter 18

THE MEETING WAS arranged at short notice for Friday evening, 2 May. The only item on the agenda was to be Operation Scene Change, the Prince Charles plan.

This time, Pedr drove to Tywyn, picking up Llŷr and Geraint at the second shelter from the southerly end of the promenade. Geraint sat in the back of Pedr's battered Maxi, tense and nervous. Yet again his mind drifted back to his earlier conversation with Melanie.

'Ger, you can't go!'

'What do you mean, can't?'

It was a fine May evening and the sea over to his right sparkled in the setting sun as Pedr drove on.

'Because… just because. Ger, I don't want you to go. Just promise me, please!'

He had stayed silent, wrestling with it.

'Ger, we've been through all this and I've, well, weakened, I know. But tonight, now, I don't want you to go.'

'It's important, I've got to go. Please don't try to make a big issue of it.'

Over on the carefully manicured golf links were strolling, club-carrying figures, and others, immobile, poised to strike.

'It is a big issue. I can't really explain, but I don't want you to go tonight – not just because we were going for a walk, but… ' But what, then?

High up on their left were the imposing white walls of the Trefeddian Hotel with its uninterrupted views across the Dyfi estuary and Cardigan Bay.

'You'll just have to trust me, Ger.'

He had visions of Scouse and the others, the flag, memories of his oath, the arguments and the necessity of striking a really effective blow for Cymru. 'Mel, I have to do it. I mean, go tonight. I'll ring you when I get back.'

A young couple, holding hands, smiling secretly at each other, oblivious to the world, heading into the Penhelig Arms for an evening of togetherness.

'Mel, why are you getting so worked up about it all? It's just a meeting tonight.'

'Geraint, I am asking you to stay here, not to go. I just want you not to get mixed up any more, please!'

He tried to hold her but she jerked away angrily. 'It's not fair, you're trying to force me and it's, well, it's important to me, and I don't see why it has to be a big choice, between LAW and you.'

Pedr drove past the entrance to the Outward Bound school and on, along winding roads next to the railway line, both hugging the narrow strip of land between the hills and wide estuary. Pennal, Cwrt, with their memories of Owain Glyndwr's efforts to establish his parliament, and onwards to turn right, crossing the bridge to Machynlleth where his parliament building still stood – a reminder of what Wales briefly had, could have kept and developed. If only, thought Geraint. He tried to forget that Melanie was English.

It couldn't end. He thought back to his one night in her house, to going home that afternoon, his mother reassuring him that it would be quite 'safe' to sleep there that night. In fact, it was his father who did not sleep there. He telephoned at ten o'clock to say that, after his meeting, he had gone back to County Councillor Martin Lewis' house in Brithdir where they were having a few drinks and consequently did not feel he should risk driving... and would be home in time to open up the shop on Thursday. Geraint thought this unusual but as his mother passed no comment, he said nothing. On Thursday evening, his father had returned home at the normal time and surprised his wife with a bunch of flowers, apologising for his absence and ignoring Geraint. Which somehow meant, hoped Geraint, that he was at least softening in regard to his antipathy to Melanie. He spent the evening behind the newspaper and glued to the television.

Passing the clock tower in the town centre, they headed on along the Aberystwyth road for Carl's farmhouse. Llŷr was puffing away as usual and Pedr was delivering a thoughtful monologue on whether Plaid Cymru could win any more parliamentary seats.

How would Melanie spend the evening? They had intended going to the promenade and perhaps along the beach towards Aberdyfi. She had told her parents that Geraint had had a gigantic row with his parents and that was the reason for his hasty need of hospitality that evening. She refused to elaborate on what the row had been about, though she reckoned her parents suspected. In any case, they had gone on seeing each other, feeling closer than they had been for a long time. Until this meeting came up.

They were the last to arrive. Carl greeted them and handed each one a steaming great mug of tea. They milled around chatting, attacking a mound of ham and tomato sandwiches on the long, scrubbed table. Scouse was engaged in deep conversation with Guto Evans of Corris, Mair laughing at something one of them had just said.

'So, how's life?' Llŷr asked Carl as they stood looking out of the window across the yard.

'Well, thank God for this good weather,' he said. 'So

far, this year has been bloody awful. You know, all the rain, much colder than usual. Lambing figures down and the ewes, you know, are using all their energy just to keep warm and I'm spending good money on feed because the grass just isn't growing like it should.'

'Is Carl moaning again?' Scouse clapped Llŷr on the shoulders and laughed. Geraint, standing near them, thought that Scouse must, therefore, know a little more Welsh than he had thought.

'Well, you would be moaning if you was farming here, isn't it?' said Carl in English.

They sat down around the familiar table, Llŷr appropriating one ashtray, Pedr the other. Despite his tumultuous affairs of the heart, Geraint felt a renewed excitement. Action at last.

Scouse broke the silence. 'I don't need to remind each of you how vital security is this evening. What we are going to discuss must remain within our heads and must not be mentioned or hinted or boasted about to anyone – lovers, wives, mothers, girlfriends.' His gaze swung round them, pausing on Guto, and rested on Geraint, who blushed and nodded, thinking with guilt about what he had already divulged to Melanie but consoling himself with the thought that she would not have told anyone else. In any case, she didn't know anything of importance.

'We've marched in public, shown the flag, been away for weekends for weapons practice, and I have undertaken special missions on our behalf. But tonight is the most important meeting we have ever attended.' He looked round the room again and raised his voice. 'So if anyone has had second thoughts about what we are aiming to do, doubts had better be voiced now.'

Silence, apart from the double click of a lighter.

'I think we are all united,' said Carl.

'Geraint?' Scouse was looking at him. Disconcerted by the attention, he merely nodded and said, 'OK.'

'Right then, let's get down to business.'

Scouse, as usual, chaired the meeting, dominating it both by virtue of his office and personality, his accent less pronounced when being formal, thicker when relaxed. He told them that he had received information – but did not divulge his source – as to the prince's programme and travel arrangements for the rest of the month. Tapping his pen on the table, he went on: 'There are two items on his programme that are potentially useful for us. First, he is to be the guest of the Marquess of Anglesey at Plas Newydd, his Anglesey home, one weekend very soon. My information is that he is almost certain to walk from there the one and half miles over the fields to Llanedwen church, a pretty secluded spot near the Menai Straits, on the Sunday. He will also be inspecting the preparations at Caernarfon, and will probably fly back from RAF Valley.' He stopped, as though inviting reactions. Tobacco smoke was already thickening and swirling.

'How on earth did you find out all this?' asked an obviously impressed Carl.

'That's not important,' he answered, smiling at an adoring glance from Mair. 'What is important is that I don't think this is any good for us. Partly because the date is very near and partly because of the distance involved. Also, those responsible for his security might feel that much more relaxed if nothing happens to him this time – when he'll be presenting rather an obvious, and superficially easy target.'

Pedr took his pipe out of his mouth and said quietly, 'You could even say they might be inviting an attempt.'

'Oh, come on, why?' asked Mair, with a scathing look.

Pedr paused, before adding, 'To pounce on whoever makes the attempt.'

'Not very likely,' put in Scouse. 'I don't think their minds work like that. And it could be awkward if things went pear-shaped.'

Geraint coughed in the smoke, and as though glad of an interruption, Mair got up and opened a small window. She smiled at him as she sat down.

'Now,' went on Scouse, 'let us consider Thursday, May 22nd. Just before the Whit Bank Holiday weekend. Charles Windsor is due to spend the best part of the Thursday filming on location in Radnorshire. David Frost, no less, to interview him on his duties and life as prince. At the home of the Lord Lieutenant at Newbridge-on-Wye. He'll be driving the forty-plus miles in his blue MG.' Scouse stabbed the air with his pen, adding, 'And, lady and gentlemen, almost unbelievable, but I have it on the best authority, he will be accompanied only by his personal bodyguard who will ride with him in the car. I just happen to know that his name is Anthony Speed, Detective Sergeant Anthony Speed.'

Geraint heard two voices clashing: 'How the hell do you know his name?' and 'Eh? That's really his name?'

Scouse merely smiled enigmatically and Llŷr said, 'So you're suggesting we go for that, rather than the weekend in Anglesey?'

Scouse nodded.

'But surely we have a perfect opportunity at the Anglesey weekend? He's going to be walking across fields, going round Caernarfon. I mean, bloody hell, how appropriate if we can grab him right near the site of the whole blasted pantomime!'

Carl was nodding. Mair shook her head, adding, 'No. As Scouse said, it's quite a distance from here. And remember Scouse used the words "almost certain" and "expected to". So what if his plans change?'

'I appreciate Llŷr's comments,' said Scouse slowly, 'but Mair has put her finger on it. And we'd have insufficient cover to grab him from those fields, and I can tell you this: he'll have a damn sight more protection than Detective Sergeant Anthony Speed that weekend.' He paused, looking at Carl and Llŷr, neither of whom responded. 'The whole business is too near Caernarfon, too much police attention. The Radnorshire thing is much easier. A good distance from Caernarfon. Narrow roads, hedges, woods, isolated farm buildings, et cetera.'

'And it does give us extra time, vital time, to be ready,' put in Pedr, gouging out his pipe into an ashtray.

'Yes, of course,' said Mair, nodding so much that strands of red hair fell across her face.

Elbows on table, Guto sparked into life. 'So what do we do, then? Grab him while he's on his way to this Lord Whatsisname's, in his car?'

'What do you think?' asked Scouse, looking at him.

Guto shrugged and looked round, as though waiting for someone else to speak. 'OK, why not?'

There was a moment's silence before Geraint spoke, almost without realising it: 'How do we actually stop him, then?'

'Good,' said Mair, nodding at him, 'let's get down to brass tacks.'

'Hold on a minute,' interrupted Llŷr. 'Where? Just in the middle of the main road? Jump out, hand in the air? Or do we hire a pantomime cop's uniform and try to look realistic? Then what? Even if he does stop?'

'Good questions,' said Scouse, 'we're addressing the practical difficulties.' He stopped, and bent down to fish something from a bag on the floor. Putting three Ordnance Survey maps on the table, he went on: 'These two one-inch maps cover the route. The other one, two and a half inches, gives us more detail.'

He stood up and pushed two mugs and the empty sandwich plate out of the way. He opened a one-inch map, pointed to an A-road and said, 'This is part of the main road he'll have to travel over. We could do it in one or two places... bends, overhanging trees, no houses nearby. But it is an A-road. There could be other traffic around, especially holiday traffic making an early start for the Bank Holiday weekend.' He jabbed his pen at a junction. 'Here, he leaves the main road and has no choice but to take this narrow road, and just about nothing will be on it unless it's going to the Lord Lieutenant's house. Here, trees close to the road. A stream there, bridge, possible cover under, and so on.'

They crowded round, necks craning.

Llŷr straightened up and took a cigarette out of his mouth. 'We'd need to have a look at the place, suss it out, and there's the small matter of where we'd take him afterwards.'

Carl and Guto spoke at once, agreeing and wondering about the explosives and whether anyone should be invited from the television companies, what they'd ask the prince to do and say.

'OK everyone,' said Scouse, folding part of the map. 'Let's sit down and be methodical.' He looked at Mair to his left. 'To speed things up, because we don't have a lot of time, Mair and I have jotted down various headings, aspects of the plan that need working out. Mair?'

Opening the file in front of her, she said, 'Yes, thank you

Arthur. Well, first of course is the site, the actual place to bring the car to a stop. We think we've cracked that problem – it's clear on the large-scale map – and Arthur and I just had enough time to visit it discreetly this morning.'

Scouse touched her lightly on the arm. 'If I can cut across, Mair, I don't want anyone to feel they are being rushed into this. Is everyone happy with what we've done so far?'

No one responded immediately, although Llŷr leant towards Geraint and muttered, 'See? Once again loads of things already decided.'

Scouse looked over. 'Sorry, you say something, Llŷr?'

Llŷr inhaled on his cigarette and then said, 'Not really. Just that an awful lot seems to have been decided before we got here. Like the Birmingham pipeline. I thought we were going to discuss, vote, come to an agreement.'

For a couple of seconds, Scouse gazed impassively at him. Then an obviously annoyed Mair spoke up: 'Llŷr, Arthur is trying to help. Have you any idea how much work and planning he's done to make it easier for us? We'd be here for ages if we had to begin trying to decide on where and ways to stop him.'

Scouse held up a hand, saying, 'OK, Mair, thank you. Llŷr, believe me, Mair is right in that I've tried to save us loadsa time.' He paused, looking around at the others. 'As the only one with a military background, I reckon I can save you time and put my expertise at your disposal. And this is a democratic meeting. If anyone disagrees with any aspect, please speak up. You usually do, Llŷr,' he concluded drily.

After a short silence, Pedr said, 'It seems OK. I appreciate the work and planning you've put it into it. But we'd have to visit it first, wouldn't we, to familiarise ourselves with it?'

'Yeah, that's a fair point mate,' said Scouse. 'But we can't all just trundle down there in a minibus and start poking around and measuring and expect not to be noticed by someone.'

'So what do we do then?'

Scouse tapped his pen on the map. 'If you'll accept the recce done already by Mair and me,' he looked over at Llŷr, who was blowing smoke rings upwards, 'we'll meet again and I'll have photographs developed by then showing you the site. She and I will go back for a more detailed shufti. We'll be ideal because a courting couple who lose their way will be good cover.' He smiled and Mair attempted to look coy. 'Let's go through the headings first. Mair?'

'Right, how do we stop the car? Well, there's a sharp bend here.' She stood up and smoothed the map, before pointing. 'We reckon we'll manage it by erecting a "Road Up" sign and another saying there will traffic lights ahead. We'll put these just before the bend, to slow them down a bit. And then as soon as they go round it, there'll be a tractor blocking the way, someone tinkering with the engine or trying to manoeuvre a trailer or something.' She looked at Scouse to see if she was getting it right.

He nodded and took over. 'Right, Mair. Then we pounce. And just in case they think of reversing or turning, the Land Rover will come bombing up and block their rear.' He looked round at them. 'We did think of using explosives to blow up the road, but I think that would be, well, unnecessarily melodramatic if not plain noisy.'

'Yes,' added Pedr, 'the less noise the better.'

'Right,' put in Guto, 'surprise is the best weapon, yes?'

'Exactly, Guto,' said Mair. 'And we have a culvert and bushes, trees, right near the road on both sides so we should be well hidden. Not that there's likely to be any traffic on that lane anyway.'

'As for the road signs,' said Scouse, 'Carl, Guto and Pedr, Mair and I, will keep an eye open over the next few days. We're bound to come across some – and when it's dark, or nothing is about, grab 'em, hide 'em. I'll check by phone to make sure we have the right ones. Anything else we need, I'll get it unless I ask you specifically.'

There was silence, and each somehow simultaneously looked round, eyeing each other, as though in disbelief that the plans were taking shape. Llŷr broke the silence with: 'Sorry, but I have to say this. Mine the road at that spot – Scouse will presumably know how from his military days. Press the plunger. Boom. We disappear from sight. LAW claims responsibility. End of prince. End of Investiture.'

Geraint couldn't help admiring Llŷr's directness and the simplicity of the idea. However, the little conscience bell tinkled again, and he felt he did not want to be part of such deliberate killing, despite the identity of the target.

There was a silence, again broken by Pedr, speaking calmly and carefully. 'Llŷr, this is not Vietnam or Palestine. And we have agreed already on something else. What we are trying to accomplish should yield just as much publicity and even, perhaps, some glimmerings of sympathy and understanding in the head of Charles Windsor – how he's being used, what we want, and so on.'

Scouse nodded. Geraint felt easier. Llŷr looked around, as though seeking support. None came.

'How will you organise the tractor?' asked Geraint, glad of the chance to get back on track.

'Don't worry about that,' answered Scouse. 'A friend of Marcus, a farmer, lives nearby.'

'Timing?' asked Pedr. 'How do we know what time he'll pass the spot?'

Geraint glanced at Llŷr to see how he was taking another rebuff.

'We'll know the approximate time,' said Scouse. 'And it will be a matter of being in position in plenty of time and being very patient, very still.'

'And hoping it won't be pissing down,' said Llŷr quietly.

Scouse nodded. 'A dry day will help, yes. Geraint, I'd like you to go on lookout. There is a hill by the bend and an easy climb to a vantage point from where you can see the car leaving the main A-road. You'll have binoculars and a two-way radio to warn us as soon as he's on the way. Then you dash down to join us. OK?'

Geraint was so surprised that he could do no more than nod. He knew he would have to be involved somehow, and had always been worried about what sort of role he would be given and how well he could cope. What Scouse had lined up for him was pretty simple, he reflected, and he even felt a sense of relief in knowing what it was, and how straightforward it sounded. He almost missed what Mair was saying.

'Next heading is weapons. Three of us will have pistols and they should be enough to force the two of them out and control them. Someone will have to remove the copper's weapon.'

Scouse interrupted. 'This can be altered, of course, but I think the three to approach the car will be myself, Carl and Guto. I'll disarm the bodyguard.'

Geraint couldn't help wondering if Scouse was not letting Llŷr near the prince with a gun. Carl asked, 'Where will we take him afterwards?'

Scouse looked at the map. 'Problem solved again. There is a rough track nearby, dead end. Or so it looks. Half a mile up, there is a barn, half full of hay, last time we looked. A bit dilapidated, rarely used, no house overlooking it or nearby. But the point is, there's a gate into a grassy field and a Land Rover could easily make its way across that field and onto another road. We'll have two options. One, a hired van will meet us at the spot where we stop the prince; everyone bundles into it. Or, as it's better to have a plan B, we drive up the track and either lie low temporarily in the barn or head straight for the road across the field and, using the radio, calling the hired van to meet us there. And before you ask, someone reliable, from down there, will be driving the van. One of us will also have to drive our Land Rover back up here, together with any of us not needed in dealing with the prince.'

'But exactly where do we head for? Where are we going to keep him?'

'Key question, Carl. It will be a remote house about fifteen miles away. One of our members who was not arrested recently. He will be away on holiday and will not, does not, know what we are borrowing his house for.'

Again there was a silence as though everyone, even Scouse, seemed over-awed by the enormity of what they were planning; that all their words, hot air, frustration, dreams, were becoming reality.

'Go on,' said Carl.

'Well,' resumed Scouse quietly, 'we hide the van under some trees and take the pair, blindfolded, into the house. We'll be wearing balaclavas, of course, and nobody calls any one of us by name. And we wear gloves all the time. Then we get to work.'

'Demands – and publicity,' said Guto.

'And trying to make Charles see things from our point of view,' added Pedr, his pipe cold on the table.

'Yes,' added Carl enthusiastically. 'Get him away from all his bloody royal hangers-on and bigwigs and tell him plain what we think, eh?'

Guto thumped the table, saying, 'Exactly, yes!'

Smiling, Scouse held up a hand for silence. 'Right. We try to persuade him to sign a document stating that he agrees not to be invested as Prince of Wales. If he agrees, the jackpot. But to be realistic, we need to talk quietly and politely about Wales, what we want to change and why, and so on.'

'A reporter?' asked Pedr.

Mair answered. 'We arrange in advance for a television or newspaper reporter to be standing by in a convenient place. We don't give him or her any details, of course, but promise them something big, newsworthy, and tell them to bring a camera. Once we've got the prince, one of us phones the reporter and arranges to meet him or her, and we send someone to fetch him here, back of a van, blindfold, et cetera.'

Scouse nodded, like a thoughtful tutor pleased with a student.

'And after we've achieved all this?' asked Llŷr, leaning back in his chair.

'We agreed we would release them,' said Mair.

Scouse added, 'The detective will be kept separate in the house. And then we'll blindfold them both, put them in the back of the van, disguise the location by driving round and about and release them on a lonely road and zoom off.' Putting his hands behind his head, he looked round at them all. 'Any questions?'

Carl raised one hand. 'What happens to the prince's car? Do we just leave it there?'

Scouse nodded. 'Well, I'd like to haul it onto a low-loader and make it vanish, leave them all baffled even more. But

I'm not sure if we can go that far. And I'm not sure it will even matter. Once we're away and have hidden the pair, they will presumably begin searching outwards from that point and hopefully by the time they really intensify things we'll be finished and gone.'

After a few seconds' silence, Pedr said, picking up his pipe, 'Congratulations. A lot of thought and meticulous planning. I'm impressed.'

'Thanks,' said Scouse. 'A few more details to put in place, like how we all get home, but I reckon we have a damn good chance of success.'

There was a sudden release of tension and babble of voices. Geraint shouted over to Llŷr, 'Come on, it looks good!' Llŷr forced a smile and nodded.

Scouse and Mair spoke for half a minute, and then he shouted, 'Right, before you all get carried away... ' The noise died down. '... we have only twenty days. Pedr, will you be in charge of getting a reporter lined up? Don't approach him or her until you've checked with me. But you have good contacts with media people. Someone, preferably a stringer so he'll dish out to all and sundry and be able to handle a camera. No separate photographer, right?'

Pedr nodded. 'No prob.'

'Right, Mair and I will draw up a draft document for the prince to sign. Maybe he won't, but we'd be silly not to have one prepared. We'll meet again a few days before the 22nd, and then on the evening of the 21st.'

Mair turned to him. 'Time off?'

'Oh yes. We'll need to be out of sight from, say, the Wednesday night, the night before, that is, till the following evening. Pedr says he has holidays owing and can take them at short notice. He'll tell his wife something convincing to explain the night away. He has a fortunately sick relative in the south. Llŷr too can take a holiday and has no wife to worry about. Carl has no pressing engagements and lives on his own anyway. A neighbour will keep an eye on the sheep and so on.'

Carl nodded. Scouse turned to look at Geraint. 'Well, Ger lad, what about you?'

He had thought about this aspect of the plan some weeks back. He couldn't very well say he was staying with Melanie. It would have to be a geography field trip, perhaps an individual one for his own research, to prepare for a major research essay. Or even a pre-university visit to Aber.

'I've one or two ideas. Should be no problem.' He did not add what he was thinking: that with the strains and tensions of home life these days, he could probably tell them there was a geography field trip to Saturn and his mother would merely ask if he had plenty of clean underwear.

'OK, then, Geraint. Do your best to make it convincing. Think of every angle. Something simple, not too complicated. Easily verified if possible. OK?' Geraint nodded. 'Thank you all for coming today, for your enthusiasm and commitment… and let us make sure we strike a blow for Wales that will reverberate around the world and force the London government to take us seriously!'

Chairs scraped on the stone flags as people stood up, stretching. Pedr appeared by Geraint and asked him in Welsh, 'Sure you'll be all right with all this? It's a lot to take on at your age, you know.'

Geraint smiled. 'Don't worry about me,' he said firmly, feeling unusually confident. 'I've been waiting for this for ages. And Scouse seems to know what he's doing.'

Pedr looked thoughtful, adding, 'Right, then, let's get you

and Llŷr back to the jewel of Cardigan Bay – Tywyn.'

You mean Melanie, thought Geraint.

Chapter 19

O**N SUNDAY HIS** father stayed in bed late and then took almost permanent refuge behind the pages of the *Sunday Mirror* until dinner was ready. After a silent meal, Geraint wiped up for his mother and then retreated to his bedroom. He stared at, rather than read, the pages of his geography book, and then concentrated even less when he heard raised voices. It seemed to have begun with one asking the other whether he/she had paid the television licence which was due. His father said that he hadn't got time when there was a business to run and if she spent just a bit less time on committees and drinking tea with other women… Well, if he gave her the £6 then she would pay for it tomorrow. Why should he give her £6? That should come out of the house-keeping money or be saved up over the twelve months.

And then onto money in general and why couldn't they sit down and discuss it like normal, civilised people, and why did it have turn into a blazing row every time? Well there's no need to make accusations and how would he like it if he had to buy everything out of that amount a week and was it his fault if the car had needed a new head gasket last month? Didn't she realise petrol now cost 6s 2d a gallon? Ad infinitum.

And no one telephoned Geraint all day.

Nor did Melanie turn up in school on Monday. He went through the weary motions, occasionally forgetting. Not in the mood for lunchtime football or wandering the streets, he sat in a corner of the library and read his geography notes for last lesson. Siân was sitting opposite, skimming through the library copy of the *Daily Post*. She slid it over to him. 'Hey, Ger, you seen this?'

He glanced at the article. One of Prince Charles' tutors had been found dead. He read on. On Saturday, someone had discovered the dead body of Dr P Tudur Morrison, head of the philosophy department at Aberystwyth and one of the prince's tutors there. The body was discovered on the beach at Ynyslas near his car, presumably drowned. He had helped prepare the prince's curriculum and was engaged to be married. Lived ten miles from the beach. Well, well, thought Geraint.

'Odd, isn't it?' he asked, pushing the paper back to her. He wondered if it was a straightforward accident or suicide. Or was it something more? Christ, am I getting paranoid? he wondered. The guy had probably been jilted or something. Women again.

Ieuan came in, said 'Hi!' to Geraint and sat next to Siân, who smiled at him. Oh-ho-ho, Geraint thought, perhaps my birthday did produce something good after all. Come to think of it, he had seen them sitting together now and again since then – but it would be just like Ieuan not to say anything or spread it around. Probably scared of having his leg pulled.

'Where's Mel today, then?' asked Siân.

'Er, not too well. She wasn't feeling great at the weekend.'

Tuesday began with double English – and Melanie sitting with Anna. Nudges and questions from Pete didn't help, but Geraint diverted the attack by asking what he knew about Siân and Ieuan. Which wasn't a lot.

When the last bell rang, he watched Melanie. She had collected everything ready for a speedy escape and flitted out and down the corridor as quickly as she could. He gathered his own things and followed, walking the same route and keeping her in sight in case she turned round and waited. She didn't.

The rest of the week was no better. She avoided him as she had months before. When they were in the same room, the library or English, he often studied her face or the back of her head – either willing her to look at him or because he found her beautiful. Once, working in the library, he looked up and saw her eyes on him, quickly lowered. What surprised him was not that she was looking at him, but the hint of... he wasn't sure. Certainly not loathing or even anger. Perhaps concern, pity? Off-putting, he felt.

He decided that attending the branch meeting that Wednesday would at least get him out of the house – and relieve his conscience, as he had not been for a while. One of the members gave Ieuan and him a lift to Neuadd Egryn in Llanegryn; Siân and Llŷr both sent their apologies, said the secretary, when the meeting began at 7.45pm. Geraint's chair was as uncomfortable as ever, the agenda was the same as always, and although he was aware of the hard work members were putting into the usual fund-raising for head office and the election fund, and into canvassing and organising coffee mornings and getting out press releases and letters to the papers, he couldn't feel stirred by it. He was conscious all the time of the Radnorshire business, of what they hoped to achieve; it was so much more dramatic, dangerous, exciting and potentially effective. If they were ever to win home rule, how could it come from sitting on hard seats in dusty village halls?

He was pleased they went straight home afterwards, rather than to the Railway in Abergynolwyn. The house was empty, which he thought a blessing, but his mood nose dived again when he heard on the radio that England had beaten Wales 2-1 at Wembley.

He had the house to himself during most of Saturday and lolled around, picking at school work, watching the banalities of children's telly and listening to music. He could have gone to Liverpool with Pete but had declined the offer, afraid to be away from the telephone for so long. His heart thumped when the phone did ring, but it was only some English-sounding woman with a message about a meeting his mother was going to the following week. He even thought about offering to help in the shop but decided he didn't want to face people and have to wear various affable masks, to say nothing of being with his dad if he hadn't gone somewhere. On Sunday, he retreated to his bedroom while his parents ghosted around in the frosty atmosphere of the other rooms.

On the Wednesday, he was looking through the paper in the school library just before the end of lunchtime. He had been about to close the paper when an article caught his eye. The inquest had been held into the death of Dr Tudur Morrison, Prince Charles' tutor. Cause of death confirmed as drowning. Fiancée baffled; said he had been happy. He had had a lot of work on that weekend and had cancelled their date to catch up. Someone else gave evidence that he had lectured to the prince only twenty-four hours before his death. And the same person, a fellow lecturer, added that his colleague had expressed some concern about the prince's safety. But he had not explained what he meant and the witness had heard no more about it. There was no further comment on the matter.

For five minutes Geraint sat there and pondered. *Had*

expressed concern for the prince's safety. Diawl! Had he got wind of their plan? If so… And then he told himself to stop worrying. He could just as easily have been referring to students insulting the prince, or possibly egg-throwing or even some plot totally unconnected with theirs.

The time was approaching. Next week. By a week on Friday it should all be over. Geraint still felt a sense of amazement, verging on disbelief, that he was involved in it. It would be on television and in every newspaper, maybe worldwide. But if they failed, cocked it up somehow, failed to foresee something… Come off it, Geraint reassured himself. Scouse is the tops, the best. Tough. Foreign Legion training. Experienced. A real Welsh patriot, despite his accent. He would lead them into something they'd never forget, that would change the face of Welsh politics. And yet, and yet – suppose something had leaked out? Suppose Guto had had one too many at his local, and…

Still, Llŷr had told him when he'd called in the shop that things were going all right; that they would meet on Monday night for a final briefing – and he had even found time to buy him a balaclava. Meanwhile, Geraint had his cover story lined up: a geography department visit to Aber, overnight because the programme extended into the following day. His parents were so wrapped up in their own affairs that neither, he reckoned, would bother to question him further or want to check up.

Friday came, 16 May, less than a week to go. School seemed increasingly unreal, lessons mere tests of his patience. The lives of the people around him seemed so humdrum, their concerns so petty. Even Pete asked him why he was in a world of his own most of the time and fortunately answered the question himself by assuming it was love-sickness.

However, during registration, while Willoughby craned his neck to see who was present and everyone milled around shouting and chatting, a girl suddenly appeared next to him while he was rummaging in his bag. Melanie. She just said a quiet 'Hi, Ger,' and hesitated.

'Mel! Hi!' He felt an immediate knotting of the stomach muscles, together with a surge of hope. 'How are you?' A banal question, but he felt so nervous that it was all that came out.

'Oh, fine.' She looked pale, even worried. 'Listen, I think we should talk; not now, tonight.'

He struggled to interpret this. Talk about what? 'Yes, yes. When? Where?'

She stood next to the table, moving nervously, flicking hair out of her eyes. 'Erm, oh, the shelter on the prom, by the phone boxes.' He nodded. 'Right, say eight o'clock. Make sure you're there.'

'Of course I'll be there. But what's so important?'

She shook her head. 'Not now. Have to dash. History first lesson and I haven't done the reading.' And away she swirled, slim-legged, mini-skirted and as beautiful and vibrant as ever.

His mother was already home. She greeted him mechanically, peeling potatoes at the sink and said tea would be ready in half an hour.

'Aren't we waiting for Dad?' he asked, assuming he must be going to some meeting straight from the shop.

'No we are not,' she said, with unusual quietness.

'Er, anything the matter, Mam?'

She shook her head. 'Nothing you can solve, love.'

He wondered if he should try to get her to explain but

decided it was just another round in the marital battle. He went through to his bedroom, switched on the radio and tried to find some decent music. He flung off his school clothes and put on the usual jeans, shirt and sweater.

Neither seemed very hungry when they sat down to eat. His mother picked at her steak and kidney pie and chips and Geraint could do no better. Putting his knife and fork together, he said, 'Mam, is there any possibility of Dad giving me regular pocket money again? I don't have much left in the post office now and I don't like having to ask you. I can get a bit now and again at the farmers' depot, but it's not often. Though in the summer it might pick up.'

His mother did not reply, merely trying to get some peas politely on top of her fork. After succeeding, she said, 'I wouldn't think it's a good idea to bother him just yet, Geraint dear. He is still angry over... her, you know.' She reached over to her handbag on the sideboard and opened it. 'Keep you going for a bit,' she said, handing him a ten-shilling note.

At about 6.30, back in his bedroom, he heard his father come in. Noises from the kitchen signalled that his mother was going to give him his meal. Then, presumably, they sat down at the table. Geraint lay there, feeling lethargic, despite the tension. Suddenly he heard his father's angry voice. Not again, he reflected gloomily. What this time? Pie gone hard? Peas too crinkly? Newspaper not ironed? And then he could not help hearing, 'Where did you get that?' No doubt about his father's anger. Despite himself, Geraint got up and went closer to the door to listen.

Chapter 20

H E MISSED HIS mother's reply, but then his father barked, 'You went through my pockets? How dare you!'

Geraint slowly opened the door a half inch.

'It's not something I've ever done before. I just, well, I went to tidy things away when I got home, and your jacket was lying on the chair in the bedroom. And I saw this envelope sticking out of the pocket.'

'The inside pocket!'

'Does it matter which? Anyway, something made me look inside. How could you? How could you, John?' She began to cry. 'After all these years.'

A chair scraped in the kitchen. His father's voice sounded less angry. 'Look, it's not as bad as you think. She just, well, she's just being friendly. I saw her a couple of times, that's all.'

'What have I done to make you do this? Why did you do it?'

'Look, give me the letter. It doesn't mean anything, really.'

His mother had stopped crying and said angrily, 'I'm keeping this. Look at this part.' She rustled the pages. '"And next time I'll wear the black ones for you, just the way you like." And then at the end of all this, this rubbish, "Love from your naughty darling, Gail." Who the hell is she?'

He heard his father groan and then say wearily, 'It's Gail, Cen Edmonds, the MP's secretary in his Dolgellau office. We just met a couple of times when I was on council business.'

'Don't treat me like a fool! No one meets on council business and then writes like that! It was that night you spent away from home, wasn't it? So-called drinking and couldn't drive home. More like taking black underwear off her. Where? Some seedy hotel room?'

Geraint leant against the door, frozen into disbelief and anger and shame. Surely this must be a nightmare and he'd suddenly wake up.

'She's single. Has a flat in the town.'

'And how many times have you been to bed with her?'

Silence. Then, 'Oh Dilys, does it matter?'

'That's a strange question! You have a wife and son and ask that!'

'I don't mean it doesn't matter. Just, well, she was someone to talk to, you know, when things weren't too good between us.'

A plate slammed down and must have cracked or broken. 'Oh I see. Our business, our private business, discussed with some cheap whore!'

'She is not that. That's unfair. She's a well educated woman who can at least listen without flaring up all the time.'

Geraint moved away from the door and sat on the edge of the bed. I don't believe it, he thought, feeling faint. He wanted to blot it out, to muffle his ears and pretend it wasn't happening. His father. And another woman. It was so disgusting he almost felt ready to vomit.

His father was shouting again. 'Look woman, I tried and tried to talk sense into you about that, and oh no, you have to have a car, never mind we can't afford it, but you have to gad about the country and keep up your position as chairman of this and secretary of that when it would suit you better to manage on your budget and look after the home. Or come to work with me, and then I wouldn't need to employ Mair, or I could put her on part-time.'

'Oh, I see, it's my fault! I'm just to dust and cook and make sure you have your meals on time? Or I go back to the shop, like years ago, so that you can make excuses and bugger off on council business, leaving the real work to me. Anyway, it's not gadding about the country; a lot of it is raising money for people much worse off than us. And if anyone's gadding about the country, it's you, on council business – to meet some floozy and then complain about all those hours you have to put in on behalf of the council. You make me sick!'

'Well if I felt I could discuss things with you, if you took a bit more interest in council business instead of just switching off when I try to talk about it, maybe I wouldn't have found someone who does care.'

'Well if that's the way you feel, you'd better go and find your comfort there, because you're not sleeping here tonight.'

Geraint couldn't remember hearing his mother so angry, and so ready to stand up to her lord and master, which was what the relationship seemed to him too often. In a way, he applauded her – but regretted the cause.

His father sounded shocked and hesitant. 'What? Come off it! I just can't go there now!'

'Why not? She's obviously catered for your needs before.'

'But Dilys, what about, well, everyone, neighbours, people we know?'

'Oh, of course! The great Councillor John Llewellyn Rees, the important man who hopes to be chairman next year and has heard a whisper that his bloody Investiture committee work could lead to an MBE. It's that that's worrying you, isn't it?'

'No it isn't!'

The argy-bargy raged on.

I'm not staying here to endure this, Geraint decided. Going to his bedroom, he slammed the door, put on his shoes, stuffed money into his jeans pocket and went into the hall. The kitchen door was ajar and they couldn't see him. Holding his hands over his ears, he went out, kicking the door shut behind him.

It was a sunny, peaceful evening with the whirring of lawnmowers in the distance and a wood pigeon calling in nearby trees. He was panting by the time he got to the hospital corner, and slowed down. He looked at her house but saw no one. A car crammed with adults and children, and towing a caravan, trundled past towards the town centre. He waited until an ambulance came out of the hospital drive and then crossed the road – tempted to knock at her door but deciding it might make things even more complicated.

I might as well head for the prom, he thought. Walking morosely along Neptune Road towards the beach, he passed the school playing fields, noticing some lads kicking a ball around. Somehow, those far-off, innocent days seemed gone for ever, he reflected. All I want is Mel. And please, God, let everything be right between us.

Perched on the top rail of the promenade wall, he watched the tide rolling inexorably in. Along the prom were a few wandering strangers from the slowly expanding caravan population. As he realised again what his father had done, he almost retched. If only it was just rows between them; they were bad enough, but, in comparison with this, bearable. How long had he been... messing around? He had a good wife, a pleasant house, a thriving business and people looked up to him as a councillor. For God's sake, why?

Out to sea, the clouds were turning from white to grey to black.

Eventually, with one thigh numb from sitting for so long on the railing, he jumped down and walked along Marine Parade with its half dozen decaying, once grand houses. 'Please be early, Mel.' Only two cars were parked facing the sea. In one, an elderly couple – sitting, staring, immobile. There was a hint of friendly dusk falling, accentuated by the darkening clouds.

Dragging his feet, he crossed to the shelter nearest the phone boxes, one of which he had used to make that agonising call to her months previously. He sat on the sea-facing side and stretched out his legs. Lolly-ice and sweet wrappers littered the concrete floor. Leaning back, he closed his eyes. What should he do that night? If he went home, what would be going on? Was there an alternative to going home? Pete's? Ieuan's? Though what excuse could he invent? If only one of his grandparents were alive and lived near them.

His mind drifted and he lost track of time. The only sounds were the advancing waves and an occasional scuttering of blown paper. When he opened his eyes, the sky was dark and it was raining heavily. He stood up and then peered out to see if she was approaching. And then from behind him, she spoke his name. He spun round and gasped, 'Mel!'

'Hi, Ger. Sorry I'm late.'

She was wearing her unbuttoned PVC mack over her jeans and a light, fawn sweater. He wanted to hug her but held back. She sat next to him, a little out of breath, and looked not at him but at the sea. Despite the uncertainty, despite what had happened earlier that evening, he felt a strange elation. It was enough, almost, that they were in each other's company for a while.

Raindrops from her hair ran down her cheeks like streams of tears and there was a narrow band of wetness round the legs of her jeans, just below the mack.

'So?' he asked expectantly. 'It's good to see you, *cariad*.'

She continued to stare seaward for a few seconds and then turned to look at him, as though decided. 'Geraint, I want you to do something. For me, for us.'

His heart dropped. Not that again, surely. 'Yeah?' he asked flatly. Her face was close to his but he couldn't meet her gaze.

'Ger, you've got to promise me that you'll give up all your connections with that lot, LAW – now. I know I've said it before, but this time I really mean it – and, and… well, it is important. No, vital.'

Geraint sighed. Her face was in shadow but he sensed its seriousness. 'We've been through all this over and over. I just cannot do it.' He sighed again, and muttered, 'Well, not now, anyhow.'

Melanie ran a hand through her wet hair. 'Geraint, now is the time! I'm even saying please.'

Geraint stood up, tortured by conflicting feelings. He shoved his hands in his jeans pockets and felt the rain suddenly blow into his face. 'Mel, why does it matter so much? Why is it so important to you? For God's sake let me live my life my way – I'm not trying to stop you being Labour.'

'Don't be so stupid!' she snapped, her words almost lost in a gust of wind and rain. 'That's not the same and you know it.'

He was silent for a few seconds and then mumbled, 'So why this special confrontation now? Why tonight, here, in the rain?'

She gripped his shoulders, speaking close to his face. 'Listen, Ger, you claim I mean something to you. Well, if I do, trust me, and please promise me you'll resign from LAW now and tell them in the morning and have nothing to do with them from right now.'

Geraint felt as though his head was going to explode. He took her hands off his shoulders and moved out into the driving rain. Putting his hands up into the air, he shouted, 'I can't do it! And yes, you do mean something to me. A lot! But you're asking the impossible.'

She dragged him back under the roof and said, 'It's not impossible. You just do it. And... ' She hesitated. 'And this has nothing to do with whether we go out together or not. I mean I'm asking you for your own good!'

Closing his eyes, he shouted, 'No!'

'Why? Is someone else more important? Is that Bethan happy to see you get... ' She hesitated as though unsure.

'Oh, we get back to that, do we?' Geraint asked bitterly, and added, 'Well at least she wouldn't force me into this kind of choice!'

Suddenly his wet face was stinging and red. Melanie dropped her hand and turned away. Incredulous, scarcely aware of where he was or what he was doing, he started walking away. Before he had taken three or four paces, Melanie grabbed him by the shoulder and spun him round. Through the rain and tears and darkness he saw only a blurred shape in front of him.

'Geraint, they're going to arrest you all! Can't you see it? It's a set-up! That's why you have to break it off now!'

He shook his head uncomprehendingly. What was she on about? 'No... no!'

'Yes. Mike told me. Mike Barraclough. I asked him to

help me. And he's checked and we've worked it out. It's all a set-up and you're walking into a trap!'

She dropped her hands and he brushed tears and rain from his sore eyes. 'Mel, what are you on about? What's a set-up?'

'Whatever you're planning.' She pulled him over to the seat and they sat close. 'That man, that bloke with the beard. He's an… an agent provocateur.'

'What?' he felt dazed, confused, as though in a nightmare.

'You know. Oh, we've done it in history. Someone who infiltrates a group and pushes people into doing something against a government – and then bang! You're arrested red-handed.'

Part of his brain refused to focus on what she was saying. He looked seawards into the blackness. He felt his sweater becoming heavy and soggy, the thighs of his jeans warmly wet and tight on his legs. A shadowy man walked past, bent forward into the wind, dragging a dog on a lead.

'You're not making any sense.'

Melanie had to strain to hear his words. Tenderly caressing his cheek, she said, 'Ger, I'm sorry. I know how much it means to you, but it's true. You remember last year we were walking past the Caravan Club and a Land Rover came out? The man knew you and said hello. Mike Barraclough. You remember he said he'd seen you in Machynlleth with someone he thought he knew – but wasn't sure, or reckoned it just couldn't have been?'

'Go on.'

'Well, I bumped into him again one day when Mummy and I were in Machynlleth. She was in one shop and I'd gone to the ladies' and was going back to join her when I met him. He told me, just by the way, that he'd seen this friend of yours going into a pub in Talybont, and there was no doubt. He had been in military intelligence, someone he'd known when he was in the army before going to work for the Forestry and moving to Pennal. You see, Mike hadn't been just an ordinary soldier. He would not tell me exactly, but he'd obviously worked with or come into contact with this other bloke. He said he'd left the army because he became fed up, disillusioned he said, with what he was mixed up in.'

Geraint's sense of unreality deepened. He looked into Melanie's face almost as though he wanted her to smile and say, 'Caught you there!'

As he didn't speak, Melanie went on. 'Obviously I couldn't make any sense of how you could be going to Plaid Cymru meetings with someone like that. Had he left the army, or…? And if he had left, and now supported Plaid Cymru, well, it was a huge coincidence that there were two such men in this area. It didn't bother me an awful lot until I realised you were into something more than, well, more than a mere Welsh nationalist party. So after we went to Barmouth, I began to wonder.' She kissed his cheek.

'Mel, we all knew he used to be in the army. He's a Liverpool Welshman. Though he did say it was the Foreign Legion he had been in – though I suppose he might have been in both.' Scouse was their rock. He couldn't have…

Melanie shook her head. 'Mike said nothing about that. Anyway, I found out his phone number, Mike's. There was one Saturday you were going to Machynlleth again. I had enough warning to persuade Daddy to drive me there. It wasn't easy and I had to think of some ridiculous excuse. I rang Mike and luckily he was in. I'd followed you and seen you go into that hotel so I sat in the café opposite. Mike came in and I explained that I was scared of what you were mixed up in. I didn't say anything else – just that I'd be very grateful if he could watch and see if he could find out more about this bloke, what do you call him, Scouse? Mike said his name was Colin Milne.'

Geraint looked down, feeling more and more incredulous, yet with the germs of a feeling that gnawed within, telling him she was right. 'Colin Milne?' he said slowly. 'Arthur Constable is his name.'

'No. Not his real name. Oh Ger, Mike was brilliant. I was so scared and panicking. He told me not to worry and when he saw this fellow coming out of the hotel, he said he'd try to follow him and he'd be in touch. So I got the last bus back to Tywyn, 'cos I knew you always went by train.' She took a breath and looked at Geraint, who just stared over her shoulder into the corner of the shelter. 'I rang him a few days later but he said to give him more time. Then, the evening of your birthday, he rang me. Luckily I answered the phone. I met him and we sat in his Land Rover parked just down from the hospital. He said he'd tracked down this Scouse's flat and he was certainly not living there under his real name. He hung around and a man came out of the flat. Didn't look like a student, so Mike followed him and he went into the main police station and when he hadn't left after half an hour, Mike went in but there was no sign of him in the public part.'

'This is incredible.' And for a second, Geraint wondered if this trap, this betrayal, was something that Llŷr had suspected – or feared.

'Ger, Mike says Aber is crawling with… he called them Special Branch policemen… because of Prince Charles and all that. Geraint, something is planned, isn't it? By your lot? Tell me, please, Ger.'

Geraint felt himself shaking all over. 'Yes.'

'What?'

'I can't say.'

'Ger, you have to tell me. When is it?'

'Soon, very soon.'

'Oh Geraint, you mustn't! It's a trap! This Scouse, Colin or whatever, he's just doing it to trap you all. I don't know why. Presumably to discredit LAW – and Welsh nationalism.'

'No.' The word came out automatically, without conviction. He looked at her with a mixture of agony and shame.

'Mike reckons it is dangerous, that whatever you're involved in, you should get out fast. I phoned him last night, after we'd been talking about agents provocateur in history, and I just said I thought the group you were with were planning something and what did he think I should do? He said to tell you to get out and have no more to do with it and hope that when it all exploded – his word – you wouldn't be associated with them at all.'

Clinging desperately to his belief in Scouse, LAW and its ideals, Geraint said, 'You've no proof. Mike thinks this, that and the other.'

She imprisoned his left hand in her hands. 'Ger, there's something else I've just remembered.' Her voice sounded stronger, more urgent. 'Your birthday night, I asked Mike if he could be sure. He said yes. He had made a phone call to London, someone he knew and used to work with and owed him a favour. All he could get out of him was that this Colin, Scouse, had not left the army. Ger, can't you see? He is still in the army. Or some shadowy branch of it.'

Geraint's final defences collapsed. He felt utterly weak, exhausted and ready to crumple. 'Christ,' he whispered. 'This… on top of everything else tonight.'

Melanie rubbed his hand. 'What d'you mean?'

He sighed. 'Mam and Dad. Oh, Mam's found out he has been seeing another woman. They were arguing like hell when I left, Mam saying he wasn't staying there tonight. And I just walked out.'

'Oh no.' She shook her head, and then, after a few seconds, as though having struggled to make up her mind, said firmly: 'Ger, come on – home, my home; we'll be alone.'

He understood what she was saying, but she had to pull him to his feet. Later, looking back, he realised that he couldn't clearly remember the next few minutes. Holding hands tightly, they had plodded through the buffeting rain and wind, neither speaking, and eventually crunched down her driveway.

Unlocking the door, she smiled at him encouragingly and led him into the hall, switching on the light and calming a leaping Pankhurst. Geraint just stood, swaying, dripping, breathing hard. She dragged him to the lounge, flung her wet mack onto the carpet and pushed him down into an armchair. Then she disappeared behind him, reappearing a few seconds later to hand him a chunky glass with the words: 'Get it down you.' Obeying, he felt a burning but invigorating heat spreading within. He looked up at her and was surprised to be able to smile.

'Well, that's a quick improvement,' she said, standing by him. 'What's so funny?'

He emptied the glass. 'You. Your hair like rats' tails, your jeans soaked and stuck to your legs.'

'Oh, thank you – very complimentary in view of what I'm doing for you!' She leaned forward and took his empty glass. 'One more, a small one.' Behind him, she went on, 'Now as I'm sopping, as you pointed out, you can knock back that medicine, Daddy's best brandy, while I'm gone.'

Handing him the glass, she kissed his wet forehead. And away she swirled, his eyes riveted to her as he sipped his medicine.

Chapter 21

H E LAY BACK and let the luxurious softness envelop him. Closing his eyes, he felt the warmth of the electric fire penetrating his jeans. Something touched his right leg – Pankhurst nuzzling him. Opening his eyes with some effort, he scratched her ear, grateful for the affection. Only two wall lights were on, and he felt his eyes closing again as sleep beckoned.

He must have drifted off because he awoke with a jerk, hearing his name. Melanie took the glass from him and handed him a soft brown towel that seemed as big as a blanket. 'Here, now do as you're told and get those wet clothes off.'

Leaving the towel on the chair, he wrestled his wet sweater off, handing it to Melanie while he unbuttoned his shirt and gave that to her too. He looked at her, standing there, an expression of mixed concern and amusement on her face. As though reading his mind, she said, 'Yeah, and the rest – get 'em off!' She smiled at his hesitation. 'All right. I'll disappear for a few moments!'

He undid the top button on his jeans and managed to slide them off. When the towel was firmly round his middle, he shouted to her and she came in. 'Right, these are going in the airing cupboard.' And away she went. Feeling somehow more alert, he couldn't help admiring her in her bare feet, very short denim shorts with fraying ends and a white T-shirt. He rubbed his head with the towel.

He was still drying himself when she reappeared. Standing right in front of him, she said quietly, 'Oh, my poor old Ger, you are going through a lot. Come on.' After switching off the fire, she took him by the hand and led him towards the door. 'Geraint, believe it or not, we have the whole house to ourselves.'

He was only half aware of walking behind her, admiring her rear view, feeling the soft carpet beneath his feet until they were in her bedroom, lit only by a small desk light illuminating heaps of A-level files and books. She sat down on her bed, patting the space next to her. 'Come on, tell me all about your parents.'

How many times have I had fantasies about being back here? he thought wryly. But never did I envisage such circumstances. He sat down on the bed, towel clutched around him. 'Well,' he began shakily, 'Mam found a letter. He's been with some woman called Gail, the MP's secretary in Dolgellau.'

'No? You mean our Labour MP here?' She slid off the bed and sat on the floor, hand on his knee.

'Yes.'

She shook her head, adding quietly, 'Ger, I think I need a drop myself, though with a bit of ginger ale. Don't go away!'

Every second of her absence seemed like an hour, but she was soon back, offering him a sip.

'I don't know what Dad will say when he sees the shrunken brandy.'

Wishing she would put her hand back on his knee, Geraint said, 'Why did you ask to see me on the prom tonight? I mean, why not here if you knew you'd be on your own?'

The hand returned. 'Oh, I dunno. I suppose I was unsure about how you'd react. I didn't know if you'd accept what I was saying about LAW. And if you didn't and we had a row,

I thought it would be better on neutral territory.'

Geraint nodded. 'Makes sense, I suppose. Where are they, your parents?'

Rubbing his knee, she answered, 'They've gone to stay with my aunty in Ludlow – for the weekend. I was supposed to go but I more or less refused – said I had loads of work to catch up on.' She sipped the brandy. 'What are your parents going to do?'

Speaking more calmly than he felt, he said, 'Mam was telling him he could go and see her 'cos he wasn't going to stay there tonight. And he didn't seem to want to. I mean, go to her. God, I've never heard Mam so, so angry and determined.'

'Well, it's not surprising, really.'

'Yeah.'

'If you don't mind me asking, Ger, how long have your dad and this woman been sort of, seeing each other?'

He paused before saying, 'Seems to be a few months. Mam thinks a lot of his late nights have just been an excuse. She even called him a bastard.' He didn't smile, and felt incredibly depressed. Having a row with his dad was one thing; lots of teenage boys did. He could even forgive him opposing his going out with Melanie, but this... He realised that something seemed to have changed forever; it didn't really matter if his parents made it up, or whether he and Dad could talk amicably again. There could be no going back: the plinth was smashed, the statue in smithereens. In the space of seconds, his world had changed irrevocably.

Neither spoke for a while, until Melanie said slowly, 'If anything like that ever happened to me, I don't know what I'd do. I just can't imagine it.' She held his hand. 'Why? I wonder why he did it. What makes them?'

Geraint wondered too, and couldn't think of an answer. Yes, maybe you could understand a man going to a party and getting seduced. But deliberately? And going back?

Pulling his hand from Melanie's, he covered his eyes then stood up and rushed out to the toilet. He knew he was going to vomit and just wished it was over. He heaved and retched, and heaved again, his innards disgorging into the bowl. Feeling relieved, he wiped round his mouth with toilet paper and rubbed the back of his hand across his wet eyes. Managing to stand, he flushed the toilet, bent over to wash his mouth out with cold water and wobbled back to the bedroom.

Melanie was standing in the doorway looking worried. She took his hand and led him back to he bed. They stood, facing each other, Geraint still within his towel, and she said, 'Ger, I'm sorry it had to be tonight I told you everything, but I was afraid if I delayed it you might do something before I had the chance.'

He leant his head on her shoulder, saying, 'No, don't apologise, Mel. It's me. And thanks. All the time I thought you'd turned your back on me and wanted nothing to do with me. Why? Why did you go to all this trouble?'

'You idiot, Geraint Rees. If I couldn't save you one way, then I had to try another.'

'But why?' he asked, almost dreamily, conscious of her warmth against him.

'Because, you stupid great oaf,' she said quietly and slowly, 'because I couldn't get you out of my mind, because I am forced to admit, despite your pig-headedness and refusal to see sense, I love you.'

He looked at her, their faces an inch apart; two pairs of eloquent eyes speaking more than words ever could. Suddenly he felt conscious of the state of his mouth and his lips still tasted the remnants of what he had disgorged.

'Mel, can I go back to the bathroom to freshen up my mouth?'

'Of course. Use my toothbrush, the green one in the rack.'

Grinning, he went out, remembering a novel he had read, one in which the author had said that sharing a toothbrush was a sign of real love. After much rubbing, splashing water on his face, running his hands through his hair and washing out his mouth again, he went back feeling, if not a new man, at least a more alert Geraint.

There was no light on in the room. By the landing light, he padded across the carpet towards Melanie, who was standing by her desk. As he neared her, she raised her arms ready to embrace him. Geraint put his arms round her waist; the towel fell silently and he began to fumble for it but she whispered, 'Forget it.' Nervously, Geraint hugged her and kissed her gently, hoping his mouth was fresh. She pushed against him and her tongue slowly explored his mouth. Geraint felt a warmth, a security, an elation, that surprised him. And then, equally to his surprise, came tears, cascading, uncontrollable, his chest heaving. Her head on his shoulder, her hair tickling him, she said, 'It's OK, Ger love. It's OK. I love you and I'm with you.' He tried to blot out the world beyond, and hoped he wasn't hurting her as he gripped her and pulled her against him.

Gradually, the flow stopped and, weak, fuzzy-headed, he still held her tight. Melanie stroked his head and said quietly, 'Ger, darling, let go a minute. Back soon.' He swayed on his feet but a few seconds later she was back, and, before holding him tight again, slipped something under her pillow.

She pulled him by one hand onto the bed and it seemed

so natural that he should gently and carefully lie on her. '*Cariad*,' he croaked, his mind flooding with an awareness of her soft, intensely warm skin. Gradually, passion blotted out all else, his earlier turbulent feelings about LAW, his parents and the world beyond the bedroom. He couldn't remember much after that, though he recalled her gentle hands unrolling something onto his hardness and guiding him into her. Later, sweating and exhausted, yet elated, he laid his head on the pillow and exulted in his feeling of, as he thought, becoming A Man.

They lay silently, arms round each other, until an inner alarm bell dissipated Geraint's inner peace and tranquillity. 'Mel, I'd better phone home. And what about Llŷr and the others in LAW?'

Melanie murmured, 'Yes, you're right. If you want to phone home, use the one in Mum and Dad's room. Tell them you're fine and staying here. Unless, unless there's some emergency, and you've got to… '

Neither wanted to acknowledge the possibility of parting – at least not before a new day had dawned.

He walked cautiously across the room, feeling for the door. The second door he opened revealed a phone by a double bed. The electric alarm clock said 11pm. Shaking with tension again, he dialled.

'Yes?' His mother.

'Mam. It's me, Geraint.'

'Oh, Geraint love, where are you? Are you all right?'

'Oh yes. Fine. Are you all right?'

'Me? Oh yes. You… you heard it all, didn't you?'

'Yes.'

'Oh love, I'm so sorry.'

'Mam, it's not your fault.'

'Well your father's not here. I couldn't stand the sight of him tonight, anyway. Aunty Carys has come down to stay. She was very kind at such short notice, all the way from Blaenau Ffestiniog.'

'Good, good. Mam, I'm staying at Melanie's tonight. If you're all right with Aunty Carys, that is.'

His mother didn't speak and he wondered if he should explain. No, he decided, plenty of time for that. If she suspects, well, leave it at that. He was afraid she'd ask if her parents minded because he didn't want to lie to her, least of all after what she had been through that night. But she merely said, 'All right. Perhaps it's just as well.'

'Yes. See you sometime tomorrow, Mam. *Iawn?*'

'Yes, Geraint, thanks for phoning, love. 'Night.'

He put down the phone and sighed. It could be worse, he reflected as he shuffled back.

Melanie had switched on her bedside lamp, throwing a pool of golden light onto her head and shoulders as she sat up, the sheet held up for him to clamber in. He told her what had been said, adding, 'What about the other problem? My mates in LAW? I owe it to them to warn them.'

'Not tonight, surely?'

'No, suppose not. What a complicated mess! I trusted him. We all did.'

'Well, warn the others tomorrow… and then it's over. He won't go ahead on his own.'

Geraint wasn't sure how to explain what he was thinking. 'I can't just let it go at that. I dunno. I've got to see him.' She sensed he meant Scouse. 'I mean, suppose, despite what I say, he convinces them to still go ahead.'

'With what, Ger?'

'It. And… I've just thought of something. They arrested

Marcus and others. And we wondered why none of us was taken. Scouse said it was just luck, or better security.' He looked at Melanie, his brain racing. 'It more or less proves what you've told me. Obviously we were left untouched.'

He sat up in bed, sex forgotten. 'We've got to see Mike and get him to help us. And somehow tell this Scouse to pack it all in.'

'But couldn't that be dangerous?'

'No,' said Geraint, only half believing himself. 'What's Mike's number?'

'I've got it somewhere. Shove over and let me out.' Naked, she clambered across him and took a silk dressing gown from the wardrobe. She slipped it on and sat at her desk, rummaging in a drawer. 'Here.' He got up and took a scrap of paper from her.

'Come on, then,' he said, looking towards the door.

'Ger, isn't it a bit late?'

'It's not that late and it's so important.'

They sat on the parental bed and Geraint dialled. It rang for a minute, after which a gruff voice answered.

'Geraint Rees. You know, Plaid Cymru.'

'Ah. Geraint. And what can I do for you at this hour?'

'Sorry Mike, but Melanie has told me everything. I think, I mean it all fits. This chap, Scouse, Colin. He must be what you say.'

There was a short silence. 'Well, I'm glad she's finally told you. I was thinking of contacting you myself in the morning.'

'Mike, it's urgent. There's not much time. I can't explain why, but can you take us to Aber tomorrow to try and meet Scouse so I can, sort of, try to persuade him to... forget everything that's planned?'

'Mmm, I was right. Something big, eh? It's OK, don't answer that.' Mike was silent for a moment. 'Don't you think it's dangerous trying to confront this character? Why not walk away, after warning the others?'

'Because, well, he's clever and cunning and persuasive. Suppose he convinces them I'm mistaken or mad or have been got at, and the plan goes ahead? I certainly don't want *that*.'

'Yes. See what you mean. OK, tell you what. I'll pick you up tomorrow or today or whatever it is. Say 9.30. Where?'

Geraint thought quickly. 'We'll be walking along the Aberdyfi road, starting from by the hospital.'

'Yes, see you then. You can fill me in on everything and we'll try to sort something out. By the way, have you told anyone else about what you've found out?'

'No. Melanie's only just told me.'

'OK, keep it that way for the moment. 'Night.'

'Good night – and thanks, Mike.'

He sat there looking so despondent that Melanie asked, 'What's up, Ger?'

He sighed. 'Just that, well, I thought I was doing something great, something for Wales, something that would really change things the way… ' He lapsed into silence, shaking his head. She kissed him on the cheek and they wandered back to her room.

Chapter 22

'"So hand in hand they passed... " and something.'

'You didn't learn it properly, did you? "The loveliest pair that ever since in love's embraces met."'

'OK clever clogs – but look at the trouble Eve landed Adam in later!'

Melanie said quietly, 'I think it's the other way round this time.' When she noticed his embarrassment, she added, 'Sorry, Ger – forget that.'

They sat at opposite ends of the kitchen table crunching cereal, followed by thickly buttered toast and orange juice. They scarcely uttered a word, content to gaze at each other and enjoy the simple togetherness. Afterwards, he sank into one of the deep, soft armchairs in the lounge, noticing the French windows leading to a patio and the long lawn. Beyond, trees and fields.

'Make the most of it. I don't know when we'll be able to do this again!' She was leaning against the doorpost, grinning at him. Looking at her in her tight blue jeans and polo neck sweater, he couldn't stop himself from getting up and going over to hug her. As his passion visibly increased, Melanie pulled away, laughing, and saying, 'Come on you! We have more important things to do.'

'Mmm, all right,' he murmured, and gritted his teeth, excitement drooping away.

She looked out of the window. 'Shall we take a chance on the rain not starting again?'

He looked at the slowly lightening sky. 'Yeah. I haven't

got anything else to wear anyway.'

'Pankhurst can come, can't she? She can guard us – savage anyone who tries to get us.'

'Huh! Just all bark she is! Useless.' And then noticing Melanie's expression, he added quickly, 'Joke! Of course she can come.'

They closed the front door and, hand in hand, not caring who saw them, set off along the grass verge of the Aberdyfi road, keeping an eye open for Mike's Land Rover.

'What do you reckon he'll do to help us?' asked Melanie.

Geraint frowned. 'Not sure. I reckon we should go to Aber and try to find Scouse. We probably won't – but it's worth trying. And then we should tell him his little game's up and to get back to England. Then we warn everyone else. And I suppose that's it.' He held Melanie's hand tightly and guided her round a crown of fly-infested horse dung. 'Maybe I should try to get word to Marcus – even though the trial is still on.'

'Marcus – is that the boss?'

'Yes.'

They walked slowly for five minutes before they heard a horn and a green Land Rover slowed down behind them.

Melanie opened the door. 'Hi, Mike! You don't mind if one slightly insane dog comes with us, do you? She's well behaved – usually.'

Mike smiled. 'Course she can.'

They climbed in, Melanie sitting in the middle and Pankhurst clambering over them to sit behind on the floor.

'Well, good morning lovebirds,' said Mike as they moved off, Geraint feeling himself blush.

'What do you mean, lovebirds?' Melanie asked quietly, smiling mischievously.

Mike smiled through his beard and said, 'Oh, I don't know. I'd say you both are radiating a certain aura, a brilliance, that suggests, well, strong feelings.'

Grinning, Melanie couldn't stop herself saying, 'Well, we have grown – sort of, closer.' Geraint dug his elbow into her side.

Above the engine noise, Mike added, 'Oh don't mind me, folks. We Yorkshiremen are renowned for being blunt.' He glanced sideways, smiling. 'Right, I'm just going to drive a bit further on and then we can have a chat. OK?'

'Sure.'

A minute later, they swung across the road and stopped in a lay-by opposite the hillside cemetery. To the right, they looked down over the golf course and towards the sandhills. After the ignition was switched off, they sat in silence for a few seconds.

'So,' said Mike, turning to look at Geraint, 'you've got yourself in a right pickle, haven't you?'

Geraint nodded, feeling embarrassed and angry.

'It's not just his fault though,' put in Melanie, one hand on his thigh. 'All the others in the group were conned as well, though Geraint told me he thought Llŷr might have been a bit suspicious.'

'It was absolutely vital that you were all conned,' remarked Mike quietly, stroking his beard. He wore old, dark brown corduroy trousers, a red check shirt and a sleeveless over-jacket. 'Mind you, there were suspicions among the students earlier this year, not about LAW or your Scouse.' He dug a newspaper cutting out of his pocket. 'I kept this because, well, I was going to bring it up in a branch meeting, but then changed my mind. Listen. "Steffan Jones of the Aberystwyth Student Council has asked the council to investigate student fears of

Special Branch mixing with them to obtain information. He said some mature students look amazingly like Special Branch agents. There are far more students on police and service scholarships this year. These characters wander through the town, going to pubs and parties and asking questions... "'

Mike looked at Geraint. 'I think Scouse's cover is even deeper, but when Melanie asked me to check up, I remembered this.' As Geraint looked down despondently, Mike asked, 'What about your parents? Melanie told me she was pretty certain they knew nothing of all this, and that you wouldn't want to discuss it with them – not that I blame you.'

Geraint felt the tension knotting again in his stomach. 'I just want to keep them out of it.'

'OK. Let's review the situation. There are how many in the plan?'

'Er, Scouse, me and... five others.'

'And Scouse, real name Colin Milne, rank major, expert in undercover work, fluent in Russian, German and – for all I know – Welsh. Other accomplishments include unarmed combat, explosives, ciphers and sundry other useful skills. Leading a cell of LAW with a major op imminent. Am I right?'

'Yes.'

'So what's planned? Another pipeline? Public building? Or... someone in the news, someone very important?'

Geraint was silent. He might have been made to look a fool, he reflected, but he had sworn an oath, on the flag of his country, and the others had not betrayed him. 'It's soon,' he muttered reluctantly.

'But what?'

He shook his head. 'There is no doubt about this? I mean, Scouse is definitely conning us, and not ex-army, but in the British army?'

On their right, the first sweater-clad golfers ambled towards their next hole. In the distance, across Cardigan Bay, the dark huddle that was Aberystwyth.

'No doubts, Geraint. I'm sorry. I had to twist the arm of a mate I was very close to. He confirms your man is still operational.' He stared across the links, towards the white-flecked sea. 'What I can't understand is how he involved you in it, a young lad. With the sort of games he's involved in, well, it's just criminal – worse.' Mike paused, adding, 'I wouldn't be surprised if he's being leaned on to include you, though why, I'm not sure. Anyway, I won't push you into disclosing the details of what you're planning.'

Geraint scratched his head. 'Mike, I still can't fathom this out. I mean, why? What was the point of it all? All this planning, meetings?'

'Agent provocateur?' asked Melanie.

'That's the only thing that makes sense to me,' agreed Mike. He paused and then went on: 'Look at it from the point of view of the big nobs in London, the establishment, whatever you want to call them. A few years ago, England and the UK meant the same to most people outside Wales and Scotland. Then suddenly, Plaid Cymru wins its first seat in parliament, and only months later, the SNP wins a seat – and parliaments for Wales and Scotland loom on the political horizon. And we're heading, as some in London would say, for the break-up of the great and glorious UK. So, one way of fighting back, of undermining the so-called nationalism, is to give Wales its own special prince.'

'The Investiture,' said Melanie.

'Exactly,' agreed Mike. 'Everyone, well, many, will rally round, waving their Union flags, that lovely boy, Charles Windsor, will be sent to college in Aberystwyth to learn Welsh and be "crowned" in Caernarfon. At the very least, they aim to split the nationalist movement. Are you with me?'

Geraint nodded. 'Yes, that's the sort of thing we've talked about in Plaid Cymru meetings – as you know.'

'Right,' said Mike, 'and remember I'm only guessing. Just before whatever you planned was going to happen, or in the middle of it, I reckon troops or police would have swooped and thrown the lot of you into black Marias. Scouse would have miraculously escaped and then, lo and behold, charges, newspapers and media, a big trial – probably very conveniently just before the general election – and Plaid Cymru activists and others would have been hung out to dry. The party kicked in the teeth again and thousands put off voting for us; no matter it was really LAW – to the unthinking masses, there is no distinction.'

'And why me?' asked Geraint. 'They asked, invited me, to join, to be active.'

Mike pursed his lips, looking towards the sea. Then he said, 'Maybe they'd say you were indoctrinated by nationalist school teachers, you know, innocent youth driven to violence, just another twist of the knife. And after all, you and Llŷr are card-carrying members of Plaid Cymru.'

'It makes sense to me,' said Melanie quietly.

Geraint stared ahead for a few moments before saying with obvious emotion, 'How can I ever thank you, both of you?'

'It's Melanie you should really thank,' added Mike, grinning at her.

Melanie just turned and kissed Mike on the cheek. 'Couldn't have done it without you, could I?'

'Hey you two!' said Geraint, laughing. To which Melanie rubbed his right thigh until he felt embarrassed enough to stop her. 'I want to go to Aber to see that bastard!'

Mike nodded. 'I can understand that. It may not be that simple though. I mean these people don't just play around. They're not something out of Aberdyfi Drama Society.' He stopped to blow his nose. 'You sabotage their little game and... and they could turn nasty, to put it mildly.'

'So what do we do? To safeguard ourselves?' asked Melanie, taking Geraint's hand in hers.

Mike didn't answer at first. Then he asked bitterly, 'How the hell did you let yourself get mixed up in all this, Geraint?' No one spoke, and he went on more calmly: 'Hey, sorry, it's all in the past now, spilt milk. We have to be practical, and equally cunning.' Reaching behind, he extricated a portable tape-recorder from a holdall. 'First, I think we should put on tape all you know. Or are prepared to say.'

'Why?' asked Geraint quietly.

'If you explain how you got involved, the meetings, with dates, times and places, anything you know about what this Milne has actually done or planned or organised others to do, what's supposed to be coming off soon, then this could be your protection. I post it to a friend, someone I really trust. It'll be sealed and we let it be known that if, just if, anything mysterious were to happen to you, it would go to the mass media. I'm not trying to frighten you, Geraint, but... '

'But you're succeeding,' he interrupted with a laugh.

'Well, we can tell Milne what we've done – and it could be a powerful way of covering your back.'

'Do it, Ger!' urged Melanie, looking serious.

Geraint stared ahead as he spoke. 'I can't put everything on. I swore an oath of secrecy.' And he heard an inner voice saying: Don't talk nonsense! What does that matter now? Now that I, we, have been conned?

'Geraint,' put in Mike, 'the more you put on tape, the

more credible, the more verifiable, it becomes — if needed. And if we are to use the threat, it has to be detailed.'

Geraint glanced to his left, watching the familiar green lorry of the farmers' merchant's trundle past, loaded with blue plastic sacks of fertiliser. He glimpsed the driver and recognised Sulwyn, cap sideways as always, Roy next to him. He closed his eyes, wishing it would all go away when he opened them — that he had never met Scouse, that he was back in bed with Melanie, her arms round him, that afterwards he could take her home to meet his reunited, loving parents.

Eyes still shut, he said, 'OK, I'll do it.' He paused. 'But on one condition.'

'What?' asked Mike.

'That I record it on my own, without you both hearing. And Mike, do I have your word that you won't listen to the tape, nor your friend, unless it's ever necessary?'

Melanie looked puzzled, as though unsure as to why he was insisting on this. Mike smiled and said, 'Sort of compromise? OK. But remember — if it's to be of any real value, checkable dates, places, things Milne did or told you he did, plenty of "meat" and as much of this planned operation as you can.' He handed the tape recorder to him. 'Fresh batteries, built-in mike.' He groaned. 'Sorry about the pun. Know how to work these things?'

'Yes.'

'Sixty minute tape. Enough?'

'Yes.'

'Right. Begin with your name, today's date, just say Aberdyfi and then get on with it. Melanie will take this hound for a walk across the golf links, to the sandhills and back. Honk the horn twice when you've finished.'

Geraint nodded and they got out. He was on the point of

asking Mike which language he should speak in, but decided to make it Welsh and say nothing of his choice. At least, he thought, it could cut down on the number of people who would understand.

He watched them walk away, down the path, through the rickety wooden gate and over the railway track to the sandy path that crossed the golf links. Melanie's slim form contrasted with Mike's bulk and powerful frame. Not all that dissimilar to Scouse, he found himself thinking. Drawing in his breath, he pressed the two tabs to begin the recording.

At first he was hesitant and several times erased what he'd said. Then it began to flow more easily and he re-lived the meetings, giving either the exact date or explaining when it must have been by reference to other events, either in the news or at school. It took him three-quarters of an hour, and when he looked across at the golf course, he could just make out two figures walking slowly across towards him. He sounded the horn twice and Melanie's arm waved in acknowledgment.

When they had returned, Mike put the tape into a small cardboard box and in the address section, he wrote the date, signed it himself and asked Geraint to sign it. Then Mike slipped it into his bag, saying, 'Right, well done Geraint. Now.' He gripped the steering wheel with both hands and seemed to be thinking deeply as he looked down. Melanie hugged Geraint and kissed his cheek, asking, 'OK?' He nodded, feeling a sense of relief and lessening of tension. A car with attendant caravan trundled past towards Tywyn, a convoy of frustrated cars in their wake. A few yards to their right, the Machynlleth-bound train rattled past on the single track.

'Now what, Mike?' asked Melanie, her hair a little

dishevelled from the walk and her cheeks glowing red.

Mike tapped the wheel with one finger. 'See him. Both of you, if he's there. If not, go somewhere and return later... hoping to God we can see him this weekend. I reckon it's better if I stay out of sight. I can help better if I can keep my involvement secret. He's going to wonder how the hell you rumbled him, but let him. Don't explain. The more mystified he is, the safer we are. I'll drop you in a car park or side street and tell you where his flat is. If he's in, tell him anything to get inside – and then explain you know who he is, that the big plan is off and that as far as you're concerned, he can go away and never bother any of the group again. Tell him you've informed the others – even though you haven't yet – and, this is vital, a complete record of everything you know, including the forthcoming op, is on tape and in a safe place.'

'Is it safe to go in his flat?' asked Melanie. 'Can't we see him somewhere else, in the open?'

Even as she spoke, Geraint realised that, despite knowing the apparent truth, he still couldn't, as he often said in English, get his head round it. To be afraid of visiting Scouse, the bluff, military patriot, the destroyer of an English water pipe, the inspiration to them all. It still didn't make sense. How could someone wear such a mask for so long, so effectively? How could someone willingly dupe well-meaning patriots, ordinary blokes – and a woman – and sleep at night? Even if it was all true, something made it almost impossible for him to feel fear at the idea of being back in Scouse's presence. But then, how surprised would Llŷr be when he found out?

He realised Mike was answering Melanie's question. '... met him somewhere in public, you might think you're safer. But, you'd have to phone him, we don't have his number though we could get it and that would take time. And anyway, you'd give him time to organise a watch on you. You'd quickly be under observation the whole time. This way, we surprise him, hopefully, we take the initiative, and by the time he can pick up a phone or takes action, you're away.'

Geraint put his arm round Melanie's waist. Melanie said, 'Suppose he tries to do something to us, something violent?'

Geraint grimaced. 'I don't think he will somehow. Anyway, if the tape threat works, he might not dare.'

'Right lad,' said Mike. 'And I'll be watching, discreetly, and if you're not out when he leaves, or no one comes out within, say, thirty minutes, I come in.'

'Couldn't we just go to a reporter, expose it that way?' asked Melanie.

'No thanks,' said Geraint forcefully. 'I've had enough of all that – and anyway, how would I prove anything straight off? We have to act fast.'

Melanie touched his leg, adding, 'Yes, sorry, silly idea.'

Geraint kissed her cheek. 'Hey, it's all right. It wasn't silly – just that I couldn't face all the publicity.'

'Right, action!' said Mike, switching on the ignition. 'First, the post office.'

They drove the short distance into Aberdyfi and parked on the promenade. He took the packet into a newsagent's where he bought a strong envelope and sticky tape. In the Land Rover, he first taped the ends of the container, then put it in the envelope which he sealed and taped. 'I'll write the address in there,' he said, and headed for the nearby post office.

As they snaked their way out of the village, through Penhelig, under the railway bridge by the tiny wooden platform and passenger shelter perched high up above the road, Mike said, 'I had thought of wiring Geraint for sound.

246

You know, a concealed mike.' He stopped, grinning, and added, 'I'll have to stop this punning. But knowing Milne, he'd probably frisk you anyway and it would be a waste of effort.'

Through Pennal and past Mike's single-storey, stone cottage, and on to bustling Machynlleth, past the clock tower and the bird watchers' hotel, and then onto the main road Geraint knew so well – though he said nothing as they passed the turn-off for Carl's farm. His stomach had that familiar knot of tension. What would Llŷr say when he found out? And the stolid, thoughtful Pedr – even he had been hoodwinked. No wonder none of them had been arrested last year. How had Marcus and the other top blokes been duped so completely? He had often wondered how Scouse knew so much and marvelled at his so-called sources of information. He felt a nausea and opened the window a little to feel the rush of air. If it hadn't been for Melanie... Well, he reflected, there would have been no A-levels probably, and what? Borstal? Prison?

Chapter 23

EVENTUALLY THEY WERE speeding down the steep hill leading to the centre of Aberystwyth. They passed the university's new white buildings on the left and saw ahead, spread before them, the huddle of slate roofs and curving promenade.

'I reckon the best place to park,' said Mike, as they slowed down for the lights, 'is somewhere near the end of the prom, the far end from the old university buildings, so we have a quick get-away down the side street and away up the hill again.'

They pulled up outside the Glan y Don, a white hotel looking a bit smarter than most of the rather drooping, weary establishments that had degenerated into student hostels. Geraint and Melanie looked into each other's eyes, acknowledging wordlessly their nervousness and tension.

'About a hundred yards back,' said Mike, 'there's a house with a slate nameplate by the door: Llys Ceredigion.' He sounded calm and confident as he continued: 'Usually the door is open. Go in and up the stairs. Second floor landing, first door on left, marked 2A. Ring the bell. That's it. OK?'

Geraint nodded, holding Melanie's hand tightly. He looked at his watch. 'Nearly quarter past twelve.'

'Mmm, let's hope he's not in the Skinners drinking with his student friends. And unknown to them, on the lookout for anyone who needs adding to Special Branch surveillance list,' said Mike wryly. Geraint looked sharply at Mike, who smiled, adding, 'Oh yes, Charles is better protected than you think.'

'Supposing someone's with him,' said Geraint.

'Milne? Well, you say you want a word with him privately – and urgently.'

'It might be Mair, his girlfriend. Presumably even she doesn't know what's going on.'

'I guess not,' said Mike. 'But then love can be blind. Sorry you two!' he added with a grin.

'But if she is there,' said Geraint thoughtfully, 'I might as well speak in front of her too. If she's been conned by him, all the better. If not, she'll have to know anyway, and I doubt if she'd leave just because I wanted a private word. I mean, it would be about LAW, and she's just as much a member as I am.'

'OK,' said Mike, 'makes sense.' He looked at his watch. 'If no one is there, come straight back – but take a glance now and again to make sure that just by chance, neither he nor Mair is trotting along behind, just having noticed you. Which brings me to afterwards. Get back to the Land Rover bloody quick! But if you think, or know, he's after you, which is unlikely, walk on. Take the next right and immediately you do, there is a back alley on the right. Go down it and keep walking until you hear me tell you what to do. This also applies if I see anyone following you. To begin with, I shall be over the road in that shelter, reading the paper. If you're clear, I'll come right over and we'll be away. But if by the time you're near the vehicle, and you realise I'm not moving, try not to draw attention to the Land Rover, but keep walking and turn as I said. A bit complicated, but I'm trying to think of eventualities. Both got all that?'

They nodded.

'Shall we go?' Geraint asked.

'In a second. If you get inside, make sure you tell him

about that tape before you've said anything about what he should do or about dropping the plan. And tell him that as far as you are both concerned, if he is prepared to bugger off and nothing else is heard about him or the plan or that LAW branch, then you want to forget about the whole thing too. And you'll assure him that the others think the same way as well. Maybe he'll believe it, maybe not. But the tape, and the fact that someone who knows what's what has obviously helped you, and the presence of another person, all this should make it easier.'

Mike looked doubtfully at them, as though unsure of their ability to carry all this out. 'My guess is,' he went on, 'if we succeed, they'll just abandon it, cut their losses and reassign him to the embassy in Costa Rica or Vladivostok station two. Or there's always the possibility of a "relaxing" undercover tour of duty in Northern Ireland. Maybe your Scouse has annoyed someone and they gave him this assignment. It's very rare for someone to be switched from overseas work to working in the field here. Normally MI5's preserve. Though maybe he had ideal special qualities, too good to overlook.' Mike shook his head, and added, 'Or, it could be one of those little private jobs: if anything goes wrong, no one knows anything, all responsibility is denied and the operator is left right in the shit – excuse my language, Miss Wilson. Anyway, that's beside the point.'

Geraint put his hand on the door and looked at him questioningly.

'Yes, let's go – and good luck. Keep your nerve, stay calm, remember all I've said – you're the ones with the initiative. He'll be frantically thinking, but you two have the element of surprise.'

Melanie turned and stroked Pankhurst, telling her to stay

there, be good, and on guard!

Even though it was mid May, there was a chill breeze. The few people on the prom wore winter coats – a few dog-walkers, hand-in-hand student couples and a group of chatting teenage lads, astride their askew racing bikes. The mounds of faded green, tarpaulin-covered deckchairs and tattered newspapers swirling around the forlorn, still closed ice-cream stalls added to the bleak atmosphere. The incoming tide crunched and rattled the pebbles and swirled round the green fronds of the rusting piles beneath the short pier.

Geraint shivered as they walked slowly, as calmly as they could, the few yards to Llys Ceredigion. Anger – that was what gave him the courage, he reflected. Plus the comforting feeling that Mike was at hand and seemed to know what he was doing. God, that was once what I thought about Scouse, and now... Please, God, let him be in; I have to get this sorted, tidied up.

He looked at Melanie, asking, 'OK, *cariad*?' She merely smiled and squeezed his hand. Then a shivering thought struck him: if Scouse believed that they were the only ones who knew about his real identity and purpose, then wouldn't he simply try to dispose of them? And then the plan would be safe. Then he remembered that he was going to tell Scouse first about the tape and second that the others knew anyway. And anyway, for Geraint to have found out and organised this, he must realise someone was helping, someone unknown but proficient.

The entrance hall was long, dark and dismally brown; two entangled bikes leaned against one wall and the stair carpet was noticeably threadbare. Two girl students in jeans and dark sweaters squeezed past them, chattering in Welsh. They creaked their way up the flights of stairs, hearts pounding.

An unshaded single bulb cast inadequate light on the landing. There were three doors, marked in faded white paint – A, B and C – and two other unmarked doors; bathroom and toilet perhaps, he thought. Shiny, new-looking Yale locks. A bell button by the dark and paint-scratched door marked A. They stood there, breathing rapidly.

'OK?' whispered Melanie.

Geraint nodded, listening. From one of the other flats came pop music, but no sound emanated from A.

It wasn't a bell but a buzzer and seemed to sound far into the flat. Geraint's hand shook as he pressed it, and he swallowed hard. No one came. Come on, come on. Geraint willed him to appear, though part of him wanted just to run away and hide, to bury his head in his hands and pretend none of this existed.

The door opened suddenly and there he stood, with large, powerful hands, short beard and piercing eyes, wearing dark trousers and a donkey jacket as though about to go out. Scouse accent as always.

'Geraint! What the 'ell, lad? And?'

'We need to come in,' said Geraint, hoping he sounded urgent, calm and decisive.

Scouse stared at them, his mind obviously trying to work it out. 'How did you know where I live?'

Geraint shook his head and said, 'We have to see you; it's vital.'

Scouse stood back, holding the door, and they went past into a large, high-ceilinged room, obviously what was known as a bedsit. It seemed totally, well, ordinary, thought Geraint, looking round, though he wasn't sure what he'd been expecting. Certainly not a Kalashnikov being stripped down, or grenades heaped up ready or clocks being attached to bombs. There were even files and file paper, as any student would have, and textbooks strewn untidily next to the phone on an old–fashioned sideboard. Magazines were scattered across the counterpane of the double bed in the corner.

'OK, sit down then.' Scouse's voice was quiet, controlled.

They went over to the sofa which backed onto the large sash windows overlooking the seafront. They sat side by side, upright and on the edge, Scouse eying them from the door.

Geraint didn't know how to begin. He looked at Scouse, seeing the same reassuring bulk and strength. But then the anger kicked in. 'We know the truth. Who you really are: Colin Milne. And what you're trying to do.' He stopped, his mind a swirl of thoughts, forgetting what Mike had told him. All that mattered was that this man had betrayed him – and the others. An English bastard army man.

'Now hold on, Geraint lad,' said Scouse, his hands in his donkey jacket pockets. 'Where the hell are you getting all this crap from? Who's been getting at you?'

'We know who you are,' said Geraint, his hands on his knees. 'We want you to abandon the plan and just get back to where you came from.'

Scouse eyed him, not so much curiously as calculatingly. 'Listen, I don't know who's been filling your head with all this, but it's just so much crap. I'm your old mate Scouse, Arthur, and we have something special to do, something that's taken bloody ages to plan – and what the hell can I say in front of someone not connected with us?' He went over to the sideboard, leaning on it with one elbow, looking sad and pleading, though his eyes remained piercingly alert.

Melanie could remain quiet no longer. 'You've been identified by someone who knows you, who you are, what your real background is, that your name is Colin Milne and you're working as an agent provocateur.'

'That's fancy French, young lady, whoever you are, but it's all total nonsense. Yes, I was in the army, before the Foreign Legion – but now I'm a postgrad student here.'

'For Chrissake, Scouse – it's no good!' Geraint stood up, facing him. He tried very hard to stop the first tears from showing. 'You conned us all – they all know: Llŷr, Pedr, everyone. I've told them!'

Scouse stood straight, a couple of feet from Geraint, his hands loosely by his side. 'You fool!' he said quietly and slowly. 'You naïve young fool! Don't you realise what you're doing? You're blundering into deep and murky waters.'

Melanie stood up, her eyes blazing anger. 'Ger – tell him about the tape!'

'Oh.' He cursed himself for forgetting. 'Yes. I've put everything on tape: places, meetings, times, names, what you've carried out – and, and what we were going to do. So if anything happens, it goes to the press and TV.'

Scouse continued to stand there, immobile, staring at Geraint, his face a mask. Melanie interrupted his thoughts. 'We've got back-up,' she said, regretting the corny phrase she had used. 'We're walking out of here now. And you have to pack it all in. The LAW group is finished and the plan – and I don't know what it was. Geraint refused to divulge the details, but's it on tape.'

Suddenly, Geraint found himself spinning and flung against the sideboard. A foot kicked his ankles back, forcing him to lean slightly forward while his arms were held behind his back. He heard Melanie yell, 'Hey you – let him go!'

'Sorry about this, Ger lad,' panted Scouse as he frisked him. 'For all I know you've been sent here wired for sound, know warra mean like?'

Geraint was conscious of flitting hands and then within seconds he was released. He stood upright and turned to see Scouse weave and grab Melanie's arm in the act of trying to clout him with an empty but heavy vase.

'Now, now darlin', I was checking. And what about you? Are you broadcasting to the world?'

He let go of her arm and took the vase, replacing it on the wide windowsill. Melanie stood, red-faced, panting, hands on hips. 'Just you try and touch me, you… you… '

Geraint glanced sideways, more in admiration than anything.

Scouse looked from her to Geraint. 'Well, is she — or isn't she?'

Geraint shook his head, hoping he'd accept his word. 'It was too obvious. We knew you'd check.'

Scouse shrugged, and turned, as though deliberating on his next move. 'We?' they heard him say, as though to himself. For a few moments he stood, head bowed, his back to them. Then he swiftly turned and said forcefully, obviously trying to control his anger, 'Geraint, I don't know where you get all this… all this fiction from. Someone's put you up to it. Haven't I proved myself? Didn't I do, you know, special jobs like — and report back to you all? You were pretty happy then, weren't you?'

Geraint looked at his face. 'Maybe. I believed you — then. But we only had your word.'

'Well, believe me now. We have something to do that we've worked hard to prepare for. I mean, if we can count on your lady friend's silence, it can go ahead. Think of what we can achieve. Don't just throw it away on the word of… I dunno, some weirdo with a loony theory.'

'It's not a theory, though,' said Melanie, quietly but forcefully. Geraint nodded.

Scouse moved back and leant against the door. 'So who's behind this, lad? Who's the Masterbrain?' Geraint shook his head. Scouse looked at him and asked quietly, without any trace of a Merseyside accent, 'Well, is he out there now? Waiting for you?'

Geraint wasn't sure what to say but Melanie said, 'Never mind asking us questions. We've said what we came to say and now we're leaving.'

Scouse didn't move as Melanie went towards him. She just stood in front of him and stared at him. Geraint walked over to her, wondering what he would do if Scouse refused to move. He took her hand in his and squeezed it.

Scouse fixed his gaze on Geraint. 'I hope you both know what you're doing. There are people above me, my masters. People who don't take kindly to interference.' He paused, and added slowly and quietly, 'Geraint, I have to follow orders. I wasn't too happy at trying to involve you, someone so young. Remember that meeting? I asked how you felt about it. And Pedr tried to talk me out of it. But orders is orders. Once you leave here, though, you're on your own. Pity you can't finish your schooling in Patagonia.'

He moved sideways and Melanie opened the door, gripping Geraint's hand at the same time. As they walked out, he saw Scouse staring ahead, his face a mask. Geraint felt his stomach churning, his back tingled. Each step was an effort, as though learning to walk. Having shut the door, they moved slowly towards safety. Muffled pop music still emanated from nearby. As they reached the floor below, he was sure he heard a door click shut and glanced back. Nothing. He wished they could walk faster, but it seemed important not to panic. What was Scouse doing? he wondered. Phoning? Loading a pistol?

At last they reached the welcome caress of fresh, cold, Cardigan Bay air. Geraint shivered and they looked into each other's eyes. 'Fast,' was all he could mutter, at which she nodded. Still holding hands, they set off briskly. He glanced again at Melanie, face set, lips tightly compressed. What a girl, he thought.

Then he remembered his instructions, saw the Land Rover and looked across the road for Mike. There he was, sitting on the road side of the shelter, reading a paper. Geraint expected him to notice them and get up, but as they neared the vehicle, Mike didn't move, still apparently intent on the paper.

'Mel!' he muttered. 'Mike's not looking at us!'

She half turned towards him and answered, 'I know. So we keep walking, right?'

Pankhurst couldn't believe it. Rejected, merely glanced at, she stood her forepaws high up on the window and barked and barked, to no avail. Melanie willed her to be quiet but the noise continued.

They were passing seedy-looking hotels and boarding-houses, steps up to main entrances, steps down to cellar bars or cafés. Geraint felt more and more tense and longed to turn off the promenade, feeling that they would somehow be less exposed. There was the right turn. He resisted the desire to run, to hurtle round and keep running.

At last they made the turn, and a few more yards brought them to the next right turn: a long, narrow alley between the backs of hotels and whatever the buildings were on their left. High brick walls were punctuated by occasional tall wooden gates, battered bins, heaps of rubbish, kids' scribblings on the concrete road and walls.

'What now?' asked Melanie, sounding tense.

'Dunno. Just come down here,' Mike said.

No one was in sight, which somehow made them more rather than less nervous. Both wanted to look back, but their necks refused to obey. Ahead was the end of the alley and Geraint wondered which way they should turn. Round to the promenade in a circle? They were a few yards from the end when they heard someone behind them shout, 'Geraint!'

Turning, they saw Mike about thirty yards back, bending forward, his arms round something big and heavy. Even as they ran towards him, they saw him drag a limp but powerful man, his head lolling, and lay him on the concrete by the wall.

'Let's get out of here you two!' Mike straightened his sweater, ran a hand through his hair and looked again at the recumbent Scouse. 'Don't worry – just sleeping.'

They were back in the Land Rover within sixty seconds. The engine started first time, and Geraint and Melanie, faces smeared by a canine tongue, both breathed deeply with relief.

'Just as I expected,' said Mike. 'You two OK?'

'Yes, fine,' gasped Geraint, still puffed and shaking a little. 'He followed us then?'

'Aye.' Mike chuckled as they drove up the hill past Bronglais Hospital and the spacious, detached houses on the left.

'What are you laughing at?' asked Melanie, having persuaded Pankhurst to stay in the back.

'Oh, nice to know I haven't lost my touch. He never knew I was behind him until a half-second beforehand. That is, too late.'

They overtook a lumbering caravan pulled by a packed Maxi.

'So, do you want the details?' Geraint asked.

After they had both finished, Mike smiled and said, 'Well done the two of you! Just as well we didn't try to record it.'

'What do you reckon he was following us for?' asked Geraint, beginning to feel relaxed, hoping it was all over, bar contacting the others.

'Oh, I suppose it was to try to find out who you were going to meet. Pretty obvious you two didn't add two and two and get four yourselves.' He looked thoughtful for a few seconds before adding, 'Or four and a half.'

'What do you mean?' asked Melanie.

Mike seemed to be concentrating on the back end of the green Crosville bus in front. 'Well, who knows what's really behind it all? We reckon we've worked it out — but these people can be even more devious than we give them credit for.' And then he suddenly asked, 'Where are you two going to be tonight?'

Geraint looked at Melanie, who smiled and, still gazing at him, answered: 'At my house, both of us. My parents are away.' Blushing, she turned to Mike, and added, 'I mean, I just thought I ought to tell you. In case it might be important.'

Mike laughed out loud. 'Oh to be young and carefree again! Well, may you both be carefree very soon, anyway.' He zoomed past the lumbering, green single-decker bus and slapped the steering wheel before saying, 'Ah, I'm just being over-cautious. I reckon the tape idea worked. The last thing they'll risk is having such dirty tricks splashed around via the media.'

As they slowed down in the traffic approaching the T-junction in the centre of Machynlleth, Melanie broke the silence: 'Hey, I don't know about you two, but I'm famished!'

And suddenly Geraint felt the same, relishing the sense of relief and deliverance that Mike seemed to have endorsed.

'Well,' said Mike, changing down, 'I don't see why we can't celebrate our success with a quick meal of some sort!'

They were lucky to slot into a parking place by the clock just after another car pulled out. Standing there, amid the late afternoon shoppers, Geraint felt surprised that, despite recent events, he still felt a strange sense of alienation, almost as though he were floating along unseen by the scurrying, chattering people with their mundane tasks. He heard Mike say, 'Why not?' and saw him and Melanie grinning and laughing as he followed them across the road to the café opposite the hotel.

They ate burgers and salad followed by home-made ice-cream, Melanie ordering a burger on its own to take back to Pankhurst. As they drove at a leisurely speed out of town, across the bridge and turned left to head for Tywyn, Geraint found himself pondering the future. Back to Plaid Cymru activities, and put the rest well behind him? Or pack it all in? No, not that. I believe in my country, he reflected, I believe in our right to a parliament.

'What you thinking, Ger?'

He shook his head and smiled at Melanie. 'Oh, the future, what's happened.'

'And how much wiser you are, I hope,' put in Mike. 'Stick to the more boring political processes – Plaid Cymru for all its faults. Much safer. Now, what about the others in the group?'

Geraint felt a cloud cross his eyes. There was still this loose end, not one he looked forward to. 'I'll see Llŷr tonight and together we'll try to contact everyone.' And suddenly things began to seem clearer, more bright. Simpler. Plaid Cymru

– and Melanie. An end to ultimata? He hoped she'd come with him to see Llŷr, as he couldn't bear the thought of being away from her even for five minutes. His inner warmth was suddenly hit by a blast of cold air: Dad. And Mam. He'd have to check on what had been happening.

They pulled up outside Melanie's house. Geraint breathed deeply. 'Mike… '

'Yes?'

'Well, you know, thanks, for everything. I mean, without you, well… '

'Hey, forget it. Been, if not a pleasure, well, a service. A pleasure though to have saved two very nice people. Anyway, Ger, lad, you owe more thanks to Melanie, one determined young lady.'

A meeting of eyes made words unnecessary.

As they clambered out, Pankhurst leaping and bounding at being released, Melanie thanked Mike and went round to the driver's side to kiss him on the cheek. Mike for once seemed lost for words, smiled, waved and did a U-turn. They watched the vehicle become smaller and smaller until Melanie said, 'Ger, she's been patient for ages. Do you mind if we give her a quick run?'

'Sure,' said Geraint. 'I feel like some fresh air – sand, space, wind, freedom.'

They ran along the road and took the familiar turning for the beach, Pankhurst bounding ahead, slowing every now and then to check they were following. They had half an hour's lung-pounding running, chasing, stick-throwing, shouting and finally a frantic wrestle on the dry sand, culminating in a long, passionate kiss while Pankhurst tore fruitlessly after sea-gulls, sending them skyward off the beach, squawking in protest.

'Come on, let's get back,' said Melanie, breathing heavily. She shouted towards Pankhurst: 'Come on, girl, home! Food! Grub!'

Chapter 24

GERAINT COULDN'T MAKE up his mind whether he ought to go home to see his mother or just phone her. It was as though returning to his own home would somehow snap the link, the absence from Melanie being unbearable. He couldn't face the thought of dragging her into the arena, so decided he'd phone from Melanie's house. Hopefully, he thought, Aunty Carys will still be there.

His mother's relief was almost tangible, making him feel guilty at not having phoned earlier. After asking how he was, she told him his aunt was still there, was being a saint and listening and helping and she didn't know what she could have done without her, and yes she had spoken on the phone to his father… long pause… and possibly he would call tomorrow to discuss things and no he wasn't staying with That Woman but in a hotel.

'Are you sure you're not in the way there and Mr and Mrs Wilson don't mind?'

Pause. He switched to English, deliberately. 'Well, Mam, they're away for the weekend.' Melanie, holding his hand, smiled and raised her eyes. Geraint wondered what would come next.

His mother continued in Welsh. 'Oh, I see. Well, do they know you're there?'

Pause. 'No, Mam.'

'Geraint, love. Well, are you, er, I hope you're being sensible, I mean in separate bedrooms and all that.'

He looked at Melanie, wondering if she realised what was

being said. So easy just to say yes. Simpler. Kinder? Melanie – who had stood up for him, taken risks for him, given him so much. What the hell. 'No, Mam.' Silence. 'Mam. You there?'

'Yes. Oh I see. Well, you will leave everything tidy, won't you, and if you see Mr and Mrs Wilson, will you, well, sort of explain.'

'Course I will, they'll understand. And thanks, Mam.'

'What for, love?'

'Oh just… '

'You'll come home tomorrow then?'

'Yes, Mam. Whatever.'

'Right, if we sort things out, well, I'd like you to bring Melanie here soon. Anyway, bye for now. Sorry about everything – it's a mess, and you don't deserve to be in it.'

'It's all right, I understand. See you tomorrow. Love.'

I don't understand, he reflected. How could Dad ever… He put the phone down and looked at Melanie.

'Does she know? Did you say we… you know?'

He nodded. She leant forward and kissed him, putting her hands round his waist. 'Weren't you going to contact that friend of yours, Clear?'

Geraint laughed. 'Llŷr? Yes, suppose we'd better. Before we… relax. I'll phone him to make sure he's in.'

'Right, now, what the hell's going on? Why all this mystery? Your face worries me, Ger, so spill the beans.'

Geraint found it odd hearing Llŷr speak in English. The room was the usual tobacco-smelling homely chaos of books and magazines. He and Melanie sat on the lumpy, cracked, brown settee while Llŷr, in faded blue jeans and dark sweater, sat by the gas fire.

After they had completed their tale, Llŷr stared at the fire for nearly a minute, brow furrowed. Then he looked up and uttered a heartfelt '*Diawl!*' Unwrapping a new packet of Embassy, he said, 'It's... awful. I mean, I know I occasionally had just the germ of a suspicion. But now that you've spelt it all out, in detail, it's an utter nightmare. No doubts at all?'

Geraint shook his head.

'And it wasn't just us he conned. Marcus, the rest of them down there. Complete trust in him. And you didn't see Mair?'

'No.'

'Does she know?'

'I don't reckon she did. But probably now, unless she went home for the weekend, which I doubt, with what we were planning being so near.'

'The bastard!'

His face betrayed his agony and disillusionment, provoking Melanie to say quietly, 'I think I know how you feel. And I'm sorry I helped destroy your hopes, but... '

'Thank God you did!' He looked at them both, sitting close, Geraint's hand on Mel's knee.

'And this Mike Barraclough, well, I wondered about him in Plaid Cymru! *Sais*, suddenly appearing, knows just enough Welsh to understand what we say in meetings. But, well, thank heavens he moved here and did join!' Llŷr exhaled a cloud of smoke, and added, 'Scouse. I can't stop trying to work it all out. That big pipeline job over the border, well it must have been carried out just to convince us, to make us trust him. That was when I first began to wonder.'

'And,' said Melanie, 'it's obvious why you lot weren't arrested. Sort of being saved.'

'Sacrificial lambs,' murmured Llŷr.

'We need to contact the others,' said Geraint. 'But you know more than I do about how… '

Llŷr patted Geraint's knee. 'Hey, leave it to me. Just hope I can convince them. Maybe I can refer them to you if they have any doubts?'

'Yes, by all means.'

Llŷr shook his head. 'Bastards! They would have had us all well and truly by the short and curlies. And with at least two active Plaid Cymru members, an ex-Plaid councillor… Well, you can imagine the media. They'd've had a field day. Plaid Cymru could have been crucified in the next election.'

Geraint felt his cheeks going hot as he added, 'I still haven't told her, or Mike, exactly what we were planning.' He glanced nervously at Melanie, who gazed calmly enough at Llŷr.

Llŷr returned the gaze, saying, 'So how did you… Ah!' He smiled bleakly. 'A highly intelligent girl – as well as a decisive and ingenious one.'

'I was thinking of Geraint,' she said slowly, 'and adding a lot of things up.' She looked down and added, 'But the whole con trick was unjust, totally wrong. Unfair on all of you.'

After a short silence, Geraint asked, 'Scouse hasn't contacted you today, tried to see if I had told the truth about warning you beforehand?'

Llŷr shook his head. 'He must realise it's pointless. You must have been convincing enough.' He looked sharply at Geraint. 'Are you sure you're going to be safe? After all, you have blown apart the plan, smashed maybe months of preparation, elaborate planning.'

Geraint looked at Melanie. 'I guess so. Mike thinks the tape business will do it. A sort of trump card.'

'And wouldn't he like to get his hands on that.' Llŷr stood

up and said briskly, as though dispelling any doubts, 'Ah, you'll be OK. Mike seems to know his business. How about a beer or two. Or Coke?'

'Thanks,' said Geraint, 'but we'd better be getting back.'

As they went downstairs, Llŷr said, 'Well I suppose I'd better get on with phoning around. They're gonna love this.'

As they reached the door to the street, Geraint, feeling worried, looked at Llŷr. 'Will you make sure you get through to each one?'

'Yeah,' answered Llŷr. 'Don't worry, I stay on the phone either until I've spoken to each, or if one's not there, I'll do it first thing in the morning or arrange for someone to ask him to phone me.'

As they set off along the High Street, Geraint looked at his watch and said, 'Only nine o'clock. What a day.'

'I know,' sighed Melanie. 'But it's not all stressful, is it?' She squeezed his bum and he realised there was still something to look forward to. They reached her house without meeting anyone they knew – some achievement in Tywyn – though Geraint felt he no longer cared who saw them.

After the usual effusive canine welcome, they pushed their way in and Melanie said, 'I'm surprised Mum and Dad didn't ring last night. They've probably been ringing all day. Still,' she reflected, 'they know I'm a big girl.'

'Lovely and big,' muttered Geraint, glancing at her breasts.

Laughing as she faced him, she said, 'Geraint Rees, you're learning fast. Becoming a real sex maniac!'

Pankhurst having been fed, stroked, petted and taken for short a walk to do her business, they sat in the lounge, Melanie twiddling through the stations on a portable radio until she found one with pounding rock music. He was kissing her earlobe when the phone rang. 'Probably M and D,' sighed Melanie, disengaging and dashing out. Geraint followed, passion wilting, nervous as to what she might say to her parents.

Melanie's 'Oh, hi!' didn't sound like a greeting to parents, he thought, confirmed by a grinning face that mouthed Anna at him. She sat on the lower stairs and Geraint looked at her, feeling she was the most beautiful, the sexiest, the bravest and most intelligent girl he could ever meet. And his. He leant against the front door, continuing to drink in her attributes and then rolled his eyes skyward and made yakkity-yak gestures with his hands, at which Melanie shook her fist at him, smiling.

Eventually, he heard, 'Well, yes, pretty good so far. Yes, tell you Monday, well, not all of it. Just an edited version... No I am not! Yes, he is here, and looking at me impatiently.' Until at last, 'OK, Anna, must go now. See you – byeee!'

No sooner had she replaced the receiver than the phone startled them by ringing stridently again. Melanie raised two clenched fists and grimaced. 'Hello, Mummy.' She beckoned Geraint to sit next to her on the stair. When he'd settled himself, he could hear the far-away metallic chatter of a female voice.

After a lot of 'Yes, Mummy' and 'No, Mummy' and 'Sorry, Mummy', she said, 'Well I'm here now and yes, everything's all right and Pankhurst's fine.' She changed the phone to her left hand and put her right hand on Geraint's knee. 'Mummy, before you go, there's one other thing... Geraint's here... Yes, here now. He's, well, he's had a spot of bother again at home; well not him, his parents have a... domestic crisis and he's sort of sheltering here over the weekend… Yes, overnight.' Then there was more sustained metallic squawking and Melanie was silent for a few moments until: 'Well, actually, yes, he slept in my room… we slept in my room… Oh Mummy, come on, we've been through all that – it was quite safe… and Mummy, I don't regret it – and I love him.' Then she shook her head at something she heard. 'Mummy, I'll explain everything, well, almost everything, when I see you. And tell Daddy not to go mad at me, please!… Yes, see you both tomorrow night.' And that was that.

'Well,' she said, putting the receiver down, 'that's four, or maybe three, worried or wondering parents.' She went back and sat next to him and, arms round each other's waists, they sat in silence for a few moments until, standing up and stretching, she sighed, 'See, Ger? We've done it! Told 'em all! Boy, was I shaking!'

He stared up and smiled, silent for once. He admired her courage and felt a sense of ease, relief – it was out in the open and nothing could turn the clock back. He couldn't really believe the last twenty-four hours. It seemed incredible that on Monday, perhaps thirty-six hours away, they would both be expected to put on school uniform and trog off down the road with a bag of school books and files, and sit dutifully at desks, taking dictation or enduring headmasterial trivia or reprimands for minor misdemeanours. At least the following week was half-term, he remembered.

Back in the lounge, Melanie stood for a moment, a serious expression on her face. 'Ger, just come with me to check the windows and doors – everything locked and so on.'

'Sure.' Yes, he thought, I should have suggested that. Just in case. They went round every downstairs window and carefully locked and bolted the back door. Curtains tightly closed. Fire off. Kitchen needed tidying but plenty of time for that. Pankhurst with head down over paws, blinking up at them, her wicker basket just in front of the washing machine.

Melanie beamed at him. 'Right, snug as a bug in a rug. Come on upstairs.'

Chapter 25

SUDDENLY, HIS NOSE scraped the wallpaper. He hadn't realised how near to it he had been sleeping – except that he had been half awake for a few moments anyway. They'd argued about who should sleep on the outside, and he'd lost. He tried to turn over onto his back without disturbing her. He thought he had managed until he heard a whispered, 'Ger?'

'Who else?' he whispered back.

She didn't respond, nor move for a while. Then slowly she turned over, her straggly brown hair tickling his cheek. She spoke so quietly, he could scarcely understand: 'Did you hear it too?'

He lay, pondering. Hear what? The room was totally dark. Curtains shut, door presumably still ajar. Silence. The kind of total, immensely pregnant, ear-drumming, windless silence of the small hours in the country, when a bed creak sounds like a sudden rifle shot in a cavernous, empty church.

'Hear what?' he croaked.

She turned slightly towards him and, putting a hand on his chest, whispered directly into his left ear. 'Dunno. Something. Downstairs, outside. I'm not sure.'

He felt suddenly more alert – and tense. 'Well, what sort of noise?'

Exasperated, she snapped, 'I don't know!' She turned her face away as though straining to listen. 'I just know I woke up – something woke me up. And then I heard… another something, downstairs I think. But don't ask me what.'

Geraint didn't know what to say. Surely Pankhurst would

give warning if... Melanie must know that. Nervously he heaved himself up, hoping the bed would not creak. His hearing taut, he looked into the swirling atoms of darkness towards the door. He could not be sure, either; as though something moved or someone's presence was somehow transmitting itself to him. When Melanie whispered that she was scared, he knew he had to act.

Standing on the deep, soft carpet, he tried to control his breathing. Then he bent down and, groping around, managed to disentangle his underpants from something frilly. Slipping them on, he decided to try to move over to the door silently. Were there any creaking boards? Not something he had bothered to think about earlier on.

He groped in front of him like a blind man who's lost his stick but eventually gripped the edge of the door. For what seemed like hours, he stood there, feeling as though his breaths were as loud as a saw rasping through wood. And then he did hear something: the slightest, gentlest creak possible.

Downstairs? If only Mike... And then he remembered. 'Phone me,' he had said. How? Ah, extension in her parents' room. He stood, frozen, gripping the door. To move even a muscle seemed impossible. He was afraid even to move his head in case his neck creaked. But he had to get across the landing and open that door, and go across to the bedside phone.

Could he remember Mike's number? Pennal... Pennal 356, or was it 365? Or, no. 356. The code? Yes, he remembered both.

He let go of the door and took one agonising pace. His knee cracked like a shotgun going off. Another pace, silent on the carpet. And then he was there, turning the knob and praying it wouldn't squeak or be partly jammed. He pushed open the door, the bottom swishing quietly against the carpet pile. Trying to accustom his eyes to the darkness, he gingerly moved forward until his bare legs met the softness of the bedding. Moving along the edge of the bed, he felt for the small table where the phone should be. His hand knocked something onto the carpet, a hairbrush maybe. And then he felt the familiar shape.

How do I dial in the darkness? he wondered. And what about the bloody whirring as the dial comes back? He carefully picked up the receiver, deciding he could probably finger the holes and work out which one matched each number. Ready to try this, he transferred the receiver to his other hand – and then he sensed something not quite right.

It hit him like a blow to the stomach. No dialling tone. Cut off. Dead.

Strange, he thought, that a fault should have developed only a few hours after their conversations. Stop kidding yourself, Ger lad, he thought.

Feeling suddenly very cold and very naked – and very alone – he turned to get back to Melanie. Find a torch, a weapon, escape outside, anything. But get back to Melanie first.

He was about to enter their bedroom when there was a dazzling light and an explosion of violence and vice-like arms and he felt his shoulders tearing with pain, his head forced forward, and he yelled something, then more dazzling lights and pain, and arms gripping him, and he found himself being forced downstairs, stumbling, slipping, but still controlled by strong arms, the feel of a sweater, perhaps, against his bare skin.

He felt himself flung into an armchair in the lounge, the main light on, forcing him to lift his hands to shade his eyes, but the pain in his arms and shoulders stopped him and he blinked. Slowly he forced his senses to report back to the brain.

A length of wire flex suddenly cut into his chest and he found himself pushed back into the chair, the wire digging into him. He tried to loosen it but then the man behind moved round and deftly twisted the wire round his wrists and yanked back on them so each arm was drawn behind him and made fast.

And then silence, followed by quietly padding footsteps – away from him. A creak of stairs. With a sickening pit opening up in his stomach, and before he could try to warn her, he heard her shout, 'Geraint! Help.'

Her words were smothered and there was a scuffling that went further away, then silence. He couldn't find the strength to shout, but croaked, 'Mel!' Suddenly, there was Scouse, standing in front of him. Feeling utterly helpless, and shaking with fear, he asked, 'What have you done to her?'

Scouse went over to the hearth and rested an elbow on the mantelpiece. 'Asleep. A quick jab. She's best out of it. For the moment. Nothing worse than a headache and furry tongue when she comes round.' He licked his lips and added, 'Assuming she is allowed to… ' He had spoken quietly and seemed dangerously calm.

Geraint tried to look over his shoulder towards the door leading to the kitchen and laundry-room. Though what could Pankhurst do?

'Oh, if you're seeking the hound, also hors–de–combat. Temporarily.'

His chest and wrists were hurting but Geraint managed to gasp, 'If you hurt Melanie in any way… '

Scouse still leant there, looking at him. 'I don't want to.

But that depends on you, matey.'

Still shaking, Geraint looked down at the carpet. 'How did you know where to come?'

Scouse padded over and stood just in front of him, hands on hips. 'I took a chance – and it paid off. Lucky really. I drove here. Phoned your house, but your mother said you were away for the night. And then while I was planning what to do, noticed that meddling friend of yours dropping you at this place. Very convenient, just the two of you in the house.'

Geraint knew he had never felt so cold, so terrified, so helpless, before in his life. 'So why are you here?' he managed to ask, despite trembling.

Scouse bent down and put his face close to his. 'Information, matey. Quickly. That tape you mentioned. Tell me where it is. When it's in my hands, I'll be away – out of your lives.'

Geraint summoned up the strength to say, 'I don't know where it is. And Melanie's parents are due back any moment.' Pathetic, he thought, but he had to try something.

There was a pause. And then Scouse hit him across his cheek with the back of his gloved hand.

'Now listen, lad! To say I am angry is the understatement of the year. I am angry – my bosses will be angry. And we're talking about some pretty important, powerful people. Months of work, preparation, down the pan! Now you've got a choice. The tape, forget you ever knew me, mention me to no one and that will be that. Perhaps you'll both live to a peaceful old age. Mess me around, any tricks, like having a duplicate tape somewhere, and it won't just be you who'll suffer.' He grabbed Geraint by the hair and pushed his head back. 'She's attractive. If you want her to stay that way… '

He let go of him and took a pace back. Geraint heard a

click and realised Scouse was holding a flick knife.

Geraint's head was a maelstrom of chaotic thoughts. If only, he reflected, if only we'd asked Mike if we could stay with him, just for tonight. If only I was a hero in a film and had some brilliant plan to extricate myself from this. If only Melanie had been able to get outside and run.

His head was yanked back again until he thought his hair was going to be ripped out.

'The tape. Now! Try to play the hero and I drag her down here in front of you. And this knife might just make her a bit less attractive. And that will just be for starters.'

'OK, OK!'

His head jerked forward and Scouse released it. 'Well?'

'It's... it's not here. We posted it – I don't know where to or who to. Somewhere safe.'

'I don't believe you. Now if...'

And suddenly there was a flash of light from behind, somewhere by the door, and he managed to look up to see Scouse's surprised face looking over there, expression frozen. A voice, suddenly familiar, authoritative: 'Drop the knife – now! Now slowly, very slowly, raise your hands.'

Mike moved into Geraint's sight. A 35mm camera hung from a strap round his neck, and in his right hand, a pistol with what Geraint assumed was a silencer. 'You OK, Ger?'

'Yeah. Melanie...'

'She'll be all right.' Watching Scouse carefully, Mike removed the camera from round his neck and put it on chair.

Scouse stood there, hands just above his head, his expression concealing his anger. He spoke slowly and calmly, 'I hear you'd taken a job in the wilds; didn't know it was round here though. Until today. You never did know when to b discreet. Always pushy, always poking your nose in.'

Mike merely gesticulated with his pistol, adding, 'On the deck, face down, hands behind your back.'

Scouse obeyed, his face still impassive, though his words betrayed his feelings: 'They'll come after you, Barraclough!' Scouse had to raise his face from the carpet to speak.

Mike dug a pair of handcuffs out of a pocket and clicked them over Scouse's wrists. 'Knew these would come in handy one day.' He moved over to Geraint and began freeing him. 'Milne, you should be ashamed of yourself. Involving a schoolboy, a lad as young as this.'

'Orders,' said Scouse, turning his head sideways. 'Something you never got used to following.' Geraint stood up, rubbing his wrists and groaning. 'And you know your trouble, Barraclough? Morality!' Scouse almost spat the word out. 'That soft conscience of yours. No wonder they gave you the boot!'

'I resigned,' said Mike quietly. 'Go on, Ger, get upstairs and see to her. And put some clothes on!'

Geraint needed no urging, and as he hobbled away, heard Scouse say, 'You're a dead man!'

'Oh aren't we all – eventually?' retorted Mike. 'But I bet I outlive you, old fellow. I have a picture of this delightful scene, plus a short tape of the conversation, plus my own tape which I shall bring up to date and put in the same safe spot as Geraint's. He was telling the truth, you know – it's been posted to… somewhere secure. And then, of course, as you would expect, in the event of any little accident, whether motoring or biological – or domestic – picture, tapes, full details to key people plus the media. They might come heavy-handed on some editors with D notices and the rest, but not all of them will comply. And there's always abroad.'

Upstairs, Geraint found Melanie lying on top of the bed, looking as though she was merely asleep. He knelt and caressed her face, whispering, 'Melanie! Wake up! Come on, *cariad*.' Remembering what Scouse had said, he realised it was pointless. Tucking her up carefully, he kissed her on the cheek and sought his clothes. Fully dressed, he blew her a kiss and went as quickly as he could down to the lounge.

Scouse was still prone on the floor, and Mike was sitting where Geraint had been, pistol pointing at him. Mike looked at Geraint's worried face and said, 'Hey, she'll be all right. She'll probably sleep for another hour or two.'

Geraint nodded. 'I nearly forgot. Thanks Mike – again. What happens now?'

Mike smiled. 'Mr Milne is going to enjoy a little nocturnal tour of Merioneth with a navigation and initiative test to follow.'

Geraint thought he heard Scouse emit an expression beginning with 'F' and looked, puzzled, at Mike.

'I'll take him up to the wilds of the hills somewhere remote, and leave him there with the key to the cuffs chucked somewhere on the road a few yards away. That will give me time to drive off. And then our Colin can find his way to... wherever he wants.'

Sitting on the arm of the sofa, Geraint said slowly, 'Fine. But what if he, you know... '

Mike shook his head. 'I reckon I can convince him that it will be in all our interests to try to forget this sordid episode, the plot, this attempt to get the tape. Everything.'

Scouse raised his head and barked, 'They'll get you for this, Barraclough, never you fear. You won't know what's hit you. Have you any idea how high up this goes? And what the climax of the plan was to have been? The climax mark two?

No, of course you haven't,'

Mike gave a short laugh. 'Don't worry about me.' He helped Scouse up and added: 'Out. Land Rover.'

The three went out through the front door to the drive. With some difficulty, Scouse heaved himself into the back of the vehicle and sat on a side seat.

'Right Ger,' said Mike, 'let's make sure he behaves himself.'

From the front passenger side, Mike took a length of electrical flex with a prepared noose which he very quickly and deftly put over Scouse's feet, binding them tightly. Then, with another length of flex, he tied one end through the handcuffs and the other through a bracket on the inside wall of the Land Rover. Finally, he blindfolded him with a scarf.

Scouse sat silent, immobile. Conscious again of how betrayed he felt, Geraint asked quietly, 'Scouse, why? Who are your bosses? Who ordered you to do this?' He thought he could guess, but just wanted to see if Scouse would open up. Scouse turned in his direction for a second, and shook his head.

Mike slapped Geraint on the back. 'Right, back to Melanie. She'll be fine by daybreak. Then, keep her quiet, something to drink. OK?'

'Yeah.' He shivered despite his sweater.

'I'll deal with Mr M here. And I don't reckon you'll have any more trouble. Oh, and I should be able to organise your phone coming back to life.' He stroked his beard thoughtfully.

Despite longing to get back to Melanie, Geraint asked, 'Mike, how did you know? How come you were here?'

Mike gave a short laugh. 'I didn't want to alarm you but I thought something like this might happen. I parked the Land

Rover in the hospital car park – I'm friendly with the night sister on tonight – then kept watch discreetly. When I realised the scenario had begun... well, the rest you know.'

'And you taped him, us?'

He led Geraint a little further away from the Land Rover. 'No, just a thought to worry him. But I do have a pic and will update my own tape to go with yours. So I reckon that's it. I'll ring you tomorrow afternoon, right?'

'Right.' And then he thought. 'How did he get in? We locked everything.'

Mike shrugged his shoulders. 'Did you bolt the front door?'

Geraint shivered. 'Hell – no.'

'It's not difficult for the likes of him.' Mike patted his back, saying, 'OK then, I'll get off before the local bobby comes pedalling along.'

'OK, Mike – and again, thanks for everything.'

'Think nowt of it, lad. We West Riding lads have to help the Welsh. I mean we're not really English, are we? Independence for Yorkshire and the Yorkshire pudding quoted on the world currency markets.' And, giving him a resounding slap on the back, away he went to his strange cargo.

When the Land Rover had gone, Geraint shivered and went back in, double-checking all the locks and bolts. Suddenly remembering the other victim, he went through to the kitchen. Yes, Pankhurst, snoring but certainly alive, still in her basket.

He turned and headed for the stairs. 'Mel... '

Chapter 26

THE DAY HAD arrived. Tuesday, 1 July 1969. As though to mock the riot of colourful flags, bunting and costumes in Caernarfon, the skies were a dirty grey, the winds chilling.

He followed her up the steep, stony path, past a crumbling stone wall and then eventually to a semi-ruined tower. They clambered up some steps to the top of the tower and braced themselves against the wind, staring across the green countryside towards the hills and mountains.

Castell y Bere, a remote, ruined castle, was one of the few that had been built by the Welsh. It had been in ruins since being sacked by the English, the defenders slaughtered. That morning, at Geraint's suggestion, they had cycled the few miles from Tywyn, heading inland, past Craig Aderyn, and stopped to relax on the grassy slopes and explore what was left of the castle.

Tentatively, he slipped an arm round her waist, meeting no resistance. 'Wonder who once stood up here, staring down just as we are doing,' he said.

She didn't respond. The wind blew strands of brown hair across her face and she pushed them away. He swayed for a moment in a gust and instinctively held on tighter to Melanie. She glanced sideways at him, face firm, unsmiling, but not severe.

'Are you sure you won't come down to the beach this afternoon for the branch picnic? You could bring the hound, and you know most of the people who are going.'

Her voice was low, controlled, firm. 'No, Geraint. You

don't seriously think I'd feel at home, the only one not a member of Plaid Cymru? I understand why you're going, to escape from the telly and so on.'

'Mel, you're always on about how big a Labour supporter you are, so how can real socialists put up with all this... pantomime?'

'Some Labour MPs have refused to attend.' She pulled his arm away. 'Let's get down – out of this wind.'

When they reached shelter, she stood and faced him. 'Even after all that's happened to you, that awful Scouse business, well, it was just one corrupt man who thought up the plan. I mean, every country has scandals and things now and again. I bet we don't know half the truth about President Kennedy.'

Geraint put his hands on her shoulders, determined to be quietly reasonable. '*Cariad*, if we had no royal family, English anyway, none of this would have happened.'

'If, if, if!' she shouted, impatient. 'The royal family wasn't involved in what happened to you, or even the government.' She paused and said more calmly, 'Well, I admit I'm not sure about them.'

He moved his hands to her hips, and then round her waist, gently pulling her nearer, reluctant to re-enter such murky waters. 'Sorry, Mel. I don't want to annoy you, 'specially today.'

She said quietly, firmly, 'I know. But Geraint, I want to watch it on TV. It's, well, historic, not something you often see. And I suppose the Queen and Charles are OK really, you know, as people.'

'Oh.' He didn't know how to go on, at least not without opening old wounds. His hands were still round her waist but he wasn't conscious of any warmth or togetherness.

She seemed to be staring at a pair of gliding buzzards,

soaring, wheeling, emitting mournful cries. 'Geraint,' she went on quietly, 'leave it! I'm me and I don't think exactly as you do on this. OK, you're out of all that nightmare, LAW et cetera, and I'm not mad on Plaid Cymru but I understand why you're in it and I'm not pushing you to pack it in, am I? Anyway, you never know, Charles has learnt Welsh and lived in Aber – and he may well help Wales. He might buy a house to live here until he becomes king, identify with the country and stick up for it. He's probably not mad keen on all the fuss today, either – or the politicians making use of him.'

'But... '

'But off! I'm English even though I live here – and I suppose that means I don't see things the same way you do.'

She removed his hands from her and went back down to the grass. Geraint followed and they sat on the slope. The row had been simmering and festering ever since they had met earlier on. She leant against him and put an arm over his shoulder, perhaps, he thought, to atone for her hostility.

'I've never asked you, didn't want to, well, make you relive things. But what's happened to Scouse and the other members?'

He sighed. Ever since Mike had rescued them, they had deliberately avoided speculating about the organisation and Geraint's involvement, although he had followed events in the newspaper and on the radio and occasionally Llŷr had passed on some information.

'Where is Scouse now? Doing what? Answer: I have no idea. Nor do I want to know. If "they" set out to destroy LAW, they seem to have succeeded.' Geraint paused, kissed her quickly on the cheek and went on: 'Marcus and two others were at last found not guilty a few days ago, and two were cleared in an evening session only last night.' He looked down, as though pondering whether to continue. 'A Bridgend member of LAW was acquitted back in May; that left two who had pleaded guilty and four others convicted. On the radio, Gwynfor called it a show trial, saying that the offences they'd actually been charged with were so minor they should have been brought in front of a magistrate months ago.' With a shudder, he realised again that if Scouse's plan had not been stopped, he, Geraint, could have been charged with something certainly not trivial.

Melanie was nodding. 'The ones you knew?'

Perhaps this way, he thought, they were helping to exorcise it. 'Pedr and co – Llŷr convinced them that weekend – and I haven't seen any of them since. I see Llŷr and Mike usually, you know, in Plaid Cymru meetings.'

She took his hand in hers. Feeling stronger, he added, 'Despite everything, LAW slogans are still appearing on walls and bridges all over the country, though I suppose this must be by sympathisers as there are no real members left. And according to Llŷr, MAC, the shadowy other lot, the Movement for the Defence of Wales, seems to be still operating. Maybe it was their bomb discovered on a pier at Holyhead last week – the royal yacht was going to tie up there.' He thought she might let go of his hand, but she didn't. 'And,' he sighed, 'early this morning, according to the radio, a bomb blasted a postal sorting office in Cardiff.' Melanie looked at him with an expression he couldn't quite fathom. 'Oh, I know,' he said quietly, 'But you know I'm out of it all. Just little old Plaid Cymru.'

She let go of his hand and stood up. He remained sitting, deep in thought, as she strolled away. Time went by and he suddenly realised where he was, as the images of the past melted away. Where was Mel? He squirmed round and there she was, deep in thought, ambling along, fingers tucked into the back pockets of her jeans. He felt a strong urge to hold and be held. Walking up to her as quietly as he could, he grabbed her by the shoulders, twisting her round to face him. She just looked down, so he raised her chin and stared, grinning. 'I still reckon I'm fitter than you,' he said quietly.

She maintained a severe expression for two seconds and then a broad grin cracked it and she began thumping him on the chest, yelling, 'Geraint Rees, sometimes I hate you, you arrogant, stubborn… ' As he tried to pinion her flailing arms, she went on: 'No I don't! I love you, you pig-headed, Welsh… hunk!'

He said nothing, merely silencing her with a kiss. Then she asked, 'How are things with your dad?'

'Not too bad. They're still going to marriage guidance once a week. All I know is that Mam is a bit more cheerful and there are no obvious rows. And Dad is home more than he used to be in the evenings. He's lost weight. I reckon he feels guilty about the whole thing. People must know, but no one has said anything to me. One or two funny looks in the library, your Anna and that Fiona. Anyway, I ignored them.' He sighed. 'I suppose I should appreciate the fact that he even apologised to me for that… that business on my birthday. But I still can't sort of, well, relax with him or forget or anything.' He added bitterly, 'Well at least he doesn't moan about me going to Plaid Cymru meetings any more. You know he and Mam are going to the Investiture Ball tonight at the Corbett Arms?'

'So I could see you?'

'Why not?' He hesitated. 'We're thinking of having a bit of a *noson lawen* at Ysguboriau, a farm belonging to one of our members. Nothing much: a few drinks, sarnies, Siân on the harp, sing a few songs.' Taking a deep breath, he went on: 'You could come with me. No politics, I promise.'

She laughed, but it struck him as amusement rather than bitterness. 'No politics! Just a load of anti-Investiture nationalists singing songs about freedom.' She shook her head, smiling. As she didn't immediately speak, he feared he'd blown it – again. But then: 'OK, no picnic – but if the price of seeing you tonight is that thingy, I'll come if they don't mind.'

Geraint felt a surge of warmth and pleasure. She had not experienced that sort of traditional get-together and even if most of it would be in Welsh, he could whisper translations in her ear.

They walked over to a wooden fence and perched on the top, at first silent, alone with their thoughts. A relaxed silence, this time.

'We've had some interesting experiences,' said Geraint, looking at her. She laughed, nodding. He added, quietly: 'I'll never forget when you woke up after Scouse had… you know. I was so relieved. And I'll never forget holding you, while you cried.'

She leaned over and kissed his cheek. 'And then when Mummy and Daddy came home. Wow! I don't know how I stayed so calm!'

'I wish I could have been hiding there to hear it all.'

'Oh it could have been worse. The worst thing was the look on Daddy's face when he asked about us sleeping together. I think he didn't feel quite so bad when I told him you, we… took precautions.'

Geraint stared and asked, 'Yes. I meant to ask you: where did that packet of… those things, come from?'

Melanie smiled. 'Not telling you.'

'Oh come on.'

'Secret?'

'Of course!'

'I pinched it from the little drawer by Dad's side of the bed. Well, I took the packet. He wouldn't miss it as there were a few there.'

Geraint laughed out loud and couldn't think of anything to say at first. 'You are some girl, Melanie Wilson! Just as well I knew what to do with it.'

'You!' Melanie laughed at his embarrassed grin. 'If you remember, Mr Rees, I... you know... dealt with that!'

Geraint went on smiling and decided it was not the time to ask how she was so adept at it.

He looked up and noticed the grey armada of clouds that had replaced the sunshine. He buried his face in her windswept hair, comforted by the now familiar perfume. As for UK politics, he thought, if I've experienced England's secret service, its genuine James Bonds, if this is what patriotism (UK style) is all about – the Proms, 'Land of Hope and Glory', and clocks still standing at ten to three – then stuff it, thank you. Keep your honey for tea. He laughed out loud at another swirl of memory.

'Hey, you – what's so funny?' asked Melanie. 'Come on.'

'And after that weekend... school. As though nothing had happened.' He laughed again. 'Just before registration, I went to the bog and as I was standing there, Pete comes up next to me and does his. And he said, "Hi Ger! Good weekend? Haven't seen you about." So I think – what on earth do I say?'

'What did you?'

'Oh, I just said yeah, fine, nothing exciting, you know.'

She laughed too. 'Mmmm, I must admit, I couldn't

concentrate on any lessons that next day.'

They sat again in silence. Geraint felt a deep sense of warmth and peace. Melanie interrupted: 'Ger, you know what we're gonna do as soon as the exams are over?'

'Buy a double bed?'

'Go to Shrewsbury on the train – and I'm going to take you to a trendy little boutique. You'll love some of the gear there.'

'Look forward to it. But nothing too drastic. This isn't London. Mike at the agricultural place promised me some work so I should be able to afford something.' He waited while an old Fergie pulling a trailer roared past and added, 'Then… '

'What?'

'How about us getting a tent… and going camping after our exams?'

Melanie's eyes opened wide. 'Why not? But – parents?'

'We'll convince them.'

'You reckon?' She smiled and kissed him. 'Come on, let's head back… go to the caff before I go home. And you can tell me where this *nos* thing is tonight.'